THE HEART DOESN'T LIE

Jay opened the door after hearing a second soft knock. Trent stood in her doorway, tall and good-looking. Several open buttons on his blue shirt revealed his muscular chest, and the slender waistband on his wide-leg blue pants accented his narrow waist.

"Come in." Jay moved away from the door and watched as he walked into the room.

Trent shut the door and gathered her into his arms. His mouth was firm and warm against hers as he parted her lips and gave her a searching kiss. He held her close with one hand while he slipped the other over her hips and lifted his head to look into her eyes. "I went to the hotel last night because I wanted to spend the night with you," he said.

THE HEART DOESN'T LIE

Marcella Sanders

ARABESQUE

★*BET*

BOOKS™

BET Publications LLC
http://www.bet.com
http://www.arabesquebooks.com

ARABESQUE BOOKS are published by

BET Publications, LLC
c/o BET BOOKS
One BET Plaza
1900 W Place NE
Washington, DC 20018-1211

All Kensington Titles, Imprints, and Distributed Lines are available at special quantity discounts for bulk purchases for sales promotions, premiums, fund-raising, and educational or institutional use. Special book excerpts or customized printings can also be created to fit specific needs. For details, write or phone the office of the Kensington special sales manager: Kensington Publishing Corp., 850 Third Avenue, New York, NY 10022, attn: Special Sales Department. Phone: 1-800-221-2647.

First Printing: June 2002
10 9 8 7 6 5 4 3 2 1

Printed in the United States of America

One

The flight attendant's fresh voice informing the passengers that their flight was about to touch down at the Lagos African airport aroused Jay Lee out of sleep. She opened her eyes and blinked against the brilliant sunlight shimmering against the plane's half-opened window shade.

Jay let out a delicate sigh, a habitable sound that usually followed a lengthy sleep. She snapped the seat belt into place, securing herself for landing before she turned to see who was sitting next to her.

Jay had shared a seat with her boss, Professor Myers, until they had reached London, and she hadn't paid much attention to the team member who had sat beside her after she boarded the plane for their final destination. Instead, she had faced the window and closed her eyes, allowing the sound of shuffling papers and later, the clatter of her seatmate's nimble fingers stroking the keys on the laptop to lull her to sleep.

Slowly, Jay lifted her gaze, noticing a black laptop resting upon a pair of muscular jean-clad thighs, and she wondered what imposter had passed himself off as a member of the cultural research team. Certainly if any of the men she worked with had owned a pair of thick, muscular thighs, she would have noticed before arriving halfway around the world.

Jay watched as the man seated next to her strapped himself in his seat. Out of old-fashion curiosity and the need to get a better look at the gentleman sitting beside her, she allowed her gaze to travel from his thighs and finally to his muscular chest.

The outline of his muscles pressed against his blue shirt, and just enough biceps peeked from underneath his short sleeves, making Jay believe that this was a sure sign that the man lifted weights.

There was nothing more beautiful to her than a well-built man, and the man seated beside her was everything Jay Lee admired. With that thought in mind, she allowed her gaze to travel farther, observing a pair of sensual lips, neatly trimmed black mustache, and chiseled facial features.

Jay lowered her gaze thinking that she'd seen this gentleman walking through the corridor around noon once or twice since she had begun working for Myers Research Center. If he was a new member of the team, why hadn't he attended their last meeting and been introduced to the staff? Jay dismissed her wandering thoughts, and shifted in the seat, stretching her long legs out in front of her.

"Hi," Jay's seatmate spoke to her. His voice was smooth and relaxed as if he didn't have a care in the world.

"Good morning," Jay said, moving her gaze to his soft brown eyes and nodding. Yes, she had seen this man donning dark suits, Stacy Adams, and a smile that promised to melt a woman's heart. However, she noticed the few times that she had seen him in Myers' hallway he hadn't paid attention to the sexy comments and fox whistles her female coworkers had directed at him.

"Um-huh," Jay said, catching a quick glimpse of his short thick wavy jet-black hair and wondering why he was with the research team. Her boss hadn't mentioned that another person would be joining their African marriage research project.

"I didn't mean to . . ." he said. "Professor Myers . . ." The gentleman started again, and again his voice broke. He looked at her for a second before he continued. "I didn't mean to disturb you," he said.

"You didn't disturb me," Jay replied, trying not to stare at him. She turned away and raked her fingers through her short, wavy hair.

"Myers had business to attend to in London. My seat is at the back and I didn't want to sit there so I took a chance and sat next to you." He quickly explained and nodded toward the back of the plane, then gave her a smile. "I hope you don't mind," he said.

Jay swallowed. If she didn't know any better, she would have thought she was still dreaming. "No, I don't mind," she said.

He let out a soft rippling chuckle that swept through her like angelic feathers while he held out his wide hand to her. "Trent—Trent Prescott." He seemed to have been studying her as if he had some mystic message he wasn't conveying.

Jay slipped her hand in his and clasped his firm, broad palm. "Jay Lee." She introduced herself, thinking how wrong she and her girlfriend, Carol, had been when they were discussing the sparsity of good-looking men.

Trent Prescott was picture-perfect, except for one diminutive flaw: he carried the surname Prescott. Jay gave Trent Prescott a firm handshake, and tried to disregard the disturbing reminder that was bulldozing its way through her mind.

According to her grandmother, Gladys Lee, everyone on the eastern seaboard of New Jersey knew the Prescott family. They were a clan of good-for-nothing people, a family of swindlers, cheats, and murderers.

Not only were they a lazy bunch, they were uneducated and not one of them had earned a high school diploma. The family had been known to destroy anyone who crossed their wicked paths. Jay believed her grandmother because she was living proof of these facts.

"I can't wait to get off this plane," Trent said, as if he was attempting to engage her into friendly conversation.

"Me neither," Jay replied, his comment snapping her back to the present. Shortly afterward, her mind was riddled with another trail of ceaseless questions.

Her grandmother had mentioned years ago that the Prescott family had moved shortly after the tragedy. Jay wasn't sure where Gladys said the family had moved to when they left town. Hadn't Gladys mentioned that they had moved to Delaware? She let the tail end of that thought swing across her mind.

Jay dismissed her endless questions and meandering recollections regarding the severe description her grandmother had given her about the Prescott family. She was convinced that not one of these horrible, uneducated people had been struck by any inspiration for knowledge and acquired a GED. Because of the family's reputation, it was almost impossible for any one of them to have attended a college and graduated.

"This has been a long trip," she remarked hesitantly, with a burning desire to ask Trent if he was related to the Prescotts her grandmother warned her about. But she thought it was too soon to interrogate him. Jay decided that maybe she would ask him when they had finished their work and returned home. She didn't want any old memories from the past to disrupt the time she was spending in the country or the work she could hardly wait to throw herself into.

However, just in case one member of the Prescotts had managed to slip through an intellectual crack, Jay made a silent promise to keep her distance. An adjacent airplane seat and an introduction were probably the extent of her conversation with Trent.

Once she was working on her project gathering information on African marriages, she wouldn't see Trent Prescott again. Jay let out a soft sigh, an indication that she was satisfied with a solution to a disturbing problem.

"We'll be working together," Trent said as though reading her mind. His voice floated out to her just as the plane's wheels squished and squalled against the black tarmac.

"What?" Jay asked. She was almost certain that she hadn't heard him correctly until she noticed his lips tilting into a smile as if her shocked voice amused him.

"I said, we'll be working together," Trent repeated. "Do you have a problem with that, Miss Lee?"

Jay didn't know how to answer his question. She wasn't sure if she had a problem working with Trent Prescott, even as the old memories arose inside her again.

Once she inquired into his background, she would have an answer for his question. "I didn't know that you were working on the project with Rose Simpson,

Webster Nelson and me," she finally replied, hoping that she had quieted the shock in her voice.

"Are you saying that you would rather that I hadn't joined your team?" Trent asked as the captain's voice cracked through the speakers, wishing them a wonderful time in Africa.

"I didn't say that," Jay answered, noticing the frown that had gathered between his smooth brows. She rose from her seat and watched Trent raise himself to his full height and step out into the aisle removing a black leather bag from the overhead compartment.

Jay didn't miss the opportunity to take a survey of his muscular physique. Trent had to be at least six feet tall, she figured as she calculated the length of his towering muscular body with one sweeping glance.

"I thought you might have some objections about having to work with me," Trent remarked, sliding the strap of his bag over one shoulder, and adjusting his laptop computer bag on the other.

"Do I have a choice as to whom I work with?" Jay asked, knowing she couldn't pick and choose. She'd been employed with the team for a year and for the first time since she'd work for Myers Research Center, she was assigned to travel with the crew.

"No, you don't have a choice." Trent reached back into the compartment, pulling out a crimson leather bag. "Is this your bag?" he asked, holding the soft leather tote out to her.

"Yes," Jay said, taking the bag and securing the strap on her shoulder as they walked single file down the aisle and out of the airplane's cabin.

"Do you think we can work together?" Trent spoke in a low voice, and again she wasn't sure if she could work with him. Even if Trent was not a member of the family that she had been taught by her grandmother to hate, his last name would remind her of the Prescotts' evil history. As that thought winged its way across her mind, Jay wished that Trent wasn't walking so close beside her. There were a number of reasons for his disturbing presence. First, he was a handsome, well-built man. And there was nothing more attractive to her than the scent of rich, subtle masculine cologne, a golden complexion, and a winning smile.

Jay noticed that Rose and Webster were ahead of them and she quickened her pace to join them on their way to the conveyer belt to wait for their luggage. She was still unable to avoid Trent. With a few long strides, he was beside her, wanting to talk.

"Miss Lee." Trent fell in step with her and slowed to her pace.

"Please, call me Jay," she said in a voice a pitch higher than she'd intended. Usually, the men working at Myers didn't say much to her, unless they were discussing their work. Jay figured that Trent also wanted to talk to her about the projects they were planning to work on. The least she could do was be gracious enough to listen to him, and she began to walk slower so that they could talk.

"Jay, you seem to have a problem with me, and we don't know each other yet," Trent said, and Jay wondered if she was that transparent. "Just in case you have a problem with me, I want you to know that I'm not going anywhere. I expect for you to follow orders and pass in all reports to me at the end of the day. And let me make myself clear. I don't like to baby-sit and I don't like whining women."

Jay Lee stopped walking. She was aware that she didn't look her twenty-five years, and in some cases, she had to show identification in nightclubs. At any rate, Trent Prescott had to know that she was a grown woman. "Not that it's any of your business, but I am more than twenty-one years old, I don't need a baby-sitter and for your information, I don't whine," she snapped and then stared at him. *And I don't like anything about you.* She mused. *Liar,* followed the end of her thought, as she shifted her bag, adjusting and sliding the straps on her shoulder.

"I'm not finished talking to you, Jay," she heard Trent's arrogant voice behind her, and she couldn't believe that he was ordering her to stop. Or maybe, it was just that he wasn't use to having a woman walk away from him in the middle of a conversation. "I am your supervisor."

Jay stopped. She figured that he was in charge of the team after listening to him bark orders. Nonetheless, she needed her job. The goals she had set for herself depended on her savings and the money she would receive from this project. Having Trent reporting to Matthew Myers that she was too difficult to work with would mean that she would have to put the promise she made to her grandmother to reopen Lees' Bed and Breakfast on hold.

"Yes." Jay turned her attention to her new supervisor.

"If we're going to work together, you need to check your attitude."

"And which attitude would you like for me to check, the one that's not drooling over you?" Jay rendered, willing to forget her dream and promise for a moment as she recalled all the sexy comments the women she worked with had bestowed on Trent Prescott the few times she had noticed him at the office.

"No, Miss Lee—or is it Mrs.?" Trent inquired, searching her ring finger.

"Do you see a wedding band on my finger?" Jay asked.

"Just remember our discussion," he replied. "Because I don't deal well with spoiled brats."

"Spoiled brats?" Jay stood in front of him, so close she could feel his warm breath against her skin, and the electricity between them seemed to flow as they searched each other's face. He was labeling her a troublemaker just because she wasn't afraid to speak up and defend herself.

Again she remembered the project she ensured her grandmother that she would complete as soon as she returned home. With that reminder traipsing across her mind, Jay turned away to keep herself from getting into more trouble than she figured she was already in. "I'm stuck, working with a jack ass," she said softly.

"What did you call me?" Trent asked.

Jay was surprised that he was still trailing close behind her and had heard her. She didn't answer him and she didn't stop until she was walking beside Rose.

"Jay, you're not out of the airport and you already look like you hate you took this trip," Rose's clear glossed lips curved into an amused smile that appeared to make her ebony eyes and nut brown complexion glow.

"I don't have a problem with this trip. It's Trent Prescott who I am concerned about," Jay replied, watching Rose's smile widen as if being irritated with Trent was amusing. "Oh, he's so disgusting," Jay chuckled softly.

"Jay, don't worry about Trent, he's all right," Rose

said, and glanced behind her. "Trent is just blowing off steam."

"I can't imagine why," Jay said, wishing she had kept quiet. But she also had the right to defend herself. "Why did Myers make him the supervisor?" Jay looked at Rose, but addressed her question to Webster.

"Because Trent promised Myers he would work for him on this trip," Webster said. Webster Nelson was tall, dark and attractive with a muscular physique. He had a no-nonsense attitude, but he was polite. Jay knew so because she had talked to him many times at work, usually while she was waiting for Rose to join her on her lunch break.

"Myers couldn't be with us," Webster said. "We have several projects going on, and Trent is supervising the marriage project. After I assist Trent with that, I'll help prepare for the Dancing Mask project." Webster shifted his bag on his shoulder, and slipped one arm around Rose. "And you and Rose are working together."

"Webster, I know. I don't need an explanation," Jay assured him. "I just didn't know Trent was working with us." She wasn't disturbed that Trent was her supervisor as much as she was concerned about his last name. The surname had forced her to recollect her thoughts. She didn't need old memories from the past to dampen her spirit.

"Trent worked out of another center until he resigned six months ago," Webster said.

"I didn't know that," Jay said. She was aware that Myers had two other small centers, one in Delaware and another center in Canada. Jay felt a dreaded trace of apprehension move through her when she thought of Delaware, and wondered which center Trent had worked in. If he worked in Delaware, he could be related to the Prescott family. She had never before mentioned to Rose or Webster the deadly disaster that happened to her family so she kept quiet and didn't mention her suspicions about Trent. Once the project was over, she would return home and would probably never see Trent Prescott again.

However, working closely with Trent for three months would be a long time for Jay, especially since she and Trent couldn't seem to speak to each other without a heated confrontation.

"Trent's a good guy," Webster said. "But sometimes he has his moments."

"I'm sure he is a good guy," Jay said, dismissing any thoughts that she'd had about Trent.

"Jay, you can't let Trent upset you. His bark is worse than his bite," Webster smiled, showing a set of even white teeth.

Jay didn't say anything to Webster. Her reaction to Trent had been based on the past and trying to make Webster and Rose understand her feelings was not important. "If you say so," Jay said.

"I'll catch up with you ladies later," Webster said, cutting into Jay's musing, and walking off.

Not bothering to look back to see where Webster was going, Jay feared that she would find Trent trailing close behind her again. Her intentions were to stay as far away from him as possible, and to keep a distance between them until she had no other choice but to be in his presence. For some strange reason, Jay almost felt the need to apologize to Trent for being rude. She had lost her composure the second he introduced himself and mentioned his last name, which made conversation between them almost impossible.

Jay's thoughts slipped to the promise she had made to her grandmother Gladys Lee and ultimately back to the past, time that she would always remember, but had hidden in the back of her mind until today.

Lees' Bed and Breakfast sat on the crest of her small town adjacent to Atlantic City. As long as Jay could remember, the business had once been the main source of income for her grandparents, Rollins and Gladys Lee. For years Lees' Bed and Breakfast catered to tourists and vacationers who loved Atlantic City and all that the city had to offer, but enjoyed the comforts of a bed-and-breakfast. Not only that, Jay was also certain that the guests enjoyed the family atmosphere. The lodgers had gathered in the dining room for breakfast, lunch and dinner, sharing their stories and making friends with one another. Their children had entertained themselves in the game room, or watched movies that had been provided for all ages.

Shortly after Jay graduated college, her grandfather, Rollins Lee, died and Gladys closed Lees' Bed and Breakfast, mainly because the majority of the younger employees resigned and found employment in larger nearby hotels while the older employees retired. Rollins had been the glue that had held the business together and he'd had a better relationship with the employees than Gladys.

It was then that Gladys asked Jay if she would reopen Lees' in the future. Jay had agreed to reopen the business if her godmother, Barbara Hilton, who had once managed the small beauty salon in Lees', would agree to manage the bed-and-breakfast, since she was no longer working in the beauty business. Barbara had agreed to manage Lees', because she understood how much Jay loved and enjoyed her career and that she had no time or interest in operating the bed-and-breakfast.

"Do you need help with your bags?" Trent asked her as they headed outside.

"No, thanks," Jay said to him, sliding the handle of the rolling luggage upwards.

"All right," Trent replied, and Jay noticed that he was looking at her in a way that she thought was usually meant for people who knew and cared for each other.

She dismissed the unprofessional thought, not caring to think that Trent Prescott had the ability to arouse every positive and negative emotion inside her. If she wasn't careful, and let him too close, he could arouse warmth to her heart. Suddenly, another thought crossed her mind and she glanced quickly at his ring finger. Earlier, when Trent had asked her if she was married, she hadn't thought to check his marital status. She wasn't surprised when she noticed that he wasn't wearing a wedding band. He wasn't married and he was probably proud to be single, Jay thought.

Determined to expel all of her thoughts concerning Trent Prescott, Jay turned her attention to her team members, who were quiet now. Most of them were stretching their arms to the ceiling and yawning as if they needed to rest and adjust their bodies to the new time zone.

Jay knew her body needed to adjust as well, but as thoughts of the past unraveled, she found it almost impossible to think about sleep. So she allowed the thoughts regarding the death of her parents and the reason for their tragic murders to play in her mind.

Lees' Bed and Breakfast was once owned by a member of the Prescott family. One night, when Jay's father, Rollins Lee, Jr., gambled and won the business, the

Prescotts' intention was to strike out with fatal revenge.
According to Gladys, threats were made on Rollins Jr.'s
life. Jay's father hadn't believed the rumors that members of the Prescott family were angry because they
had lost their business and intended to kill him, because the family believed that Rollins Jr. had cheated
to win the game.

Jay was six years old at the time of her parents'
death. It was the first Christmas that she remembered
really well. Her mother, Audrey Lee, along with Barbara and Gladys, had made a big fuss over her being
good all year so that she would receive all the gifts she
wanted. Added to that, she was allowed to help decorate the huge Christmas tree with colorful lights. In
her childish way, Jay had imagined that after the tree
decorating was completed with the tree illuminating a
rainbow of colors, there had to be at least a thousand
red, blue and yellow Christmas lights. Coupled with
those memories, were spicy scents and sweet smells,
circulating out of her mother and grandmother's
kitchens, which she now associated with her favorite
yellow cake covered with white icing and coconuts.

But later that night, Jay remembered that Barbara,
instead of her grandmother or her mother, had taken
her to her room in her grandmother's home where
she spent many of her weekends when her parents
went out. And because of her excitement over the gifts
that she wished to receive the next day, she hardly remembered the story that Barbara read to her.

The next morning Jay remembered not seeing her
parents. Taking time out between playing with her toys,
she had asked for them. Jay recalled her grandmother
saying something to her about angels and peace. Jay
hadn't paid much attention to what was being said.

She had seen lots of pictures of angels and had heard songs being played on the radio and television about peace. She became more interested in wishing that the snow would stop so she could go outside and ride her brand-new bicycle.

Later, when she was older, Jay had learned from Gladys the horrible truth about what had actually happened to her parents. Rollins Jr. and Audrey Lee had gone out to do last minute Christmas shopping and were returning home when a speeding car struck and killed them. According to Gladys, the Prescotts' deadly promise had been fulfilled, executed in a way that was suppose to keep Gladys and Rollins from becoming suspicious that the Prescotts had kept and enforced their promised threat. Jay became a child without parents and clung to her grandmother, unable to understand why her parents would never return home to her.

At night, she would refuse to sleep and Gladys would sit in her room and read Jay stories. Other times, Gladys would ask Jay to read her a story. Jay always fell asleep after she read either to Gladys or during the story Gladys read to her. But there were times when she cried for her parents in the middle of the night and Gladys and her grandfather, Rollins, would comfort her.

Nevertheless, after the horrible nightmare of her parents' death, Gladys promised to take care of her and often reminded Jay that the Prescotts were evil people, and she should stay away from them.

Barbara Hilton, who had been her mother's friend, promised to help Gladys take of care of Jay. Both women had kept their promises, looking after her until the day she completed her education and was gainfully employed.

Jay's only memory of her parents' image would have been even more vague if Gladys hadn't bought her a small child's wallet for her seventh birthday and slipped a snapshot of Rollins Jr. and Audrey Lee inside. When she was alone at night and feeling lonely, Jay often took out the small, pink child's wallet and looked at her parents' picture.

Her mother's fair, flawless complexion, bright ebony eyes and beautiful smile often brought a special peace to her. It was comforting knowing that she had her parents' photograph to look at when she was contemplating and worrying about her problems. It was during those times that Jay would often look at her father's picture. He was dark, with clear, laughing eyes and a smile that held a hint of mischief, one that often made Jay think when she was older, that maybe Gladys Lee was right when she told Jay that her father may have been full of the devil.

"Let's get out of here." Trent interrupted her thoughts once more, as the bus pulled up to the curb.

Jay moved passed Trent, making her way to the waiting bus that was taking them to the suburbs of Nigeria, where she and the others would spend most of the first two months of winter and the first month of spring studying the preparations for marriages, weddings and the ceremonies that were important rituals for African marriages.

Jay boarded the bus, inhaling the scent of worn brown leather, and took a window seat. She shouldn't have been annoyed when Trent sat next to her, but she was. Again she reminded herself that she had no other choice but to conduct herself professionally if she wanted to keep the job she loved. Hitched to that reality was the fact that she wanted to continue working in her profession whether she kept her promise to re-open Lees' or not.

"I'm sorry if I was rude to you," Jay apologized to Trent, hoping to break the icy tension that now suddenly was flowing from Trent like a chill on a frosty night.

"As long as you understand that you have a job to do, and that I expect for the job to be done well, we definitely can work together. You understand?" His voice was cool.

A smart remark tittered on the edge of Jay's lips, but instead of asserting herself, she quietly nodded. She would work and report to Trent, and hopefully in her spare time, she would find out if he was related to her family's enemy.

She snatched another glance in his direction. The electricity that she had experienced between them while they were in the airport had returned and was replaced with a warm sensation that she would rather not contemplate, so she ignored the amiable emotions sweeping through her and heeded the warning whisper that reminded her that she would be wise to keep a close check on her heart and her emotions.

Jay dismissed her mental counseling. She was in Africa, the country she always dreamed of visiting. Anyone would probably have strange emotional reactions, especially if they were sitting as close to Trent as she was. So, without hesitation, she blamed her feelings on the foreign air and her happiness for having fulfilled one of her dreams. She assured herself that her disturbing sensations had nothing to do with the fact that Trent Prescott was the handsomest man she'd seen in a long time.

Jay cast another glance at him. Trent appeared relaxed and at peace, resting his head against the leather seat, his eyes closed, as if he didn't have a care in the world. Adjoined to those observations, he appeared to wear his authority like a cloak of armor, proud, strong, and in control.

Jay reached inside her bag and took out her sunglasses, shading her vision from the early morning sun, before she turned her attention to the open dry scenery that rolled into view.

The sunburnt pasture looked as if a strong wind would rip the dry grass from its roots and scatter it to the far ends of the field. As Jay observed the light sandy winds blowing against the Arcana trees, she realized that her love life was as dry and disheveled as the fields and pastures. She played with that thought while turning to steal another glimpse at Trent and was satisfied when she didn't experience any warm reactions.

"Is this your first trip out of the country?" Trent asked.

Jay guarded him carefully, noticing that his head was still resting comfortably against the back of the bus seat, but then slightly tilted toward her and from underneath half-lifted black lashes he held her gaze.

"This is my first trip with Myers," she answered him.

"I know this is your first trip with Myers," Trent said. "I meant did you ever travel before this trip, like a vacation out of the country?" Trent rolled his head further to the side and continued to look at her through his narrow gaze.

She was determined to keep her composure because she wouldn't have been the least surprised at him if he had decided to pick another fight with her. "Yes," she answered him as calmly as she knew how without adding any extra information.

"Where did you go?" Trent asked as if her travels were important to her trip and her work in Africa or maybe he was just trying to be polite. Jay wasn't certain of his intentions.

Jay smiled, remembering her trip to Canada the summer Gladys decided that she was going on a fishing trip. While she, Jay and Barbara were in Canada on a vacation that was not exciting to her, Gladys planned to teach her how to fish. At the end of their vacation, they were going shopping for school clothes. "I went to Canada," Jay said, still smiling and noticing Trent's narrow gaze at her.

"What city?" Trent asked her and closed his eyes as if the sun was too bright for him.

"We went to Montreal," Jay said. It had been a long time since she had thought about the vacation she hadn't enjoyed. Gladys was determined to choose her school clothes and Jay was determined that she was old enough to pick and choose what she wanted to wear. Gladys finally decided that she could choose a few outfits for herself as long as the dresses and skirts weren't too short and the slacks and jeans weren't too tight. At the age of sixteen, Jay could hardly imagine wearing outfits that were not as stylish as the girls living in her neighborhood who she went to school with.

"Did you enjoy yourself?" Trent opened his eyes, unveiling a soft brown gaze that seemed to search her soul.

"The trip was okay," Jay replied. "But I could've skipped the fishing lessons." She chuckled.

Trent's hearty chuckle reached out to her and she stilled herself and the warm previous reactions she had experienced toward him earlier that morning.

Jay would never forget her two weeks in Canada.

Over half the time she was bored because she never got to do what she wanted to do. She couldn't go to the movies because Gladys thought the film she wanted to see was too sexy. And she wasn't allowed to go out with the teens she had met while she swam in the hotel pool. "I remember that vacation," Jay said, shaking her head.

"It was that bad, huh?" Trent asked, while a hint of jolliness played around the edges of his mouth.

"The vacation wasn't bad, but it wasn't that good neither," Jay slipped her fingers together and pressed her hands against her flat stomach and relaxed against the seat's back.

"At least you learned how to fish," Trent stretched his arm across the back of the seat.

"No," Jay said, and turned away from Trent's soft gaze. She wondered where he spent his summer vacations. "Your vacations were probably fun." Jay unwound fingers and waited for a few seconds, but he did not say anything to her and she looked at him and wondered if he was paying attention.

Trent shrugged his broad shoulders. "I didn't have vacations because I had to work." Trent's lazy gaze held hers and she turned away. "If your vacation was just okay, I have to assume that you were very young," he said, and Jay didn't think he wanted to talk about himself.

"I was sixteen, and going on vacation with my grandmother was not my idea of a fun trip," Jay said, observing how he had closed his eyes again and said nothing. She couldn't believe how strict and overprotective her grandmother had been when she was growing up. She glimpsed at him, noticing another smile playing around his mouth.

He looked at her and took a deep and unsteady breath. "I believe you'll enjoy yourself while you're here," he said, touching her arm as if he was comforting her because she hadn't enjoyed her childhood vacation.

Jay laughed. He was right, but she didn't see how he could compare her vacation years ago to her working trip in Africa. His fingers were warm and firm against her skin and Jay shivered under his touch. "I believe I'll enjoy myself," she said, determined to keep her promise and distance herself from Trent. She looked down at his hand on her arm. His hand was wide, not too soft and not too hard, but firm enough to circulate the uncontrollable shivers that had been resting peacefully inside of her. Jay decided that Trent's touch was a friendly gesture and had meant nothing more to him. She covered his hand and patted it lightly. "I'm sure I will."

"I'm sorry," Trent apologized, after she had eased her arm from underneath his hand. "I didn't mean to touch . . ." His voice faltered. "I'm always interested in knowing about other people's travels," Trent finished.

At least she and Trent had two things in common, she believed, thinking that he must love his work and the opportunity to travel as much as she did. "I've always wanted to see the world," Jay replied softly.

"Then you chose the perfect career," Trent replied, and resumed his previous position, resting his head against the back of the bus seat.

"Hey, Trent, get back here, man. I need to talk to you." Jay recognized Webster's voice.

Trent got up and headed to the back. "What?" Jay heard Trent ask.

Instead of straining to listen to the conversation, she took a small square piece of sugarless gum from her bag and peeled off the wrapper as they rode into the residential community. She carefully viewed the homes, and chewed the gum slowly, allowing herself to recall her last relationship with Austin Carrington.

She and Austin's romance had been like the gum, with all the flavor, but the sweetness in their relationship was unreal. She began dating Austin during her college years. Her grandmother thought he was the perfect gentleman and she approved of him. Austin's family were pillars of the community and decent people. According to Gladys, Austin Carrington could do no wrong. Little did her grandmother know that Austin was a swindler and would blackmail anyone to get what he wanted. Not only had Austin been unfaithful during their relationship, he wanted nothing out of life but a job that provided him with nice clothes, shoes, an expensive car, and a rent-free apartment.

Six months before she left for Africa, Jay had broken off her engagement to Austin. She had discovered him in a club with his lover. He had pleaded with her to forgive him and she refused, knowing that she could not spend her life with Austin because he had no respect for her, himself or their relationship.

When she told Gladys that she couldn't marry Austin because she was no longer happy, Gladys was angry. She reminded her that Austin was the right man for her and that Jay was making a mistake.

Jay didn't have to think twice about Gladys's evaluation. If Austin was the right man for her, she knew that she would never find Mr. Right, and by the time she boarded her flight to Nigeria she had stopped missing him and healed from her hurt. She had made plans to spend her life single forever.

The bus seat sagged under Trent's weight as he sat beside her again, drawing her back from her memories of her withered relationship with Austin.

"We're finally home," Trent said, leaning close to her, stirring another swirl of new emotions inside her.

She refrained from looking at him this time and made a promise to herself that she would work, but stay away from Trent Prescott as the bus pulled up to the curve in front of the white gray trimmed two-story house.

Eighteen hours ago she had been a levelheaded woman with plans to move forward with her life, enjoy her career and spend her spare time once she returned home reopening the bed-and-breakfast. She had ultimately come to terms with her fate and had thought she had locked away her passion for the affairs of the heart. After her relationship with Austin ended, her heart had ceased to swell when she had been in the presence of an attractive man. She had been poised and polished. But Trent threatened to unwrap the lining that she had sealed her heart and she stole another quick glimpse at him. She should have asked him if he was related to the Prescotts, but instead of speaking her thoughts aloud to him, she had listened and answered his questions and wished that her heart would be still when he looked at her. Jay mused, thinking how they'd had an unpleasant beginning. She gathered her bag and assumed that maybe Trent's attitude had changed because of her apology. She had been right in her decision to say in so many words that she was sorry and afterward she learned that Trent was easier to talk to than she expected. Although the pestering thought continued to nag her and she wondered whether he was her enemy. Jay decided then that she would find out if he was a member of the enemy's family. Soon, she would have an answer to her question.

Two

As soon as the bus stopped in front of the house, Trent collected his overnight bag from underneath the seat and shouldered his laptop, cursing himself for sharing a seat with Jay Lee for the second time that day.

While Trent waited for the bus attendant to unload his bags from the bus's luggage compartment, he tried to guard himself against every thought that crossed his mind relating to Jay. Nonetheless, he lost the battle and allowed himself to think about her anyway.

The woman was like a magnet dragging him to her and he didn't like what being around her was doing to his emotions, which could have only sprang from his past romantic experiences. Jay was different from any woman he had ever met in his travels or while dating.

Jay Lee was sassy and outspoken and hadn't seemed to care that he was her supervisor. On the flip side of that, she was beautiful. Most of the women he knew were just the opposite of Jay Lee, attractive, but not for speaking up and defending themselves if they were confronted, as though they feared that he wouldn't like them. Jay hadn't seemed to care if he liked her or not. She said exactly what was on her mind and hadn't minced words when she tagged him for being a jerk.

And swaying on the wings of that, he had never believed for one second that she would ever fall over herself just to be in his presence.

However, he had strained to keep check on himself and his reactions to her. He had lost that battle because he was the one who was almost drooling. Trent found himself wanting to know every personal thing about Jay Lee. He wanted to know about her past and all of her future plans, and knowing whether she had a boyfriend back home wouldn't hurt, he thought, realizing that the last thing he needed while he was in Africa was having Miss Lee stampeding his heart like a herd of wild elephants.

Trent headed toward the house that he and the team would be sharing for the duration of their work. He lifted his eyes to a stack of clouds, thanking the heavens he'd had the good sense to reserve a hotel room in town because there was no way he could stay in the same house with Jay for three months and maintain a professional relationship with her.

As he neared the porch, more visions of Jay played tag with his reflections. Her short hair was shaved close in the back and the longer wavy top was perfect for her. Her amber complexion complemented her full blush red mouth. Trent swallowed and licked his lips, remembering her tempting smile and how he wished he knew her well enough to kiss her. He let the thought vanish. It was too soon for him to think about kissing Jay. Trent had to admit that he liked everything about Miss Jay Lee. Even the fashionable wide-legged blue jeans she was wearing made her round hips set out from her narrow waist. Shaking his head as if the quaking movement would diminish all of his visions of her, Trent wheeled his luggage inside the house.

He had just stopped at the entrance of his bedroom and was about to unlock the door when Jay stopped at her bedroom door across from him and he let out an agitated groan. As soon as everyone was settled, he was moving to his hotel room in town. He shuffled through the ring of keys on his key chain, remembering the employees' roster that Myers had given him. Myers had circled Jay Lee's name in red, telling Trent that this was her first trip with the team. Trent found the right key and unlocked the door and let himself in.

No sooner had he walked into his room and set his luggage and laptop on the floor than the telephone rang. No one but Myers could be calling him at this time of the day and was probably checking in to make sure they had arrived safely.

"Yeah?" Trent answered the call. Sure enough Myers was on the other end of the phone. "Myers, we're fine, and I promise you that no one will miss the meetings," Trent said, while he continued to listen to the professor dish out orders.

Trent raked his fingers through his hair. "You told me once before that this was Jay Lee's first trip," he said as held the receiver between his shoulder and ear while he unbuckled his belt. "Myers, Jay will be fine. She's working with Rose," Trent said. It was just like the professor, Trent mused, tacking on extra responsibilities, telling him to make sure he escorted Jay when she went out at night. He already had a full schedule, and he would have loved to spend his evenings alone or free time with someone other than one of the team members. Now, he was stuck with orders from Myers to baby-sit Jay. *And you can hardly wait to take her out.* Trent dismissed the thought. "Hold on, Myers," he said, laying the phone receiver on the top of the

dresser and pulling his shirt over his head before tossing it toward the bed and missing it by a foot.

"What were you saying?" Trent asked the professor
once the central air was blowing against his bare back
and chest. "Jay will get the same instructions." Trent
paused. "I promise you, I will make sure she is not
alone. But, I think that she can take care of herself,"
Trent added, and listened to Myers again. "Okay, I'll
call you." Trent finished his conversation with Matthew
Myers on other research business and hung up.

He propped both hands on his hips. His feelings for
Jay were an indication that he'd been working too
hard, or he maybe it was because he hadn't had a serious relationship in a while. Therefore, what he
thought was threatening his buried passion was only
his imagination. Reckoning with those thoughts, Trent
reminded himself that Jay had made herself clear that
she hadn't liked him much. She probably had good
reasons, Trent decided, recalling how hard he had
been on her when they first met.

Trent crossed the room and opened the blinds, letting in a stream of yellow sun rays, along with a perfect
view of the Nigerian suburban community.

Like always, he found himself caught in a tangled
web when he had let Myers talk him into working three
months with the team since his resignation from a supervisor's position at Myers Research a year ago.

His property investment business had prospered
since he no longer worked full time for the research
company. Myers hadn't liked that Trent had resigned
and had made him feel guilty, reminding him how he
had taken Trent under his wings in the early days. The
least Trent could do was to fill in for him on the marriage project for three months. Trent could hardly re-

fuse the man who had played a huge part in his life, giving him an opportunity that he might never have been able to achieve without his help.

So, he left his growing business in the hands of his small competent staff, thinking that while he was doing Myers a favor, he would also get a chance to relax and Nigeria would be work with the added benefit of a well-deserved vacation. He could not have been more mistaken.

The minute Myers made him feel guilty, Trent should've told him to go to hell, and gone ahead with his plans to move his business to New Jersey instead of traipsing off to Nigeria. If he had done that, he wouldn't be in Africa putting up with Myers' abuse.

Trent kicked off his shoes and pulled off his socks, before discarding his pants and headed to the bathroom for his shower, all the while blaming Myers for everything that had happened to him, beginning from the time he boarded the plane until he met Jay Lee.

Trent pushed his telephone conversation with Myers to the back of his mind and mentally prepared for the meeting he was expected to have with the team after lunch.

He discarded the remainder of his clothes, turned on the water and stepped into the shower, allowing the cool water to soak his body as he thought how marriage was the last thing on his mind.

The idea of holy matrimony had quickly vanished when he had arrived home from a business trip and discovered his ex-fiancé Sonya with her lover.

At one point, his trust for women had escaped him and he was left with no hope but to stay a bachelor for life. It was his best friend Webster who lectured him on trust. All women were not dishonest, Webster told him, and the least Trent could do was start dating again.

So Trent began dating. Evenings spent in a nice restaurant sharing a meal with a lovely lady, dancing and sometimes attending a play were fine with Trent, but the minute his date began to make sexual advances, he froze. He couldn't trust himself enough to accept the affection offered to him.

Hours ago he had met Jay, and his hopes began to rise again along with his libido. Still, the questions lingered in the back of his mind: Was Jay like his former lover? How many women were as unfaithful as Sonya? She had been prepared to marry him, knowing that she had a lover, and the whole idea of her plan still made him sick.

Trent stepped out of the shower, dried and then shaved. Just as he was pulling on a pair of jeans, he heard the door across the hall close with a firm thump. Jay was either returning to her room or leaving, and he hoped she didn't have sightseeing plans before he had a chance to meet with the team.

He needed to stop her if she was going out, and as much as he didn't want to, he knew he had to apologize to her for his actions earlier that morning. He had lost his temper, barked orders and gotten upset when she told him off. He had thought his reasons were valid. She had lifted a part of him from a dark place and he didn't like the feeling.

Trent closed his pants and pulled on a fresh T-shirt, before opening his door, crossing the hall, and knocking on Jay's door. After the second knock and still no response, he was beginning to believe that Jay had left. He was about to go outside and look for her when she opened her door.

"Yes?" Jay stood in the half-opened door.

Trent caught himself staring at her, and for the first time in many years, he was at a loss for words. She was wearing a short shirt that was a fraction away from being a brassiere and that unveiled the flatness of her stomach and her narrow waist. "I need to apologize." He finally managed to speak after a couple of swallows that seemed to loosen his vocal cords.

"What are you apologizing to me for?" Jay tilted her head to one side and looked at him.

Trent watched her dark red mouth tilt into a faint smile and he wanted to reach out, pull her to him and kiss her. But instead, he lowered his gaze, observing her firm, shapely legs, that were partially covered by a pair of denim shorts. Ten candy-red toenails complemented her smooth bare feet. "I'm not usually crabby," he said, hoping she would forgive him for his rudeness.

"You could've fooled me," she said.

"Can I come in?" Trent asked, hoping Jay wouldn't slam the door in his face. For a moment, her faint smile faded, and she looked as if her intention was to do more than to slam the door in his face.

"Come in," she offered, pushing her hands inside her shorts pocket.

He walked in, taking a quick survey of the room and inhaling the scent of soft perfume. "I didn't mean to make you uncomfortable or to come off as if I'm trying to make you lose your job," he said, shifting his gaze to the vanity near the window that was supplied with enough cosmetics to last through the winter months.

"I was beginning to think that maybe I had signed on to work with a tyrant," Jay said, going over to the bed and taking a piece of luggage to the closet.

"No, you didn't, and again I'm sorry," Trent said.

"Your apology is accepted. If you will excuse me, Mr. Prescott." She held the door open for him.

"Wait." Trent couldn't believe he was asking her to wait. Was he losing his mind? "Everyone calls me Trent," he said, scanning the room.

"Trent, I'm very busy," Jay said, still holding the door open for him.

"Let me make it up to you," Trent continued. He was positive now that something was wrong with his mind, and that his actions had nothing to do with Myers asking him to make sure all the women were safe. "Will you have dinner with me tonight?" Trent asked.

"Hum . . . I don't know. I'll have to think about it," Jay said with more enthusiasm than he expected.

"All right," Trent said, wishing he could remain planted in her room for the rest of the day. "Will I have an answer before six this evening?" he pried, refusing to leave until she gave him a definite answer that would confirm she was accepting his dinner invitation.

"I said I'll think about it." Jay drew the door open wider and waited for him to leave.

"I'll see you at the meeting," Trent said, and walked out into the hallway.

Once inside his room, again he prepared for the meeting with the team. Trent was sure he'd lost a brain cell or two while traveling to Africa because he had not intended to ask Jay out to dinner. If he didn't know any better, he would think Myers had set him up with Jay. He slammed his fist into his palm. "Old bastard!"

Myers had been his anthropology professor and at one time, his college advisor. Before he graduated, Trent had the opportunity, through a program, to travel a couple of summers abroad with Myers on excavating assignments, and later, after the professor opened the research center which provided universities and colleges with the knowledge he'd acquired from his cultural research trips, he'd hired Webster and Trent along with a few others to work and travel with him.

Several years later, Trent decided that he could help more in America. With the money he had earned from his trips around the world, he bought dilapidated buildings in cities and sold them to low-income buyers at a cost they could afford, making it possible for men and women to own homes and businesses without paying top price.

Later, he'd ventured further, buying commercial property in upscale urban neighborhoods and then renting at a price that he knew customers could afford.

Trent hadn't just happened upon venture buying and selling by accident. His family had managed to lose everything they owned, and he had his uncle to thank for that disaster. He was eleven years old when his uncle managed to lose the last piece of property that he owned. And since his father worked at the business that his uncle lost, his father was out of work, and for a while Trent and his family had struggled to survive. Trent, his sister, and their parents were almost left homeless. If it hadn't been for his father's army buddy, they would have probably slept on the street at least for a short while.

But Trent's father, who was a determined and strong man, reckoned to rise from the fall and took a job helping to restore old buildings and homes. Trent remembered those days when he assisted his father, working on the weekends and after school once his homework was completed. He should have been out playing basketball with his best friend Webster Nelson, or listening to his favorite music. But he couldn't afford to play, and taking a summer vacation was a luxury he and his family were unable to afford. Trent remembered promising himself that once he became a man, he would never be poor again.

Two years passed before his father, Christopher Prescott, had saved enough money to purchase a home for the family and a year later before his father purchased a small apartment building. It was a building that Trent had help to restore and his father was able to purchase the building from the owner at an affordable price.

With that task accomplished, his father attended night classes, learning to manage his growing business. He encouraged their mother, Flora Prescott, to do the same, and promised to disown Trent and his sister if they didn't graduate high school and get into college.

Trent didn't need to be threatened. It frightened him to be poor. He remembered worrying at his early age about where his family would live once the business was lost, a concern that only his parents should have thought about. It was then that Trent decided that a life of poverty was not for him and unlike his father, he would depend on himself for his well-being and not rely on the promises of others. Thoughts of owning his business stayed with him over the years until finally he slipped off the anthropology trail, cutting himself a successful path to riches and a prosperous life.

Trent gathered his attache case and headed for the door, thinking he should at this moment be in a city buying and selling properties instead of traipsing around Africa supervising a marriage research project, and thinking about Jay Lee who probably wasn't giving him a second thought.

He left his room, and gave a firm tap against Jay's door. She was required to attend the meeting, and she had better not be wearing those shorts and top. He toyed with that idea, along with visions of Jay's round firm thighs and her nonchalant attitude when he stopped by her room earlier to apologize for his bad behavior.

Trent reached the area at the side of the house and found most of the staff seated on the grass instead of the lawn chairs and picnic tables near the lagoon behind the house. He noticed Jay among the crew wearing the shorts and top. She wasn't dressed any differently from the other women, it was just that she bothered him in a way that he would rather not think about.

Trent opened a folder, took out the meeting's agenda and proceeded to remind the team of the rules, while at the same time taking careful measures to avoid making any eye contact with Jay. "You guys need to listen because I'm not repeating myself," Trent said when he noticed that several of the members were holding a conversation among themselves. He went over the house rules, which were not complicated. Everyone was required to keep their rooms tidy, breakfast was served every morning at six, and the bus and boat schedules were on the table in the foyer.

Trent informed the team that he would not spend every night in the house because he had a hotel room in town. If anyone needed to contact him, he would give them his card and telephone numbers.

"Of course, he would have a hotel room in town," Sonya Smith spoke up but Trent chose to ignore her.

"Jay Lee is the newest member to the team and she's working with Rose on the marriage project," he reminded everyone as he caught a quick glimpse of Jay raking her fingers through her short wavy hair.

"It's too bad all of us didn't get the chance to work with Rose and have lunch with the brides-to-be." Trent recognized Sonya's voice again.

"Girlfriend got it made in the shade, right, Miss Jay Lee?" Sonya's friend was seated across from Jay and offered a snide comment.

Trent noticed that Jay ignored the women's comments as she listened to him go over a few other details, such as reminding the team to be careful, and warning the women that having an escort while they were out at night was essential unless they wanted to be mistaken for streetwalkers by the police and hauled off to jail. Renting automobiles was another issue he brought to the team's attention. If anyone chose to rent an automobile while in the country, Trent warned, they should guard against swindlers, whose con was to sometimes oil the brakes on an unsuspecting motorist and charge a healthy price, to repair the damage. Just before he ended the meeting, he reminded the team that exchanging money on the black market was a definite no-no.

With that done, he walked over and joined Jay under the Red Flame tree. "Have you made up your mind about dinner tonight?" He planted his hands on the tree's trunk just above Jay's head, and towered over her, preventing her from moving and forcing her to look at him. He hoped that she wouldn't refuse him the opportunity to share a meal with her.

"Trent, I think I'll stay in tonight," Jay said.

"Are you sure you want to stay in tonight?" He asked her, realizing that Jay probably wasn't aware that team members usually went out on their first night upon arriving in a new country or state. Then he decided that maybe Jay didn't want to go out with him period. "After a nap, everyone goes out the first evening," Trent said.

"No, I wasn't aware of that." She looked up, her gaze settling on him. He hoped that she hadn't noticed the ruggedness that had captured him by surprise.

"Then we'll talk later," Trent promised her and headed toward the back of the house and sat on the porch steps. He tried to turn his attention to anything but Jay. He listened to the humming roar of a speed boat's motor and the faraway cries and laughter of the African children in the Nigerian community. But it was not long before his mind went back to thoughts of Jay. He suspected that she might have been tired from the trip, as they all were, but he couldn't deny the fact that he actually wanted to go out with her. It had been a long time since he had met a woman that interested him enough to ask to dinner without Webster hassling him to get back into the game, which was common for his best friend since Webster Nelson didn't mind his own business. Webster had even questioned him while they were in the airport about the fight he had picked with Jay. Trent didn't have an explanation, at least not one that he wanted to share with his longtime friend. However, he was certain that he liked Jay Lee, and was almost sure she had refused his dinner invitation because of his attitude toward her this morning. It had occurred to him that Jay had dismissed the heated discussion between them at the airport.

Trent rested his elbows on his thigh as he watched Sonya stand on the bank near the lagoon. He covered his face with his hands. Sonya was an obscure memory from his past, wherever he went, she followed. She was determined to keep herself in his thoughts whether his thoughts of her were good or bad. It seemed not to have mattered to her, but he was also a determined and patient man, willing to wait for the right woman with whom he would enjoy spending time with. He had once tried to have a life with Sonya, but she had rejected him in ways that he never knew could be so painful.

Today, he was wading his way back from the heart-wrenching agony and not because his choice was very thought out, but because in his soul it felt right being be close to Jay Lee and wanting to know her. He planned to take one step at a time.

Three

In the week since they had arrived, Trent hadn't kept his promise to talk to Jay later and she hadn't seen him all week. But Jay understood, because everyone had been busy, especially she and Rose. She hadn't had the time to check Trent's background and had been too exhausted in the evenings to find out if he was related to the Prescott family that had murdered her parents. She had been exhausted her first night after they had arrived in Africa, and afterwards it seemed that all she had done was work, eat and sleep. When she was finished with her work at the end of the day, she dropped her report inside the case on the wall next to Trent's bedroom and turned in for the evening.

But she had no complaints about her work. All week Jay had enjoyed herself, visiting the young women who were preparing for marriage in the neighborhood. The women had shown off their new up-do hairstyles that were symbols of womanhood, individuality and beauty.

Scarring the skin was another important ritual that many of the women chose, especially those who were keeping to their cultural traditions. Thin incisions were etched into several of the women's cheeks and dusted with dark powder, another indication of a woman's beauty, womanhood and her individuality. Jay noticed that even the women wore scarification at the top of their breast, not only for beautification. The thin-etched incisions were symbols indicating that the African women promised to keep secrets close to their breasts.

She also met young women who had spent up to eighteen months living in fattening huts and they were pleased with the weight they had gained. The young women's ankles and necks were fleshy with rolls of excess plumpness, which was the ramification of the ritual that allowed them to feast on fattening foods and rich milk to assure themselves that they would give birth to many healthy babies once they were married.

Jay was amazed at their culture and tradition and she enjoyed talking and listening to them speak about their dreams to have a wonderful family. Many of the women Jay talked to owned clothing and gift shops, or restaurants, but most intended to continue working after they were married. Then there were other women who had different opinions as to how they wanted to spend their lives. At the first chance, they had moved to the city or to another country. However, the sense of family for these women was also strong and they were aware that marriage brought about more relatives, which often meant more wealth.

The end of the work week finally arrived. Jay sat beneath one of the Red Flame trees that stood on the side of the house. Its long limbs were clustered with bright red leaves and reached out across the grass, fanning her with a cool breeze.

All of her worries about Trent seemed to have faded, leaving her calm and more peaceful than she had been in a long time. Jay was certain that her worries concerning Trent were less annoying to her because she hadn't had time to think about anything other than her work.

So, she sat on the rich green grass noticing the plants and Red Flame trees surrounding the side of the house with a beauty that seemed to sooth her heart and soul. She was content and she intended to savor every moment while she was working and living in Nigeria.

"Good afternoon," Trent spoke to the team, beginning the meeting and drawing Jay out of her peacefulness.

Jay noticed that Trent's khaki pants and shirt, and his matching khaki cap made him look as if he had just returned from a safari. He took off his sunglasses and slid them into his shirt pocket.

"Hey, baby." Sonya Smith's seductive greeting brought on a round of whistles and applause from the team members. Everyone, except for Jay, and Sonya noticed that Trent ignored her greeting.

"From the reports I've received, I'm pleased that every one of you has been working hard. Thank you." Trent scanned the crowd and Jay's eyes locked with his for a moment before she looked away. "Your care packages are outside of your rooms," Trent said to the group.

"Did we get anything good or different, Prescott?" asked a young man that Jay had seen around the office many times.

"Man, you know it's the same old stuff . . . antiseptics, Band-aids and stuff like that," someone offered.

"Please do not forget the birth control pills and the condoms," a woman said, between chips of laughter.

"I don't know what Matthew Myers is thinking about. He's acting like folks 'round here is going to be making love." Another one of Jay's female team members remarked in a loud voice which raised more chuckles from over half the team.

"Speak for yourself," Sonya said.

Jay remembered Myers' discussion during one of their meetings just before the trip. Myers had charged that he realized, on nights when lovers were together, passion usually arose and he wanted everyone to return home healthy.

"You never know," Trent said, "you might need that stuff."

Jay caught him looking at her and she turned away. She hadn't given sexual protection and birth control a second thought when Myers broached the subject. Her plans were to work, and besides that, the men that she had worked with for a year were nice and friendly, but she had never thought once about dating any of them.

"Can I have my meeting back?" Trent said and Jay noticed his serious expression.

"Of course you can have your meeting, and me too." Sonya exclaimed.

Trent didn't say anything to address Sonya's flirting comment. He simply moved onto the next subject, telling the women and men to watch for purse snatchers, and that it had been reported to him that a few of the women from the team had been seen walking alone at night. Again, he warned the women to be careful. Trent ended that part of the meeting with a suggestion that the team would support the children in the neighborhood who often sold gum, candy and other treats in order to earn spending money. With that said, he opened the floor for comments.

"Prescott, we understand that it's warm weather over here, but these women need to wear more clothes."

Jay didn't overlook Trent's sweeping gaze and she assumed that he might be thinking her shorts-set was a little too skimpy.

"What do you think we're wearing now?" Jay couldn't help herself, but she had to comment.

"Next to nothing," another man answered.

"Ah, shut up." Rose said, pulling at the edge of her green shorts.

"Yeah, well," Trent said, and changing the subject, began discussing the proposal parade, reminding the team members of the time the event would begin, and who would be stationed in which particular area. He expected perfect camera shots, and notes at the end of the day. "I don't want to see any mistakes."

Jay studied Trent's warning carefully. The educational videos were being designed for university and college classes, and he wanted only the best work.

After much discussion on behavior and conduct, the meeting was adjourned. Jay and Rose were assigned to visit two young ladies. One woman was planning her wedding, and another woman would be getting married.

Jay and Rose discussed their assignment, when Rose asked Jay afterwards would she go out with her and Webster for drinks and dinner at the Green Spot Club. Jay was telling Rose that she would give her a call if she decided to go with them, when Trent walked over and stood beside her.

"Instead of you calling me, I'll call your room

around five, and you'd better say yes." Rose flashed Jay a friendly wide grin, and began moving toward the house.

"Okay," Jay said, hoping she would be finished with her research in time to enjoy an evening out with her teammates.

The crowd thinned and Jay started walking toward the edge of the slopping yard that led off into a lagoon surrounded by bunches of colorful flowers, green plants and trees. She allowed the peaceful flow of waves lapping against the water to relax her and instead of going to her room as she had planned, she sat on the edge of the bank listening to the boat transporting passengers to the city. As she listened to the timbre clamor against the sweet sounds of exotic birds, Jay still couldn't believe she was living her dream. She allowed the flow of water lapping against a cluster of rocks to calm her senses even more, delivering her into total peace.

"Can I talk to you?" Trent cut into her serenity as he squatted beside her and braced his back against the tree.

"It depends on what you want to talk about," Jay said, turning away from the peaceful water and gazed at Trent, then reminded herself that staring was impolite.

"Can we go out tonight?" Trent asked her.

Jay reached her fingers to the nape of her neck and smoothed down the short, even hair. "I'm really not sure if I'm going out tonight," she said, lifting her eyes to meet the softness in his brown gaze. "Maybe we can go out another time, Trent," Jay said. "I did promise Rose that if I went out tonight, it would be with her and Webster."

"Three's a crowd," Trent said, removing his cap and placing it onto his knee.

"I know, Trent, but I'm not sure if I'm going with them," Jay said, feeling Trent's knee rest against her thigh. His fresh soapy scent fused with traces of aftershave also reminded her that he was sitting too close to her. And even though she was about to investigate him in order to learn if he was related to the Prescott family that she disliked, she was still attracted to him. Jay looked straight out at the water, attempting to deny herself the truth about her emotions and hoping he was not related to the Prescott family.

"I don't think you want to go out with me, Jay," Trent leaned away from her then and watched her through a narrow gaze. "Am I right?"

Jay studied him without opposition, after all, she didn't know if he was the enemy or not, but she hadn't missed the seductiveness in his eyes either. "I would love to go out with you, Trent," Jay said, meaning every word. "Ooh, but . . ." Her voice tapered to an ebbing flow.

"Jay, 'ooh—but', is not the answer that I'm looking for." Trent's hand touched the top of her thigh.

Jay took in a deep breath and let the shiver from his touch lose its effect on her. If he touched her again, she didn't know what she would do. "If you stop by the Green Spot Club tonight, I promise to have a glass of wine with you and maybe one dance." She stood up from her comfortable seated position and started to move away from the tree, when Trent stood and blocked her from moving farther.

"Okay, a glass of wine and one dance," Trent said, moving in closer to her. He then took a step back, freeing her to leave him. "And I'm not asking you out

because I want to make sure that you have an escort."
Trent's smile lifted the edges of his black mustache.

"I know, because you don't baby-sit," Jay reminded
him.

A soft chuckling sound arose from the deep part of
his throat and floated out to her. "We had a rough
start, but I want to get to know you," Trent said.

"Our first meeting was not a pleasant one," she
agreed.

"Which means that we should start over." Trent suggested to her, and raising his arm, rested his hand on
the tree's trunk, blocking her once more from leaving
him.

"Maybe . . ." Jay stopped talking to Trent and
looked at him. Why should she waste precious time
and money searching for Trent's hometown and the
family he might have been related to when she could
ask him.

"What?" Trent held her gaze, appearing interested
in what she was about to say to him.

"Where're you from?" Jay asked him.

"Now I know your reasons for not wanting to go out
with me," Trent folded his arms across his chest.

"Really?" Jay asked and waited for him to tell her
the name of the town and state he lived.

"Yeah, you don't want to go out with me because
I'm not a home boy." Trent's amused smile threatened
to annoy Jay, but she was making progress. If he didn't
live in New Jersey, he probably was from Delaware and
she had been right all along. Jay felt anger singe
through her and she calmed herself.

"That's not the reason," Jay said, wanting Trent to
be serious instead of playing games with her.

"What's your reason, Jay?"

Trent didn't sound any less amused than he had been earlier, which was beginning to annoy her even more. However, Jay had no intentions of giving up on finding out who he was and it made no difference if he told her or not. "Just answer the question," she said.

Another warm chuckle arose from him and floated out to her. "You're serious."

"Yes, I am serious," Jay said, when Sonya Smith interrupted them.

Jay knew she should have penned Trent down and asked if he was related to the Prescotts who had once lived in New Jersey when she had the chance. She had waited too long and now the only recourse was to search for the Prescotts. "I'll see you later," Jay said, her hopes diminishing because she hadn't learned whether or not he was related to the family. Nevertheless, all arrows were pointing to Delaware where she was certain Gladys said that the family had moved.

"Jay, if you're not at Green Spot when I get there I'll stop by your room tonight," Trent promised her and took her hand in his and squeezed it lightly while talking to her.

She didn't need him stopping by her room tonight, even though she knew he was responsible for the team, she was sure she would get through the night without a visit from him, and she wished he wouldn't touch her.

Jay moved away from Trent and headed inside the house through the back entrance leaving him and Sonya to talk.

"Uh-uh, uh!" Jay lamented once she was walking down the hall to her room. *I will give just about anything if Trent's not related to the family because I really like him.* Jay admitted that thought while she lifted the box sitting outside her door and carried it inside, promising herself that she would open it later. Right now, she had more pressing business to attend to.

Jay turned on her laptop and went to work, searching and digging into the past to learn the truth. Jay felt that she was on a scavenger hunt as she began her search in Delaware, foraging through a list of surnames beginning with the letter *P* until finally she found T. Prescott. *Oh yeah!* She pondered in relief, reveling for a second in her satisfaction, then all too soon she calmed her joy. It was too soon to celebrate. Her work would be complete when she could verify that she was speaking to one of Trent's family members.

Jay's exhilaration subsided, and she rankled with the irritation that had begun to course through her, from remembering the distress she had observed her grandmother suffer over the years because the memory of her son and daughter-in-law's death had been almost too painful for Gladys to bear. As Jay grew older, she repressed her need to mention her parents to Gladys even when there were things that she wanted to know about their deaths that hadn't made sense to her.

"Jay." She heard Rose outside her door, and went to see what she wanted.

"Hi. What's happening?" Jay asked.

"I stopped by to make sure you were still going out," Rose said, gesturing a finger backward and Jay suspected the Green Spot Club was in that direction.

"Yes," Jay said. "What time are you going?"

Rose checked her watch. "We're leaving in an hour, or an hour and a half."

"I'll meet you out front," Jay said, satisfied that she had time to make a few telephone calls before she dressed for the evening. She hurried to the telephone to call the number she had found in her search.

After several unanswered rings, a man finally answered the telephone. He sounded old and jaded and she felt her heart hammering in her chest, hoping that this man was Trent's father answering her call. "I'm calling for Trent or Mr. Flint Prescott," Jay said, remembering that she had once heard her grandmother mention years ago that Flint Prescott had been her father's main enemy. She considered that if she asked for both men she would at least get one of them because she knew Trent was in Africa.

"There's no one here by those names," the man said. "You have the wrong number."

"Are you related to the men?" Jay asked, hoping she hadn't hit a dead end.

"No, I have never heard of the men before," the man said.

"Thank you." She hung up and looked at the clock. A sense of defeat swept through her and the milestone she thought she had accomplished was simply a turning point to continue her search. Her obsession to find the Prescotts or anyone related to him and also being successful in her quest was beginning to agitate her. She was beginning to wonder if the gentleman had been honest.

Jay suspended the thought. It was getting late and she wanted to go to the club with Rose. But regardless of her promises, and her need to know, she admitted that she couldn't suppress her feelings and the instant attraction that haunted her about Trent. *Ah-he's so fine!* She allowed herself a pleasurable moment to reflect slowly on how she had been drawn to him even before he had introduced himself to her.

Jay got off the bed and went to take a shower, stopping at the closet to take a brown low-back dress off the hanger, realizing as she surveyed the dress, that it might need ironing. She was unable to shake off Trent's image playing in her mind and how without warning, her passionate feelings were sweeping her heart of any ill feelings she was entertaining regarding Trent just because his last name was Prescott.

Jay carried the dress to her bed and placed it on the yellow floral bedspread, and went to the shower, telling herself that Trent Prescott probably stood too close to all the women he talked to. This was probably a habit he had acquired long ago, and again she reminded herself that it was her own starving passion that was turning Trent's easiness into a big deal.

Jay was sure that if she searched further, she would have found the Prescotts somewhere in Delaware before the day ended. But the search from Africa to the states was getting expensive. She made a mental note to call Barbara and ask for her assistance in finding out where the family had moved when they left New Jersey.

With plans to forget about the past and enjoy her evening, Jay put on the dress, and was about to zip the back when the telephone rang. Rose wanted to know if she had brought along a fingernail clipper and if she had, she would be down in a few minutes. Jay hung up before taking the nail clipper from the manicure box, then reached back to zip the dress when the zipper stuck between the brown material. Fearing that she would rip the dress if she tried to pull the material over her hips to free it, she decided to wait for Rose.

Three minutes hadn't passed when she heard the knock on her door. This was just like Rose, always on time. Jay grabbed the nail clipper and hurried to the door. "Trent!" Jay hoped her surprise at his unexpected visit didn't show much, as a new surge of warmth sailed through her, and for good reason, she mused, admiring how handsome he looked dressed in dark pants and a shirt. His expensive shoes were buffed to a perfect shine and his hair looked as if it had been cut only minutes before.

"Were you expecting someone?" Trent asked her, holding out a schedule for the proposal parade to her.

"It's none of your business, but I was expecting Rose." Jay took the paper he handed her. "Will you do me a favor and pull the material out of the zipper for me?" She turned her back to him before he could answer yes or no and waited for him.

Trent's fingers stroked her bare skin and Jay closed her eyes, as he fiddled with the zipper and the material until finally he had freed the material from the zipper's trap. "Thank you," Jay said, allowing herself to give him another admiring glance while she inhaled his manly cologne. "What's the name of your cologne?" She asked him a question that she didn't mind asking since she loved a man that smelled good.

Trent held his head close to her and whispered the name of the fragrance to her, so close to her lips she could smell his mint breath. "So, who are you waiting for?" he said, still close to her, making it hard for her to speak.

"I told you before that it's none of your business," Jay said playfully with a smile.

"I'm telling you, baby, everything that goes on around here is my business." Trent backed away from her then, and reached out and touched the side of her face.

Jay looked away from him because she was too uncomfortable with his magnetic gaze and the way being in his presence made her feel.

Before she could tell him that he could not have

been serious because whoever visited her was her business, she heard Rose knocking outside.

"Hi, Trent," Rose spoke while Jay handed her the fingernail clipper.

"Rose," Trent spoke.

"So, you're not going out with us?" Rose asked Jay.

"Yes," Jay said. "I'll see you in a few minutes." She glanced at Trent.

"Jay, don't make us late, we would like to get a good table," Rose said, her eyes switching from Jay to Trent.

"Rose, I am not going to make you late," Jay replied, and waited until she left and then held the door open for Trent. "I'll see you later for that dance and drink," she promised him.

"I'll be there as soon as I finish," Trent said, touching her waist with a warm stroke, igniting familiar passion she always felt when his fingers grazed her. But Jay kept her feelings to herself. She was in no position to love a man like Trent Prescott. Or was she?

"What're you working on?" He asked her, and started walking toward her computer.

"I was working on a personal project," Jay said, rushing to turn the laptop off before Trent saw the list of names she had pulled to the screen, and at the same time, wishing she could ask him if he was from Delaware. Tonight she would inquire, and hopefully she would have her answers to the one question that had nagged her since she had been in Nigeria.

"What's the project?" Trent asked.

"Nothing that you need to know about right now," Jay said.

If she told him without proof to back up her accusations, that she suspected he was a member of the family that had murdered her parents and walked away without spending time in prison for the crime, he would probably be insulted and think she was crazy. Jay didn't want to think of all the other awful possibilities that could arise and cause her mental pain if she learned that he was related to the family. But because she had no proof, she was unable to share her suspicions concerning his background, leaving her powerless to answer his question. Jay turned off the computer. "Trent, I'm meeting Rose and Webster outside in a few minutes," she said, going to the closet for a pair of brown heels and then to the vanity for her comb.

"Have fun, Jay, and be careful," he said as he walked out of her room without looking back at her.

Jay locked the door behind him realizing that Trent Prescott posed a problem for her heart. He was relentless, asked too many questions, and was determined to stay in her life whether she wanted him to or not. She didn't bother to apply any other make-up except just enough lipstick to add color to her lips.

Ten minutes later, Jay walked into the Green Spot Club with Rose and Webster. She hated being a third wheel, but going out with them was better than staying in her room.

The Green Spot Club reminded Jay of the clubs back home. Dim lights encircled the bar and dance floor while soft white lights illuminated the dining area, casting an inviting glow over the diners as they enjoyed their meals. Harmonious sounds of slow jams filtered through the room, intermingling with gushes of laughter, conversation and ice cubes clattering against glasses and fusing a gay atmosphere to the surroundings. The ambiance of closeness engulfed Jay and she felt as if she had returned home, joining her brothers and sisters in an old fashioned family reunion.

Jay, Rose, and Webster were about to place their orders when she looked over the top of her menu and noticed Trent walking toward their table. Her heart went through its regular round of flutters, making her heart palpitate like a teen with a bad crush on a teenage boy who wouldn't give her a second thought.

"It's about time you showed up," Webster said as Trent pulled up a chair and sat across the table facing Jay.

"I know I'm late," Trent said, and cast a brown gaze at Jay. As much as she tried to ignore his tender glances, she was finding it impossible to avoid him.

"I was beginning to think that you weren't going to join us and help Jay celebrate her first night out in Nigeria." Rose directed her comment to Trent, then she turned to Jay and chuckled softly.

"Jay," Trent spoke to her and his voice sounded as if it held a sensual challenge.

"Hi," Jay said, giving Trent a friendly smile when she spoke to him.

All through dinner the four of them made light conversation until their tete-a-tete turned to Rose and Webster's engagement and Jay noticed that Trent was almost too quiet. Finally, Webster shifted the subject, and soon the four of them finished their dinner in silence while they enjoyed the music.

"May I have this dance?" Webster asked Rose when they were finished eating. Without speaking, Rose got up and she and Webster headed out to the dance floor, leaving Jay and Trent alone.

The attraction Jay felt for Trent was strong and she knew she couldn't wait any longer to find out who he was. "I'm still interested in knowing the name of your hometown," Jay said, now that she had the time to pump him for information.

"Why do you want to know?" Trent asked, a hint of seriousness appeared to sparkle in his eyes.

Jay reached across the table and touched his hand and she stroked his skin lightly, not because she was coaxing information from him, but because she wanted to feel his skin against her own.

"Is it a secret?" She let the smile play across her lips as she drew her fingers away from his hand.

"No, it's not a secret," Trent said. "I live in Canada, but I'll be moving to your town soon," he said, getting up and moving around the table and sitting in a chair beside her. He lifted the wine bottle and filled their glasses with more wine.

Jay finally had the answer to her question and she was beginning to feel guilty for suspecting him to be a member of the enemy's family. "Did you ever live in Delaware?" Jay asked him, thinking it was wise to pry further.

"Well"—Trent spread his hands—"when I worked for Myers full-time, I'd stop by his office in Delaware and help out, and once when I was a kid, I visited Wilmington."

Jay was beginning to feel confident and she felt herself vibrate with joy. If she had known that the answers to her questions were this easy, she wouldn't have wasted an expensive telephone call to Delaware, disturbing innocent people with her concerns. Still, another endless question hammered her, but she ignored the query playing at the edge of her thoughts. It hadn't been long since she had called the Prescotts in Delaware and the gentleman had assured her that he did not know Trent or Flint Prescott. At last, she was satisfied. Maybe if nothing more, she could at least speak to her supervisor without thinking the worst about him.

"Why do you want to know?" Trent asked her.

"I was curious," Jay said, not wanting to get into the old family feud that she should have not even considered when she heard Trent's surname. Of course, it was only natural that she was suspicious of him. "I told you that I was in Canada and you could've told me that you lived there," Jay said.

Trent pressed closer to her and reached for her, folding her hand into his. "Maybe I should've told you, but you didn't ask," he replied. His voice was smooth and steady.

The music stopped and soon after, another old slow jam began playing. Without asking if she wanted to dance, Trent stood and drew Jay up with him, and together they walked out onto the dance floor. They were like a couple in love as he slipped his arms around her, drawing her to him. It didn't make sense to her to deny the familiar tremor as his fingers grazed her back as if they had danced before and for the first time in a long time, Jay felt lighthearted and she was enjoying herself. She slipped her arms as far around his wide back as she could and held him tight.

Trent let out a muffled groan and pulled her even closer to him, touching his lips to her cheek as an electric shiver vibrated through her. "You should be careful how tight you hold me," he whispered in her ear.

"Why?" Jay leaned back and asked Trent.

He drew her close again. "Because . . ." Trent's low voice rumbled against her cheek then ebbed to a silent flow.

To Jay, the music ended too quickly as she and Trent ambled back to their table and talked about everything from how nice it was to work on the projects to how it was to be in Nigeria and when another old song played that they both loved, Jay and Trent danced again.

Later, she and Trent danced several more dances in between drinking a couple of glasses of wine until he asked her if she was ready to go home. Jay wasn't exactly ready to go. She could've danced with Trent all night, but not without hoping that their relationship would be more than just supervisor to employee. Instead of wishing she could enjoy more of his company she found Rose and told her that she and Trent were leaving for the evening and that she would see her tomorrow.

Jay relished the night breeze while she and Trent walked back to the team's house. His arm encircled her as they walked quietly beneath the star-studded sky and for the first time in a long time, Jay Lee cherished the evening and hopefully the beginning of a new friendship.

"Have you ever been married?" Trent asked her, as if he had waited to ask her that question long after he had scanned her finger for a wedding ring the morning they first met.

"No," Jay said, remembering clearly the scene they had made with each other that day. "I have never been married," she said, realizing that if her state of matrimony would have been left to Gladys Lee, she would've been Mrs. Austin Carrington, and would probably be expecting their first child by now.

"Do you have any children?" Trent asked.

"No." Jay stopped walking and looked at him. "Do you have children?" she asked, wondering if he had ever been married.

"None that I know of," he said, with a warm chuckle

that floated out against the night. Then with more serious conviction, he answered her question. "No."

"I don't see a ring on your finger, but that doesn't mean that you're not married," Jay said, running her finger across his ring finger.

"No, I'm not married," Trent said.

The closer they came to the house, the slower they walked. Jay didn't want the evening to end and to think she had almost allowed her questions and fears concerning the past to deprive her of an evening that she would probably remember for a long time. It seemed that something special was happening to her since she had found good friends like Rose, Webster and Trent.

Trent stopped and turned to her, his arm still encircling her waist. His eyes felt like a magnet, holding her still with their compelling command. "So how does your boyfriend feel about you being this far away from home?" His voice was warm and smooth.

The rippling sensation coursing close to Jay's heart was not surprising. It was if someone had waved a magic wand and she had fallen under Trent's enchanted spell. "I don't have a boyfriend. Does that answer your question?"

Trent smiled. "Are you serious?"

"Yes," she said, feeling his arms tighten around her as they began to walk again.

"I'm sure the woman you left back home is anxiously waiting for you," Jay said. She couldn't imagine anyone as fine as Trent without a lover, although it was possible.

Again he stopped walking and held her at arms' length and in the dimness of the night, they held one another's gaze. "I don't have a lover waiting at home for me." Trent slipped her back into his arms.

This time, they didn't speak to one another until they were standing at her room door with Trent towering over her. "It was fun," she said, turning away from him and unlocking her door.

"Maybe we can go out again," Trent said.

"Maybe," Jay turned and smiled at him, and watched the corner of his mouth tip into a smile. "Who knows, you could be free to escort me home often," Jay teased him.

"Myers is serious when he says he wants all the women to be escorted. He means well, but this has nothing to do with Matthew Myers, sweetheart," Trent said, folding her into his arms. His lips touched hers and brushed her like a delicate feather, until she parted her lips and allowed him entry to explore her with an intoxicating kiss. The warmth that Jay felt when he touched her, swept her with a sensation that she was unable to explain.

Trent lifted his head and without warning, he slowly reclaimed her lips, deepening his kiss with a passion that Jay never knew. "I'll see you tomorrow." Trent smothered her lips with another kiss and Jay felt a quaking shudder as his mouth left hers and then planted tiny kisses on her cheek and finally he returned to her lips, giving her one quick kiss.

Jay backed out of Trent's embrace and didn't watch him cross the hall to his bedroom. She felt as if she was spinning as she walked inside her room and quietly closed the door. She had expected that she and Trent would be good friends, but never once had she thought their friendship would be developed so soon. She undressed and prepared for bed, daring herself not to think about Trent Prescott. Before she wrote Barbara Hilton, Jay sat on her bed for a long time, unwilling to recover from the unexpected passion she and Trent had shared that night. She had to tell her that she met Trent Prescott, but that he wasn't related to the people Gladys knew.

Dear Barbara,

On my way to Africa, I met Trent Prescott and I wasn't sure if he was related to the Prescott family from New Jersey. As you know, Granny told me that the family moved to Delaware. So I checked and didn't find anyone related to this man, even though the person I spoke to had the same surname.

Finally, I ask Trent Prescott and he told me he lived in Canada. We went out tonight and I had a wonderful time. I wish that you could meet him.

I intend to call Granny as soon as she returns from her trip. If she calls you and I know she will, give her my love. Take care and thanks in advance for the search. It should be interesting to know what happened to the Prescotts.

Stay well and I expect to hear from you soon.

Love always,
Jay

She sent the letter and then wrote her grandmother, omitting to mention that she had met Trent Prescott because she knew that her grandmother would be upset at the mention of his last name. Instead, she wrote that she had arrived safely and was looking forward to enjoying her work. Jay figured that by the time the letter reached her grandmother, Gladys would have returned from her trip since the mail in Nigeria was usually slow in getting to America.

Jay was exhausted, but she was unable to sleep. Her

surprising evening with Trent was keeping her awake. Jay knew she had to get to sleep because tomorrow was a busy day. Nevertheless, her mind was flooded with memories of Trent and his smoldering desirous passion.

Her thoughts began to waver, and the last nagging question that she had while they were at the club and didn't ask him haunted her, and she wondered again if Trent had ever lived in New Jersey. With that thought in mind, she decided that she should ask him if he ever lived in New Jersey or if he had lived in her town. What if she had made a mistake and had moved too fast, Jay wondered.

Finally, she began to drift and doze in and out of sleep, her thoughts wavering back and forth to the time Gladys had mentioned to her that the Prescotts were worthless. Was the family really worthless? Her thoughts turned to questions and she opened her eyes. It was still early in the evening and not quite midnight and she wondered if Trent was asleep.

Jay got out of bed and put on a pair of jeans and T-shirt determined to take Trent up on his offer and visit him in his room. But her visit had nothing to with work, but to find out if she had eaten, danced, and kissed her family's enemy.

Jay stepped out into the dimly lit hall and knocked on Trent's door and waited for him to let her inside. After a few seconds, she decided that he was probably asleep. Tomorrow she told herself, she would ask him everything that she should have asked tonight instead of acting like the love-starved woman that she was.

Trent stood on the front porch, looking out into the night as if the velvet darkness held the answer to his questions. Was he ready for another serious relationship? When he kissed Jay tonight, he thought that he was ready. Was he moving too fast with Jay? He didn't know.

Trent knew that he wanted Jay Lee from the first time he saw her. All the pain he had suffered seemed to have diminished and his wounded heart had finally healed, and every instinct inside him told him that he and Jay were right for each other. He headed to his room, stopping for a few seconds in front of Jay's bedroom door and he wondered if she was asleep. His masculine power coiling inside of him was a warning that instead of knocking on her door, he should pack a bag and go to his hotel room.

With that thought in mind, Trent walked into his room and grabbed a duffel bag, and packed the necessary clothes he needed for tomorrow. Sleeping across the hall from Jay threatened to cause a sensual problem for him. He pulled the blinds down over the window and headed outside. The night was still early and if he hurried, he could get the boat into town.

As he headed down to the docks, he reminded himself of the long day he had tomorrow. The proposal parade was a ceremony that he had once dreaded. His apprehensions once ran rampant through him like a widespread epidemic and he was afraid that the ritual would probably bring back old memories reminding him of his broken engagement to Sonya. His break up with her had been painful. Her disrespect and ability to lie as easily as if she were speaking the truth hurt him even more. He had arrived home earlier than intended and found her in a compromising position with her lover. He almost hated her for insulting him. She had made a mockery out of their love, relationship, and ultimately, their agreement to marry.

However, he hadn't missed the opportunity to evaluate the part he had played in their break up. Trent considered the agreement they had made with each other once they knew they wanted to get married. Sonya would stop working for Myers and help expand the business he was beginning, while he worked and traveled for Myers Research Center. He had been happy with his life decision and he thought that Sonya was happy too. During their break up, he learned that Sonya had a secret. Her lover was not just her lover, but the man that she had never divorced. She had pleaded with him that she planned to get a divorce and maybe she had been honest. But Trent couldn't understand or believe Sonya. She had promised to marry him without telling him that she was married and planning to get a divorce. He doubted Sonya planned to divorce the man now, and he had no idea how she thought they were going to be legally married.

Not only had she lied to him, she had used him. He had showered Sonya with gifts from faraway places, and called her every night before she went to bed. But the night he had come home unexpectedly . . . Trent let the thought fade. Sonya had made it clear to him that she would never accept that their relationship was over. She had made a mistake, and he was being unfair not to forgive her.

Sonya knew he had one last trip to make for Myers, and she was also aware that he was leaving Canada and moving to New Jersey to open the business that they had planned to own together before he broke off their engagement. Sonya had talked Myers into giving her a transfer to New Jersey, and placing her on the team's trip to Nigeria. To make sure that they were together, Sonya had conveniently saved a seat for him next to her. After all, this time she was determined to make him understand that she had made a mistake and wanted his forgiveness so that they could move on with their lives. He flatly refused and because of his decision, he had ended up sitting next to Jay.

Right after the meeting he'd had with the staff in the yard, Sonya had cornered him and asked him for his forgiveness. He had forgiven Sonya almost a year ago, even when his emotions were almost paralyzed, making it seem impossible for him to move on with his life because he had lost the will to trust himself to be in a serious relationship with a woman again.

Sonya had argued with him, giving him the same excuses as to why she had invited her husband over to her apartment. According to her, she was asking him for the divorce again and one thing led to another, and it wasn't her fault.

Trent understood that no one was perfect. He had made his share of mistakes, but there was no valid excuse for what Sonya had done, and not only did he not trust her, he didn't love her anymore.

Trent had given consideration to Sonya's actions and imagined if she had been placed in the same situation she had put him in. *Most likely, if she had arrived in town earlier than expected and found him in a compromising position, Sonya would have kicked him out of her life too and never forgiven him.*

Now that he had met Jay, Trent was beginning to feel whole again and it was time that he stopped licking his wounds and get back into the game.

Four

Jay pulled the covers over her and was not surprised that sleep did not come. Her mind was filled with Trent who was not a mystery to her anymore. Or was he? After her relationship with Austin, she promised herself that she was not getting involved in another relationship for a long time. But like it or not, thanks to Trent, she was about to change her mind. Jay turned over onto her stomach and began to doze, only to have thoughts of Trent Prescott to interrupt her much needed desire to sleep again.

Trent might have been a lady's man, Jay mused drowsily, and she didn't need that type of man in her life again. Austin had taught her how unserious some men could be in relationships. Instead of sleeping, Jay lay awake, unable to suppress the bothersome thoughts about Trent, and reveling in the satisfaction he had left her with tonight. He had managed to rekindle the very part of her soul she no longer wanted to acknowledge. To make matters worse, she couldn't seem to get the vision of his face out of her mind.

Trent Prescott was like an old song bringing back memories of the evening they had spent together. His kiss had reawakened the passion that she had put to rest when she broke off her relationship with Austin. Jay smiled and allowed the sweet memories of Trent Prescott to play in her head like the old love song they had dance to tonight.

Trent Prescott had made an impression on her the first time she saw him on the plane and tonight she knew she could like him more than she thought she could even after the upset they'd had in the airport.

Maybe it was because she hadn't had a date since Austin, or maybe it was his smooth charisma that worked like the wave of a magic wand drawing her out of her shell. Finally, she gave up on getting to sleep and tossed and turned while her memories wavered to the past.

She had worked tirelessly through the years at Lees' Bed and Breakfast. By the time she was sixteen, she was assisting with every chore. She helped to prepare meals, made certain that the game room was neat, and that the game pieces were in order for the guests' children, polished furniture and worked the front desk, filling in wherever she was needed.

Jay remembered hating her chores, but loved listening to the guests' conversation after she had helped serve their meals. Afterwards, she would stand quietly at the station near the entrance and listen to quiet and sometimes ostentatious conversations. Most of the guests were regulars during the summer months, but seemed to have enough money to travel to other states and even to foreign countries for a week or two during the winter. Jay never forgot the African man who was married to the American woman. The couple talked extensively, sharing information on the one month a year in Nigeria they spent together.

It was then that Jay knew that she wanted to visit

Africa, but first, she had to figure out how was she going to get there. According to her grandmother, by the age of sixteen, Jay should have been thinking about the college she wanted to attend instead of dreaming about traipsing off around the world.

"Girl, one day your dreams are going to get you into trouble. What you need to do is go to college and become a teacher, and then find yourself a husband." Jay didn't mind the suggestion to teach, but her hopes and dreams were to travel the world, and meet people with a culture different from her own. As far as getting married, Jay wasn't sure that she wanted to marry. Even at the age of sixteen, she wasn't dating. Gladys was forever keeping watch over her, chasing away any boys in the neighborhood that had stopped by to talk to her. Gladys's arguments to Jay were that the girls and boys were too fresh and had no business dating in the first place.

It seemed that her grandmother knew every boy and young man in town, as well as their families.

One summer morning, just before noon, Jay stood at the edge of the bank that led to the bed and breakfast and talked to Elfin Mack, a teenage boy that she knew in high school. He was one of most popular guys in town, and he seemed to like her. Their conversation had been about her trip to Canada that summer and the upcoming school year and how she didn't feel any different about turning seventeen a few days before.

Then Elfin had asked her to go with him to the concert that following Saturday night. Jay knew that she couldn't accept Elfin's invitation because she wasn't allowed to date. Asking her grandmother for permission to go on a date with a schoolmate would only bring on a lecture about the evils of dating, and how young folks should be chaperoned on dates. Added to that, there would be a lecture on how the young men in town were just out to get girls in bed and the next day, gloat before moving on to the next available girl. Jay decided that asking her grandmother was useless and accepted Elfin's invitation to the concert, making arrangements to meet him two blocks down the street from her home.

Friday evening, when all the guests were out or enjoying the live band in the basement club of the bed and breakfast, and after Gladys had gone to bed early, Jay asked Barbara would she relax her curly hair before she went to bed that night. Barbara agreed but warned Jay that Gladys was not going to like her new hairstyle. Around midnight, Jay's long thick hair was straight. A row of ringlets circled and hung past her shoulders and for once since she was a teenager, she felt attractive.

"Jay, you know Gladys is going to be upset, but you're a young lady and I personally think you should look as nice as any other teenage girl in this town," she remembered Barbara saying to her. Jay loved Barbara. She had been her mother's best friend, and after her mother's death, Barbara had taken on the mother role. However, Jay thought her chances to attend the concert were better if she didn't tell Barbara about her plans. Her grandmother couldn't help but notice the change in her hair, but if she found out that she was planning to attend the concert, Jay knew she wouldn't be allowed to go.

Jay remembered how guilty she had felt when she decided that it was best not to tell Barbara about her plans and flirted with the idea of telling her godmother again before she went to bed. Her intuitive feelings warned her that if she wanted to go to the concert, she should keep her secret date to herself. Jay finally agreed with her instincts, and decided that all her grandmother and her godmother didn't know wouldn't affect them.

However, her next problem was figuring out how she was going to get out of the house without Gladys and Barbara seeing her.

Fortunately for Jay, Gladys had a church meeting to attend, and afterwards, she had plans to visit with her girlfriend. Barbara had gone shopping, and her grandfather was busy with late afternoon chores, giving Jay the opportunity to go to her room in their cottage behind Lees' and choose an outfit for her concert date. She remembered choosing a pair of slacks and top that Barbara had bought for her while they were on their vacation.

By the time Gladys returned home and went in to take her usual nap after her day out, Jay got dressed and hurried two blocks down the street to meet Elfin, feeling guilty because she was sneaking off to enjoy a tiny bit of life.

That evening after the concert, she and Elfin stopped off at a diner for a late night snack. Jay had never enjoyed herself so much in her teenage life. The music playing in the diner was the same popular music she played on her stereo in her room, but at the small diner, the music sounded better, and added to that, Elfin was a perfect gentleman. They had enjoyed themselves so much that they had talked until close to two A.M.

Several minutes past two, Elfin drove her home, stopping in front of Lees' Bed and Breakfast and giving her a slow kiss on her lips, assuring her that he would call her later that day. Jay got out of the car and suddenly stood in front of her grandmother.

"This is what you do while I'm asleep and why did you ask Barbara to relax your hair?" Gladys Lee was furious. "Get yourself in the house and don't come out again until I tell you to."

Jay heard the tires on Elfin's car squeal against the pavement. The scent of burnt rubber scorched and reeked the early morning air. Jay had never been so embarrassed in her life and she protested, attempting to make her grandmother understand, but Gladys Lee was not hearing excuses. "I'm trying to raise you to be a decent woman, and you're out with the worst boy in town. That boy's granddaddy was a disgrace to decent men in this town. He stood on the corner every weekend in front of the bar, talking up under women dresses when they passed by. A woman couldn't walk to the store in peace without him making vulgar comments, and you're out with his grandson?"

Jay tried to defend Elfin, telling Gladys that he was a nice young man and he didn't deserve to be held accountable for his grandfather's actions.

"Uh!" Gladys disagreed with Jay. "Just remember this. Nuts don't fall far from the tree."

Jay didn't expect to see or hear from Elfin again, and she didn't expect to receive his promised phone call either. But the next evening after she had helped to serve the guests their dinner, Barbara gestured for her to come to the kitchen. She had a call from a nice-sounding young man. Jay felt as if she was walking on air, as she made her way to the kitchen to answer the call she suspected was from Elfin. She could almost hear the nervousness in his voice as he spoke to her, asking her if her grandmother was around, and apologizing for leaving in a rush. Elfin thought that it might be a good idea for him to stop by and speak to her grandmother. He really wanted to be Jay's boyfriend. Jay was about to tell him that his suggestion was a good one, but she didn't think that her grandmother would agree, when she heard the telephone extension lift then she heard Gladys's voice.

"No, you can't stop by and talk to me about Jay and nothing else. You stay away from my grandchild!"

Without saying good-bye, Jay set the receiver back into the cradle. Her eyes burning with tears of embarrassment for the friend she had lost because of Gladys's strict attitude.

"Jay." She felt Barbara's comforting hand stroking her shoulder. "Your grandmother is old and set in her ways. She thinks she's protecting you, and in her own way she's doing the best that she knows how."

Jay couldn't agree with Barbara because she was lonely and had no friends. Her life was surrounded with work at the bed and breakfast, school, and lonely summers and holidays.

"I don't know why I can't have friends?" Jay remembered asking Barbara as her pent up tears began to flow freely.

"Listen to me, Jay," Barbara consoled her. "If you think about it like this you might feel a lot better. You have one more year in high school and then you're off to college. You'll meet people and make a few good friends. Before you know it, you'll be having fun and enjoying yourself. You'll see," Barbara told her.

Jay had to smile because Barbara always had a special way of making her see her life in a positive and different light.

"By the time you graduate and start teaching . . ." Barbara started.

"I'm not going to be a teacher, at least not right now," Jay said. It was not because she was rebelling against her grandmother's choice of career for her as much as she wanted to study other traditions and cultures and see how others in the world lived.

"That's all right, Jay, you can be whatever you want to be," Barbara agreed with her.

Jay was aware of her choices, and she had made up her mind that she would travel and earn a salary that would supply her with all her wants and needs.

For the rest of the summer, Jay spent her days and weekends alone and when she returned her senior year in school, Elfin was involved with another girl. He was polite though, speaking briefly to Jay when they passed each other in the hall.

Jay snuggled underneath the sheets, wondering what her grandmother's reactions would be if Trent turned out to be a member of the Prescott family. She quickly dismissed the thought. What if Trent was one of the Prescotts and she decided to date him regardless of what her family thought? Could she go against the warnings and accusations made against the Prescotts and date him anyway? Jay wasn't certain as she glanced at the clock, noticing the time was close to midnight. If she didn't get to sleep, she would be exhausted by morning. With that thought in mind, she fell into a sound sleep.

Trent's kisses missed her lips, making a trail to the hollow of her throat as a strangling lamenting sound escaped her. His fingers inched down the center of her back, sending scorching passion through her and she raised to meet his kisses

*which made her heart dance, and overflow her with a reckless
burning desire.*

*They aroused each other to heights she had never known.
While she stroked his taut masculine body, Jay secretly promised herself that she and Trent Prescott would stay together
forever. She captured his lips with a sedating kiss, while she
explored every inch of his body with mastering strokes dragging
to surface a round of snarls . . .*

"Jay Lee, are you going to sleep all day?" Jay flinched
and sat up in bed at the sound of Rose's voice outside
her bedroom.

"I'm awake," Jay called back, shaking away the
dream she had just had about her and Trent. She
rolled out of bed, crossing the room to the shower and
touching her lips. Her dream had been so real it felt
as if Trent had kissed her, which reminded her of the
drugging kisses they had shared last night.

In less than thirty minutes, Jay was on her way up
the hall to the dining room to join her coworkers for
breakfast. She noticed Rose patting the empty chair
beside her. "Thanks for waking me up," Jay said, sitting
down before glancing around the room for Trent.

"Did you stay up all night?" Rose lowered her voice
to a whisper, making it impossible for anyone to hear
her question except Jay.

"No," Jay said. "I got to sleep late." She glanced at
Rose, suspecting that she might have thought that she
and Trent had stayed out all night. "Good morning,"
Jay said.

"Good morning." Rose passed Jay the coffee.

"Where is Trent?" Rose whispered to Jay.

"I don't know," Jay said, unwrapping the flatware,
and spreading the white cotton napkin on her lap before pouring herself a cup of coffee and taking a small

serving of bacon, toast and jelly. She glanced around the room again, noticing Sonya Smith giving her an unpleasant look. "Maybe Trent stayed in his hotel room," Jay said, and asked the woman next to her to pass the orange juice.

"And you didn't go with him?" Rose asked.

"I'll go with him the next time," Jay teased and chuckled softly.

"Did you enjoy yourself last night?" Rose asked, as she nibbled at the edge of a strip of bacon.

"I enjoyed myself," Jay said, not going into the details on how she and Trent's evening had ended.

"I was hoping you did." Rose dropped the bacon she had been eating down and picked up her coffee cup.

Last night, Trent had made Jay realize her strong need to start enjoying herself again. She had also realized that he could definitely become a very special person in her life. "Why is she looking at me?" Jay asked Rose as she caught another glimpse of Sonya's ogling gaze.

"Forget Sonya. She's probably upset because you and Trent went out last night," Rose said.

"Oh yeah." Jay caught another glimpse at Sonya and if Sonya eyes were daggers . . . Jay dismissed the thought and poured herself a glass of orange juice. She would have remembered if Trent mentioned that he and Sonya were lovers. While Jay ate breakfast, she remembered the scene she'd witness the day of the meeting when Sonya was talking to Trent.

"Is there anything going on between her and Trent?" Jay pumped Rose for information.

"No," Rose said, setting the cup down and wiping her mouth with her napkin.

Jay believed her. However, she planned to ask Trent about his relationship with Sonya. "Then what's the big deal?" Jay asked, hoping that Trent was the honest man she wanted him to be.

"Sonya and Trent were engaged." Rose lifted up her cup and sipped coffee. She then placed the cup back on the table and smiled at Jay. "But last night was the first time I've seen Trent that happy in a long time. I think you and Trent make a perfect couple." She smiled at Jay.

"We're just friends," Jay said, still not knowing if a romantic relationship with Trent was right. She tasted the scrambled eggs and decided she needed more pepper.

"Friends or not, you guys look good together," Rose said.

"Thank you, darling," Jay chuckled, "Pass the pepper," she said to the woman that insisted that everyone call her Peaches.

"Pass Trent's Ice Princess the pepper, Peaches," Sonya said, giving Jay another ogling gaze.

"Here Miss Thing," Peaches said, pushing the pepper down to Jay with such a force, the container toppled and rolled to a stop.

"What did you call me?" Jay asked Sonya, returning her and Peaches' heated glances.

"Jay, ignore them." Rose nudged her with her elbow.

"She just called me a name and Peaches might as well have thrown the pepper at me," Jay said.

"Be cool, Jay. Sonya wants Myers to send you home," Rose warned her.

Jay understood well that Myers didn't like conflict amongst the team when they were traveling. This had been her first experience, but she had heard of team members being sent home because of their conduct.

Jay heeded Rose's warning and finally sprinkled her eggs with pepper before pouring herself another glass of orange juice. Jay finished her breakfast, yet she had no intentions of being coaxed into a fight with Sonya Smith and her friend Peaches. This was the day of the marriage proposal parade and Jay intended to work as well as enjoy the occasion.

Several minutes later, Jay waited with the others outside for the bus that would take them to the parade. It was clear to Jay now as she caught the woman's evil glances that Sonya had assumed that she and Trent were lovers. It seemed to her that once people of the opposite sex were seen together, they were automatically assumed to be a couple. Jay pulled on her sunglasses, adjusted her bag on her shoulder and banished all thoughts of Sonya.

The bus's brakes squealed as it pulled up to the curve in front of the house and Jay noticed Trent getting off and heading toward her and Rose.

"Good morning, ladies." As Trent spoke to them, his eyes never left Jay.

"Hi," Jay said to him as she inhaled his fresh soapy scent. "I stopped by to visit you last night," she said. Trent hadn't opened the door for her when she wanted to ask him if he had lived in New Jersey.

"I stayed in town last night," Trent said as they took their seats on the bus. Trent told Jay his reasons for staying in a hotel room. Sometimes there were problems on the road leading to the team's house and he couldn't get home at night. To assure himself a room to sleep, his first task was to make reservations at a hotel before he arrived in the country. He had learned that lesson when he took his first trip to Nigeria a few years ago. "But last night, I had other reasons for staying in town," he said. "Did something happen?" Trent turned to Jay and searched her face and Jay couldn't help but remember her dream.

"I had a few more questions to ask you," Jay said, when Webster sat in the seat across from them and got Trent's attention.

"Can we talk tonight?" Trent asked Jay.

"Yes," Jay said, preferring to find out what she needed to know when they were alone.

Jay settled down for the short ride to the parade site where she would finally witness young women that were positive about the choices that they were making in their lives and how important it was for them to become married women.

"She makes me sick!" Jay overheard Sonya farther at the back of the bus.

"Sonya, we didn't have this kind of trouble before you joined our team. So why don't you be quiet before Myers hears about your attitude and fires you." Jay recognized the older gentleman warning Sonya.

"We'll see who get sent home." Sonya shot back.

Jay closed her eyes and reclined her head against the seat, ignoring the wry comments and nasty remarks coming from Sonya as the bus eased away from the curve. It wasn't at all uncommon for someone working on Myers' team to be sick of someone they didn't like.

Jay tuned out all conversation, thinking what a wonderful opportunity she would have to actually watch the women perform, as her fore-parents had hundreds of years ago as they marched to the beat of drums in hopes of being chosen for marriage.

She felt the worn leather sag underneath Trent as

he shifted his weight before he ended his conversation with Webster and turned back to her.

"It must be nice to have a special place to go to," Jay said, wondering if Trent kept his special room for a special friend or maybe he had never stopped seeing Sonya. That thought added another question to her list of questions to ask him.

"When I stay in the hotel room, baby, I have very good reasons."

"I can imagine," Jay said.

"Having a room in town keeps me out of trouble," Trent said, reaching for her hand and squeezing it lightly before pressing her palm against his chest. Jay felt the strong beat of his heart and the warm flow of heat that ran through her.

"So why didn't you tell me that you were once engaged to Sonya?" She asked and waited for an answer while she studied him as if his eyes held the answer to her question.

"We'll talk about that later," Trent said, giving Jay's hand another squeeze.

The bus driver stopped at their destination and Trent got up. "We'll talk tonight," he leaned down and whispered to her.

Jay watched him walk away from her and out onto the dusty road as the team members got off the bus. Jay gathered her bag, and pulled on her cap while she waited for a space to open up so she could get in line and get off the bus. She could see Rose was farther up front, motioning to her and showing the spot from the window where she would be standing.

"Girl, you can't tell Miss Thing that she don't have it going on," Jay heard Sonya.

"I couldn't tell you nothing either, if you were sleeping with the supervisor," Jay heard Peaches speak up.

"We'll see about that too," Sonya said.

Jay heard Sonya and her girlfriend, but ignored them. She had better things to think about, like the parade she was about to attend.

"It is a shame when grown women who have left home don't know how to behave." A much older woman said to Sonya.

"I know you're not talking to me." Sonya snapped at the woman.

"Yes, I am talking to you, and I'm not saying that we get along all the time on this team, but we do have respect for one another."

"Oh be quiet," Sonya said. "I was talking to Jay Lee."

Jay refused to involve herself in the petty bickering among the two women who had hounded her all morning. She wondered if Trent Prescott was worth it as she turned back to look at Sonya.

"Yes, I'm talking to you, bitch." Sonya said loud enough for everyone on the bus to hear.

This was the last place that Jay wanted to get into a confrontation with anyone. As far as she was concerned, the grounds were sacred and blessed with the joys of the women who were following a tradition that she would never know, and Sonya was picking a fight with her. However, Jay planned to stay in control and if she could do that until her job was complete, she would be a happy woman.

Jay moved toward the front to catch up with Rose as she watched the gathering crowd through the window assemble along the roadside.

"You need to be careful how you chose your boyfriends," Sonya said. She had pushed her way through the crowd and was standing behind Jay. Jay observed the tortured expression on Sonya's face. She had no shame in her conduct. It seemed to Jay that Sonya was determined to take her frustrations out on her.

Jay retained strict composure, unwilling to lower herself to the woman's standard. As she continued to inch toward the front of the bus, Jay tried her best to ignore the abuse, but she couldn't keep quiet any longer.

"Yeah, I'm talking about you," Sonya said as Jay turned again to look at her. The line had stopped moving and it seemed to Jay that everyone was anticipating the worse.

"All right, Sonya. Don't lose your job." Jay recognized a male team member's voice from the back.

Sonya fanned the man off with one hand, and pointed her finger in Jay's face.

"Get your finger out of my face." Jay's tone was slow and even. "And from this minute on, I will not be another ice princess or another bitch!"

"Or what—you'll report me to Prescott."

Jay made a clicking sound with the tip of her tongue against her lips. Her assignment meant everything to her and she was not going to do anything to ruin her chances to stay in Nigeria. If Sonya couldn't stand to see her and Trent together, she could go home.

"You are one ridiculous sister," Jay said as she got off the bus. She moved through the dusty street until she found Rose, a space to set her bag, and an advantageous vantage point from which to view the parade.

Jay stood underneath the old Red Flame tree that was probably as old as Africa itself, and watched the men who had arrived to choose the young women for their brides.

Drumsticks pelted against the top of brown cattle hide covered leather drums, filling the air with shimming rhythm. The rich reverberation echoed against the clear sunny sky, and Jay felt her soul tremble.

These were young ladies that were around the age of fifteen and sixteen years old, their cheeks decorated with beautiful traditional scarification. Some of the women's skin appeared to have been beaded with small notched scars and dusted with dark powder, a tint more ebony than their rich mahogany skin. Everything was perfect, Jay decided, watching the women's short, flimsy blue, violet and crimson outfits swing with the movement of the hips. Their breasts taut and firm, jutted in an outward fashion as they lined up along the dusty road. Their brown feet pranced against the dirt, circulating gusts of dusty powdered soil around their jeweled ebony ankles.

And with pride, they marched in place to the rhythm of the drums. The air shimmered with excitement, while laughter and merriment pealed from the crowd and a sense of ambience swept over Jay as if she were in her rightful place.

The young ladies began to march, moving through the street, swinging their hips, clapping their hands and giving two sound spanks to their back sides to the rhythm of the drums.

Jay looked away from the festive ceremony knowing that she wouldn't have missed this parade for anything, when she glanced across the road and noticed Trent looking in her direction. Memories of last night flooded her, but she dismissed them. Nothing should have been more important to her than the parade, so she turned her attention back to the women as they paraded along the dusty street. She admired their graceful movements and their strength and maturity that they had no doubt learned from their mothers.

The parade finally ended and Jay suspected that most of the women, if not all, would soon be married, and sometime later she would witness the rituals of holy matrimony. Jay stood in awe, impressed with the entire ritual that celebrated a gentleman choosing a woman that would become his wife. They would unite together as one and grow to love one another.

Jay didn't know what the future held for her and Trent. She wondered if the answers to her questions tonight would be answers that she wanted to hear or would she learn that there would be no space for him in her life.

"Jay, what was happening with you and Sonya on the bus?" Rose eased closer to her where they were standing beneath the tree, interrupting her thoughts.

"I couldn't let Sonya talk about me in that way without saying something to her," Jay said. "She was talking about me as if I wasn't there."

"I tried to get back there and stop her, but no one would let me through." Rose said, looking out across the street where Sonya and her girlfriend were standing.

"Thanks for wanting to help, but I didn't need any assistance," Jay said remembering Rose's earlier advice to be cool.

Rose laughed. "Jay, I don't know. But the parade was nice."

"Yes, it was," Jay said, as she and Rose moved closer to watch the men gathering with the parents of the young virgin ladies who were anxious to be chosen. Jay could hardly wait to witness the marriage ritual.

The day had come to an end and Jay, Rose, Webster, and Trent and the other staff members headed back home. Jay was hot and sticky from perspiration, exhausted from the heat and not having slept much last night. As she thought how much she needed a nap, visions of hot water and lots of soap held Jay's attention and she could hardly wait to get home and into her tub.

It wasn't long before she was home relaxing in her bath, shutting out the day and all it had to offer. But in spite of it, thoughts of Trent invaded her memories and she became impatient and anxious to learn what fate held for her. She shut off her thoughts and lifted herself from the cooling water, wrapped herself in a towel and shortly afterwards, she took a nap, waking an hour later in time to get dressed for her evening with Trent.

Before she pulled on the black flare-tailed dress and stepped into her heels, Jay applied her make-up, combed her hair, then checked her e-mail.

Hi Jay,

It's good to hear from you and know that you arrived safely. I hope you enjoy the work, and while you're there, have a nice time with your new friend, and stop worrying about the Prescotts. I don't know what happened to the family after they moved out of New Jersey years ago. Gladys said they moved to Delaware, but I didn't find anyone related to them in that state.

Anyway, Jay, you know as well as I do, that it's Gladys who's keeping this story alive. You know how I feel about that rumor. I really don't think anyone in the Prescott

*family was responsible for your parents' death. I believe,
as it was reported years ago, that a drunk driver struck
and killed them and I don't believe as Gladys said that
this man was sober and was paid off by the Prescotts to
commit murder.*

*It just so happened that a member of the Prescott
family was in the area that evening and no one can tell
Gladys different.*

*I'm so glad that you didn't ask your grandmother for
information about the family. It would only upset her,
and I will have to listen to the story again. Now you
know I love Gladys as if she were my mother and I loved
your mother like a sister. But I am too old to listen to
Gladys fuss about something that happened nineteen
years ago, especially when I believe that most of what
she's saying is not true.*

*I'm feeling that you're really interested in this young
man. If that's true, enjoy yourself. I'm sure if Trent is
from Canada, you have no need to worry. So have fun
because I'm sure Trent Prescott is harmless, honey.*

> *Sincerely,*
> *Barbara*

Jay saved the e-mail and turned off the computer.
She would take Barbara's advice and free herself from
needless worry and not ask Trent if he was related to
the Prescotts that had once lived in New Jersey. She
would enjoy her evening with her new friend and forget about the hatred that her grandmother held onto
all these years. Jay realized only after she had met Trent
how much her grandmother's hatred of the family had
affected her, and over the years, she had become para-
noid at the mention of the Prescott name.

Jay opened the door after hearing a second soft

knock. Trent stood in her doorway, tall and good-looking. Several open buttons on his blue shirt revealed his muscular chest and the slender waistband on his wide-leg blue pants accented his narrow waist.

"Come in," Jay moved away from the door, and watched as he walked into the room.

Trent shut the door and gathered her in his arms. His mouth was firm and warm against hers as he parted her lips and gave her a searching kiss. He held her close with one hand while he slipped the other over her hips and lifted his head to look into her eyes. "I went to the hotel last night because I wanted to spend the night with you," he spoke just above a whisper, answering the question she had asked earlier that day.

Jay felt his strong masculinity and she pulled out of his embrace and crossed the room to get her purse. Tonight, she would make him talk to her about his engagement to Sonya Smith and what type of relationship he wanted to have with her now, if any. Then she would decide, regardless of her feelings for him, if she would continue to allow their friendship to reach another level.

"Let's go to dinner," she said, walking past him on her way out of the room, when Trent reached out and took her hand in his.

"All right," he said, falling in step beside her. They then walked to the Jeep he had rented.

Once they were inside the Jeep, Jay turned to him. "How long were you and Sonya engaged?" She asked, wanting to get the subject out of the way. Jay wanted to enjoy her dinner and night with Trent and had no intention of discussing Sonya and Trent's broken engagement later that night.

"Sonya and I were engaged for about four months,"

Trent said, turning the key in the ignition and easing away from the curb.

"How long has it been since you and Sonya changed your minds about getting married?" Jay was curious, figuring that their break up couldn't have been that long ago since Sonya was still angry, especially at her.

"It's been a year," Trent said, glancing away from the road and at her.

"All of a sudden you didn't want to marry her—why?" Jay pried further, her intention to clear the emotional blemish that threatened to destroy her new relationship with him.

"No, I just didn't come home one day and decide that I wanted out of the engagement." Trent drove slower now through the neighborhood, taking his time and glancing at Jay every once in a while as he explained the problem he'd had with Sonya.

"So, you lived together?" Jay asked, remembering how she and Austin had shared an apartment.

"Sometimes we lived together, but not often. Anyway we weren't meant to be married," Trent replied, and cast a side glance at Jay. She waited to hear why he didn't think that he and Sonya were meant to spend their lives together. It seemed clear to her and all the team members that Sonya thought differently than Trent.

"I can put up with a lot, Jay, but I won't deal with lies and infidelity," Trent said, and this time he didn't look at her and she noticed a stubborn hard muscle flexing in his jaw.

"Do you know for a fact that Sonya cheated on you?" Jay asked, and waited for Trent to answer her and when he was taking longer than usual to reply to her question, she touched his thigh. "I am waiting for an answer."

"Baby, my imagination wasn't working over time . . . I walked in on her." The tightness in Trent's jaw softened and he appeared relaxed again.

Jay tapped the edge of her nails against her purse, wondering if she had understood Trent clearly and suspecting that he could have been jealous and had read more into Sonya's relationship with her friend than was true. "Walking in on two friends is not exactly a reason to break off an engagement, Trent," Jay said, picking up a CD case off the floor and reading the titles to the songs. It was no wonder Sonya was angry. She probably still thought there was hope for her and Trent. But what Jay most wanted to know was what were Trent's feelings for Sonya, because she couldn't allow herself to get caught in the middle of a relationship that would lead to nothing but pain for her.

"Baby," Trent said, casting a quick glance at her, then turned his attention to the road again. And Jay listened to him as he told her how Sonya had lied to him about everything in their relationship.

"I understand," Jay said. She had recognized the pattern and even though Austin had never been married, he had been dishonest in their relationship.

"Do you?" Trent asked as he changed gears and accelerated the Jeep faster.

"Yes," Jay said, sliding the tip of her nail across the corners of the thin wrapper, opening the CD pack and sliding the disc into the CD player.

"How?" Trent asked, and Jay explained to him her reasons for not marrying Austin Carrington. She and Trent agreed that they were better off without people like Austin and Sonya in their lives.

Jay was satisfied that her questions had been answered and the possibilities for a meaningful relationship between her and Trent promised to flourish into a love that never ended. The rich tremor of Luther Vandross filled the Jeep and the sweet silence between them.

Trent parked across the street in a crowded parking lot from the hotel and restaurant and turned to Jay. "It was the hardest relationship experience I have ever gone through, but it's over and it's time that I moved on." He pulled her to him and she accepted his drugging kiss before they crossed the street to the hotel and took a table in the dining room.

Classical music, piped through wall speakers, permeated the restaurant as Jay and Trent sat among beautiful couples eating their dinners while drinking wine and reading their menu. Jay hoped that she would find something to eat that she liked. To Jay, the food wasn't that good in Nigeria, but she would manage. She chose the creamed chicken breast and mixed vegetables, asking for a small portion, while Trent chose the steak with all the trimmings.

While Jay and Trent ate their dinners and finished off a half carafe of wine, they discussed the proposal parade. Jay was still excited that she'd had the opportunity to witness the traditional ritual. She could hardly wait until she and Rose interviewed Emma, a young woman who had agreed to give Myers Research Center an interview on a civil wedding.

Jay slid her plate aside and sipped the white wine, and glanced around the dining room, seeing many familiar faces from the team, Sonya being among them. She understood why Sonya was angry at her now, but what puzzled her about Sonya was why hadn't she moved on. Jay dismissed the thought, and realized that the last time she saw Austin he had high hopes too, thinking that they would reconcile and get married.

However, Jay was like Trent. She had no time for games and dishonesty. Austin was a part of her past and hopefully by the time she returned home, she would find him involved in a serious relationship with some deserving woman.

While she and Trent finished their wine he told her about the arrangement he had made with Myers. "After this project is completed, I'm not working for Myers anymore," Trent told her, and drank the last of his wine.

Jay lifted her glass and looked over the rim at him. "Why?" She asked.

"I started a business a few years ago," Trent said, telling her about the properties he bought and sold.

Jay wasn't surprised that Trent wanted to work for himself. He didn't seem like a man that wanted to take orders for the rest of his life without having control over his work. Besides, she had watched him since they had met and noticed that Trent had the air of a businessman. However, she was surprised when Trent told her that he was moving his office to New Jersey. Nevertheless, Jay was pleased to know that she and Trent would see one another often once they returned home. "Business is not good in Canada?" Jay asked him.

"Yes. But after Sonya and I broke up, I wanted to leave, and I decided to move closer to my friends, Webster and Rose."

Jay glanced across the room at Sonya and Trent followed her gaze. Jay was beginning to understand why Sonya might have taken a job transfer.

"I'm ready to go dancing if you are," Jay said, gathering her purse and pushing away from the table, as the waiter stopped and placed their check on the table.

"Wait," Trent said, paying the young man before he could walk away.

They pushed their way through the crowded dance hall, a large building that was not far from the restaurant and hotel they had just eaten their dinner. A circle of scarlet red, lime green, canary yellow, and turquoise lights swirled to the rhythm of the music over a huge dance floor. Women dressed in mini or medium length flare dresses and wearing three inch heels or higher, were being spun on the dance floor by handsome men. The dance hall reminded Jay of discotheques from the seventies.

Trent reached for her hand, sliding her palm into his before he swung her around in time with the music. Jay's black flare-tail dress swirled up around her thighs as they danced to one song after another, hardly giving her and Trent time to recuperate from their last dance. Jay loved every minute of the fun she was having dancing with Trent.

Finally, after a long while dancing to fast music, the beat slowed to a soft romantic pace and Trent gathered her close to him on the crowded floor. She felt the beat of his heart, inhaled the fine scent of his cologne and savored the sensual touch of his hand as he held her close. "Let's go home," Trent whispered in her ear after a couple of slow dances.

Jay stood on the tip of her black heels and planted a warm soft kiss on Trent's lips, understanding his full meaning of wanting to go home.

Twenty minutes later, Jay unlocked the door to her room and flipped the light switch, illuminating her bedroom with a warm glow. At that moment, she understood clearly the full meaning of Myers warning when he filled their care boxes with everything they might need, including the sensual protection that he had warned them could be handy when lovers hungered for passion in the early hours of the morning. She removed a box of condoms from her care package and dropped the sensual supplies on top of her floral bedspread.

Without warning, Jay had found herself involved with Trent. And all the jokes that had been made about Myers making certain everyone had birth control pills and condoms to protect themselves was no longer a laughing matter. However, fate had dealt her a beautiful winning hand and she was left to revel in the ardent passion she had to offer Trent and he to her.

Trent cupped her face in both his hands and towered over her, kissing Jay hungrily before raising his head a fraction of an inch. "I'm staying with you tonight," he spoke soft and low against her lips, while he walked her backward toward the bed.

"I didn't say that you could stay with me tonight," Jay sat on her bed, pulling him down beside her.

"Can I stay the night with you?" He asked, reaching behind her, pulling down the zipper of her dress, and sliding the black material away from her shoulders.

Jay stood and pushed her dress over her hips and threw it onto the chair. Standing only in her black heels and silk light-blue bikini underwear, she leaned over and kissed his dimpled chin, the hard side of his jaw and finally his mouth; luscious, firm and warm. Jay's clouded mind returned to her memories and she

believed that Barbara had been right in her letter. Still
the small voice inside her whispered a message that
she didn't want to hear. What if Trent was her family's
enemy? The question rang through her mind and she
quietly pushed her nagging worries away. All of her life
she had never gotten exactly what she wanted and tonight and forever if possible, she would make choices
for herself.

Trent stood and held onto her waist with both wide
hands, while Jay's fingers slowly worked the buttons on
his shirt, revealing his flat hard stomach. Jay stepped
out of his grasp, while Trent discarded his shirt and
the rest of his clothes. Then she gathered him to her
and like a woman starved for love and passion, she
smothered his firm mouth with kisses, while he eased
his fingers underneath her brassiere strap, peeling
away the silk and unveiling her sculptured firm breast.

As he slowly undressed her between kisses, Jay mar-
veled at his body through a slanted narrow gaze. She
wasn't surprised by Trent Prescott; he was all the man
she expected him to be.

Without warning he lifted her and they lay on her
bed. He kissed every inch of body, igniting a flame inside
her and she felt as if she was in a fevered delirium when
he lightly stroked the v of her thighs. Jay Lee's senses
reeled and skidded. Her mind was clouded and she felt
hot all over as deploring cries escaped her. She felt his
lips against her stomach making a slow and fiery path
to her inner thigh and Jay knew that she would never
be the same again. She wanted to speak, but no words
came to surface, except his name which slipped off the
edge of her lips before she heard herself cry out in pure
wanton pleasure.

Jay found her strength and slipped away from Trent

and covered him. She caressed him slow and gentle, her soft touch against his narrow hips and then moved along his thick muscular thighs. With her fingers, she scribbled an imaginary design through a curly black veil, building a flame inside him. Trent groaned as if his blood was pounding and she stroked him even more, until low, lamenting sounds escaped him as if electric currents charged and coursed through him.

"Not now, baby," Trent reached out and grabbed her wrist, dragging her down beside him and wrapping her in arms and in a tangled web of passion. Jay withered under the slow burning fire building inside her and succumbed to him, allowing herself to enjoy more of his intimate caresses. Trent moved away from Jay to the box of latex, masking his masculinity for their security. With slow, even unhurried patience, Trent Prescott gathered her round hips to him and they fused, melting into a throbbing world of bliss. They moved together in pure harmony, rising to a level of raw sensation that inched through her, and together they clamored, a mixture of muffled snarls bounced against the quietness of the night. Jay and Trent clung to one another, reveling in a golden light of rearousing passion.

The next morning, Trent was still stretched out on the length of Jay's bed sleeping soundly when her ringing telephone awoke him.

After the telephone rang several times, Trent reached out to touch Jay, but instead he touched an empty space and a note on her pillow. "It's too early for anyone to get a telephone call on a Sunday morning," Trent grumbled and read the note before he answered the telephone. *Went to get breakfast. Be back in a few minutes.* He crumpled the paper and answered the telephone.

"Yeah," he answered, his voice hoarse from sleep. "You have the right number if you want to talk to Jay," Trent said to the woman on the other end of the line. "No, she's not here. Who's calling?" Trent sat up and rubbed his eyes. "All right, Barbara Hilton, I'll tell Jay that you called," he said. "Is this an emergency?" Trent asked Barbara. "All right, I'll tell Jay that everything is fine at home. You're talking to Trent," he said, when Barbara asked him who was she speaking to.

Trent lay the receiver back into the cradle and pressed his back against the headboard, letting his reflections drift to last night. Jay Lee was a sweet woman, he mused and got out of bed and went to the shower, grabbing a towel from Jay's closet on his way. Several minutes later, he heard Jay and smelled the strong scent of coffee filling the room.

"I can't stand the food here," Jay said, sorting through the bag, pulling out hash browns, sausages, hot cakes, maple syrup and orange juice and setting the food onto the dresser. While they were out last night, she had noticed a sign that advertised a fast-food restaurant inside the Hilton hotel. She had paid too much for the breakfast, but it was worth every dollar she had spent.

"You went into town?" Trent asked her as he rubbed the towel over his wet hair.

"Are there any fast-food restaurants in this neighborhood?" Jay asked, and noticed Trent's annoyed smile, suspecting that he didn't like his questions answered with a question.

"Just make sure you're careful when you go out

alone," Trent said. He had stopped towel drying his hair and had focused his gaze on her.

"Wait a minute," Jay said, raising her hand. "I know how to stay safe. And furthermore, we need an escort only at night." Jay gestured to the window. "So, don't start." She reached inside her shorts pocket and pulled out the keys to Trent's Jeep.

"You had a call from Barbara Hilton," Trent said, dropping the towel on a nearby chair and opening a carton of orange juice.

"Did she say what she wanted?" Jay asked.

"She wants you to call her, but it's not an emergency," Trent said, bringing the juice up to his mouth and taking a long swig from the carton.

Jay sat on the edge of the bed and dialed Barbara's number. When her call finally went through, Barbara's line was busy. She hung up and planned to return Barbara's call later.

Barbara Hilton realized that she was still holding the telephone receiver in her hand when the dial tone buzzed impatiently. She hung up and knew that Jay would be all right while she was in Nigeria. It was when she returned home that worried her. Jay would know how to handle her problem. Right now, she was happy and Barbara would do nothing to spoil her happiness.

Five

Later that day, Jay finally got her call through to Barbara. After learning that her grandmother was fine and Barbara and her husband were in excellent condition, she had to ask her godmother what message did she have for her.

Barbara laughed lightly and promised Jay that she had been thinking about her and just wanted to hear her voice. She told her that Gladys was visiting friends, and she hoped Jay was enjoying her work.

Jay had known Barbara most of her life and she had never known her godmother to call her just to hear her voice. But Jay understood that she was far away from home and she was glad Barbara had taken the time to call her.

They talked for a few more minutes. Jay told her how happy she was that she had received her e-mail and how she wanted her to meet her friend now that she had talked to him. Jay said good-bye to Barbara and hung up.

Jay and Trent enjoyed one another's company for the rest of the day, playing several games of monopoly that he had borrowed from the recreation room and drinking wine. When they were tired of playing the game,

Trent was careful to protect them before they made love again, igniting a smoldering flame, then slowly skidding back to the real world. Afterwards, they slept.

In the early evening, Jay and Trent went out for dinner, and as they were driving closer to the house, she asked him had he ever lived in New Jersey. He was about to answer her question when he received a call from Myers and had to talk to him until they were in front of the house.

"Jay, I have a meeting with Myers. I'll see you later tomorrow," Trent said, after he had asked Myers to hold. He gave her a soft kiss, and waited until she was inside the house before he drove off to his meeting.

Jay went to her room and prepared for her next day's work. She and Rose would be interviewing Emma. She was a young woman who had chosen to have a more western civil marriage than a traditional Nigerian marriage. There were a few questions Jay had in mind to ask Emma concerning her marriage. She made notes of what she wanted to ask and then made plans for the traditional wedding that she was invited to observe along with Rose, before she made herself ready for bed.

She lay awake, her thoughts going to Trent. Her feelings were beginning to grow stronger for him and Jay knew that she was falling in love.

The next morning, Jay was up early, dressing in a long skirt, short sleeve top, a pair of comfortable walking shoes and a wide-brimmed straw hat. Jay Lee was ready for her day and everything that it promised to her, except for the cream of wheat being served for breakfast. She had noticed a small shop down the street that served breakfast during the weekdays.

She grabbed her bag and hurried out to find Rose,

hoping that she hadn't already eaten and would have breakfast with her.

Jay stopped at the dining room and didn't see Rose seated among several of the team members already eating breakfast. It was six-thirty and Rose was usually on time. Jay headed out toward the front to look for her when she ran into Sonya.

"Why don't you go home?" Sonya said, blocking Jay's way out.

"Why don't you get out of my way?" Jay said, feeling certain that her personal and business life were heading in the right direction, and that not one of Sonya's spiteful remarks could take away her happiness.

"Jay, when I finished with you, you're going to be so sorry that you got in my way," Sonya said, her voice held an icy chill that reached her eyes.

"Don't you have a dancing mask project to prepare for or something?" Jay asked Sonya. She was determined not to get herself caught up in Sonya's outcries for attention.

"Don't you have something better to do than throw yourself at Trent?" Sonya asked, and continued to block Jay's path.

An early morning argument had never been one of Jay's favorite activities to indulge in, and arguing over a man was at the bottom of her list of things to argue about, especially this morning. "Sonya, get out of my way!"

"Are you ready?" Rose walked out on the porch and stood beside Sonya. "Good morning, Sonya."

"If you think so," Sonya said and strutted away.

"Sonya—please," Rose chuckled. "She should've stayed home and worked in the office. What was she talking about anyway?"

"Her favorite subject—Trent," Jay said, as she and Rose walked out into the yard.

"That is a worrisome woman," Rose said as they headed to the picnic tables. "Let's stop at the shop while we're going to Emma's home and buy a gift for her," Rose suggested.

"Sounds good to me," Jay said. "I need to get a gift for the wedding tonight anyway and maybe I should buy gifts for my family and friends," Jay said.

"Did you eat breakfast?" Jay then asked Rose.

"No, I don't like the cereal," Rose said.

"I saw a shop yesterday that serves breakfast. Let's go there," Jay said, when she noticed the cameraman that was accompanying them to the interview with Emma and the wedding later that day. "I have a better idea," Jay said, calling the young man over and learning that he hadn't had breakfast either because he didn't like hot cereal. Jay and Rose offered to buy him breakfast if he would go to the shop for them and he agreed.

While they waited for their breakfast to arrive, Jay and Rose sat at the table on the side of the house comparing the questions they had each listed to ask Emma about her civil marriage. Emma had met the groom-to-be while she was studying in Europe and was marrying for love. Her civil marriage was almost as if she was going to the justice of the peace, but for Emma this was an important process. Afterwards, she would have an expensive church wedding.

It seemed like an hour had passed before their food finally arrived. While Jay and Rose ate breakfast, they discussed their weekend. Jay listened more than she talked as Rose told her the plans she had made for her and Webster's wedding. Then Rose changed the conversation. "I'm glad Trent is finally happy." She looked at Jay.

Jay lowered her gaze. She was also happy, but as much as she liked Rose, Jay didn't want to discuss her and Trent's relationship with her. "He's nice," Jay said, wishing her girlfriend, Carol was with her so they could really talk about their boyfriends.

"Is that all?" Rose asked Jay as she broke the edge off of the toast.

"Yes," Jay said and smiled, before glancing at her watch. "I think we should be going," she said, changing the subject. Rose was the best friend she had at Myers, but as always, Jay didn't like talking about her personal life unless she was talking to Barbara or Carol.

With the cameraman walking slowly behind them, Jay and Rose talked quietly about the weddings they were assigned to observe as they headed to Emma and her family's home. For long periods of time, they were quiet. The quiet spaces left between Jay and Rose's conversation were filled with the swishing sound of Jay's long flowing skirt, the chirping sound of African spoonbills, and Jay's recollection of Trent and their deepening love affair.

They neared a small store not far from Emma and her parents' home. Jay and Rose stopped to go inside to purchase a gift for Emma before they continued their walk to the young woman's home. Jay also bought a gift for Gladys, Barbara and Carol and a gift for the young lady that she and Rose were observing in their next assignment later that day.

A short time later, Jay, Rose and the cameraman arrived at Emma's house, and were greeted by an older woman, Mary, Emma's mother. Mary was a friendly dark-brown woman with a pleasant smile and bright eyes.

"Welcome to our home," Mary said, her long full black dress sprinkled with tan and green spots, flowed gracefully around her ankles.

"Good morning," Jay and Rose greeted her.

"Good morning, and come in," Mary spoke fluent English, as she ushered Jay and Rose into the living room where her daughter was seated smiling up at them.

"This is Emma," she introduced her daughter. "Emma, this Jay Lee and Rose Simpson." Mary smiled at them. "Mr. Prescott told me that you would be here to interview Emma for your research project. We are happy to assist you."

Jay and Rose gave Emma their gifts before they sat down. They watched Emma admire the multicolored wrap Jay had given her. Jay looked around the living room, admiring the beautiful art pieces, and loving the elephant set on a shelf that looked as if it had been glazed with gray gloss.

As soon as Jay and Rose had composed themselves, Jay began her interview. The first question on Jay's list was the type of marriage Emma had planned for herself.

"I am going to have a civil marriage," Emma said, then added, "The first part of my marriage will take place at the registry office." She paused and smiled as if she was proud of her choice before she continued. "At the registry's office, I will receive a certificate of registration, and because I am having a religious marriage, I will have an expensive wedding in church," she said. Emma's dark eyes seemed to illuminate with pride as she explained how she hadn't participated through the rituals in the traditional proposal parade.

Jay was curious now, since she had just gone to a proposal parade and watched the young women dance in order to be chosen by a man as his wife. Although, Jay understood that Emma's wedding was more western than the traditional weddings that the young ladies from the proposal parade hoped to have. "You gave up all of your tradition?" Jay asked, thinking that Emma's marriage would be regular, but at least she understood that all the ladies didn't follow the old traditions anymore. "You didn't participate in the proposal parade?" Jay asked Emma.

"Oh," Emma laughed. "I danced and flirted in the marketplace," she said between quips of laughter. "The young men sang songs showing that they are interested in choosing a wife. But we—the young ladies," she said, planting her hand on her chest, "we sang songs to the men too and we danced up to the man we want for our husband, we stop in front of him and he knows he has been chosen." Emma was serious, but laughed in good humor.

Jay nodded. She was certain that it was the man that always chose the wife, but Emma assured her and Rose that she had chosen her husband and reminded them that the traditional marriages were changing.

"You see, I was going to school in Europe when I met him." Emma explained. "He was there visiting relatives. Now, we both are from this country, but when we saw each other, we knew that we were to be married. So," Emma said smiling. "When we were both here, we went to the marketplace where the young people were having a marriage dance and I chose him to be my husband."

Jay had noticed that Emma was slender, and had assumed that Emma hadn't stayed in the fattening hut for three to eighteen months, eating fattening foods, preparing her body to give birth to healthy babies.

"No," Emma said. "I made a choice that I would not go into the fattening hut." Emma shifted in her seat as she confirmed what Jay had suspected and now learned to be true.

"Does this mean that you will not receive a bride price?" Jay asked Emma's mother.

"The traditional customs are changing, but there will be a bride price," Mary said. She and Emma's father would receive a dowry from the groom's family. They could receive a large amount of money, or land and other valuables.

"I always thought the African culture practiced polygamy," Jay said, wanting Emma to explain, realizing many people thought polygamy was practiced by everyone in Nigeria.

"My marriage is going to be a monogamous Christian marriage," Emma assured Jay and Rose as she looked from one to the other. "As a wife I will have more security and freedom." Emma nodded as if agreeing with herself. "I will definitely be a 'ringed wife,' " the young woman smiled, going on to explain that she would be regarded as an elite woman. "I am about seventy-five percent sure there will not be a cowife in my marriage."

"Seventy-five percent?" Jay perked up and sat on the edge of her seat. Emma wasn't sure if she had to share her husband with another woman or not.

"Yes, because in my religious marriage we are marrying for love. You know, like the westerners. Our husbands don't usually take on an outside wife or a cowife."

"Cowife?" Rose sat back and crossed her legs, seeming more interested as the conversation of multiwives was being discussed.

Emma smiled, and Jay sensed that she was serious. "An outside wife or a cowife, is a woman who my husband could choose to have a sexual relationship with for several years without marriage rites or the payment of bride price. She may have children for him, and he may support her financially for many years, but he has no responsibility to her."

"How would you feel if your husband decided to take on a cowife?" Jay asked.

"Jay, we'll have a certificate of registration and I can get a divorce," Emma stated flatly.

Jay couldn't hold back her smile, thinking that Emma had taken careful measures to secure herself. "A divorce," Jay said. Emma was educated, with a degree in business administration and already owned a mask boutique. She sold African masks, greeting cards, and expensive jewelry. Her plans were to become a mother in a few years after her marriage. Emma knew there was no guarantee that her husband wouldn't take on a cowife.

"Emma, what will make your husband decide to take on another wife?" Rose asked, seeming even more concerned about Emma's marriage status than Jay.

"Sometimes the men find that it's easier to return to the traditional ways of marriage," Emma clasped her hands together.

"You'll have no choice but to accept his decision," Jay said.

"No, I will divorce him immediately," Emma replied. "I would like for both of you to attend my wedding," she said, inviting Jay and Rose.

"Divorce?" Rose asked as if she thought this procedure was impossible for Emma.

"That's why I chose to have a civil marriage," Emma said, and chuckled lightly.

"Thank you, Emma," Jay said, closing her folder.

"Lunch is ready," Mary said, when an older woman who introduced herself as Ida stood at the door of the dining room and motioned Mary.

Jay, Rose and the others settled down for lunch, eating coconut bean soup served with *Ugali,* a thick cornmeal mush rolled into balls and eaten with their fingers. This was Jay's first experience with a genuine African dish. Her girlfriend Carol once attempted to make a Nigerian meal, but her cooking was horrible. But the food Jay was enjoying today was delicious.

While they ate lunch, Emma and Mary answered Jay's questions on the importance of family. Even though Emma and her family had mixed the tradition in their family, their values were never changing. "I intend to hire my relatives to help me with my new business," Emma said. "We always help one another."

"Family is important to us," Mary agreed with her daughter, as they finished eating and waited for the dessert. They were looking forward to the additional family members that would join their circle of relatives after Emma was married.

Minutes later, Ida appeared from the kitchen carrying dessert. The round thin bread looked like large cookies. *"Chapati majis,"* Ida said, serving the dessert that was sprinkled with sugar and folded in half. Jay had never tasted any dessert so delicious. She enjoyed the sweets with a cup of tea.

Once lunch was over, Jay and Rose knew that they would return. The family was friendly and were looking forward to seeing Jay and Rose again at Emma's wedding.

"Now Jay, I think if I lived in this country I would choose the type of marriage Emma is choosing. Because if Webster and I ever married, I would divorce him too if he took on a cowife," Rose said as she and Jay headed home.

Jay laughed "You're something else, but I agree," she said as she and Rose and the cameraman waited for the local bus to take them to their next assignment. She wondered what Trent's views would be on the subject of cowives.

Doris Abuja was friendly, but shy and not as outspoken as Emma. Her powder blue smock dress, draped with a thin brown shawl hung loosely over her plump body. Gold jewelry adorned her neck and ankles and her hair was pinned up in a style of her choice.

Doris had graciously accepted the gifts that Jay and Rose gave her and then sat quietly listening to her mother, grandmother and aunts as they followed the old marriage advice tradition. The women explained that Doris was never to take her and her husband's family business to the relatives. She was the center of her family, and her husband and children were important.

When the women finished with their advice, Doris walked with them into the kitchen and stirred the boiling pot, a ritual that symbolized her desire to become an excellent housewife.

Jay watched Doris intensely as she stirred the substance in the pot. When Doris was finished with her stirring, the women exited single file to the back.

Jay noticed a man holding a sheep by a rope which was hooked to a catch around its neck. Doris walked to the animal and touched its head.

The animal was her gift from the groom and afterwards, would be taken and slaughtered, cooked and served as an offering at the wedding dinner.

The offering of bride price had been made, alloting Doris's family a large sum of money and a few acres of land. All that was left to do now was toast the bride and her new husband with a glass of palm wine and enjoy the food. Jay and Rose drank a small glass of wine and ate fruit before they had to leave, and were unable to stay for the main course of meat that was to be served with vegetables and later dessert.

"Sisters, I hope you will return for the party," Doris's mother offered, inviting them to share in an evening of dancing and celebration for Doris and her husband and his family, who were now their new relatives.

"Thank you," Jay said, and wished Doris the best with her new marriage. Doris's marriage was a traditional polygamous one. She was the second wife to her husband and a much younger woman than his first wife. Doris would add additional children to the already large family.

Nevertheless, Doris was proud of her new family and the home that had been built for her.

"Congratulations," Jay said to Doris.

"Thank you," Doris said, speaking up for the first time since she was married.

Jay walked out into Doris's yard after they had said their good-byes and headed for the house. Their weddings and interviews were finished until the end of the week.

Trent closed the lid on the small box that held the gift he had just bought for Jay. It was the end of the week and he could hardly wait to see her.

Tonight they were invited to the wedding and marriage celebration and after the festivities, he intended to spend the rest of the evening with Jay. He slipped the small box into his pocket and left his hotel room, dressed for the occasion and the evening he planned to spend with Jay.

Six

"Give me a second," Jay said when she heard a second knock on her door. She lay the comb down and opened the door for Trent. Her breath caught in her throat as she admired him in his dark suit. But as always on the weekends, he looked as if he had just stepped off the page of a fashion magazine. "Where have you been?" She asked him.

"I've been with Myers all week," Trent said, moving inside Jay's room.

"I'll be ready in a few minutes," she said, giving him a kiss when he tried to stop her with the touch of his hand on her waist. Jay rushed to the small jewelry box that held the few pieces of jewelry that she had brought with her on the trip.

Trent moved over to her, taking the small box from his pocket. "Be still," he said, setting the box on the vanity top while Jay sorted through her jewelry.

"Wait, Trent, I'm looking for earrings."

"Will you be still," Trent said, hanging the necklace around Jay's neck and fastening the clasp.

"Oh, Trent," Jay pressed her finger against the tiny diamonds circling the ruby. "It's beautiful. Thanks."

She wrapped her arms around Trent's neck and gave him a slow kiss.

"You're welcome," Trent said, giving her the matching earrings when she let him up for air.

"I love it," Jay smiled into the mirror, admiring the jewelry while she put the earrings on. "And I love you," she said.

Trent folded her in his arms. "I missed you," Trent said, kissing her softly, first on her neck and finally her lips, deepening the kiss, causing Jay to hunger for more and she melted against his strong chest.

He raised his head and lowered it again, making a trail of warm kisses down the side of her neck. Jay allowed the shivers to race through her thinking how she was lucky to have met Trent. He lifted his head again.

"I missed you, too," Jay said, stroking her fingers across his strong jaw. She pulled out of his embrace and went to get the only black party purse she had brought with her. The black bag wasn't overly decorated and went well with the outfit she was wearing and the necklace set Trent had given her.

"Let's go before we end up staying here all night," Trent said, pushing his hands into his pockets and towering over Jay while she removed a few small necessities from her work bag and slipped them into her black purse.

Jay shut her purse and went to get the door after hearing a soft tap on the door. "Paul," Jay said to the cameraman who had worked with her and Rose all week.

"This is for you." He held out a box to Jay.

Jay thanked him, noticing that the package was from

her girlfriend, Carol, and intended to open the parcel when she returned home that night.

"You're looking nice," Paul said, giving Jay a sweeping admiring gaze.

"Thanks," Jay smiled up at him, wondering what Carol had sent her.

"If you need a ride to the wedding you can ride with me," he said. "I rented a car."

"She's going with me," Trent crossed the floor to the door and stood next to Jay.

"Okay," Paul said, backing away from Jay's door. "I'm sorry."

Trent shut the door firmly. "How well do you know him?" Trent tilted his head to one side and spoke with an air of impatience.

"Trent, he's the cameraman that worked with us on the marriage project." Jay set the box on the bed, thinking that Trent couldn't be jealous but then maybe he had reasons to be apprehensive considering the problem he'd had with Sonya. "I'm ready when you are," Jay said and walked out of the room with Trent close behind her.

The ballroom in the hotel where the wedding was taking place was decorated with blue and silver colors. The bride's low-cut pastel blue gown displayed lines of dark incisions etched across the top of her breasts, and her hair was swept and rolled into an elegant style. Bearing all signs of grace, she prepared to take her place in society as a married woman. The groom was equally as handsome, Jay observed as the gentleman stood next to his brother, uncle and father. The trio of men were part of the marriage ritual. The groom's father stood tall in front of the men. He would escort the bride and his son home, assuring the family that he approved of the woman his son had chosen for a wife.

The bride price had already been paid. The ceremony had been much like Ida's marriage ceremony. The difference was this woman's celebration was being held in a hotel ballroom instead of the groom's home. She had been told of her duties as a wife. She would never go to her family with the problems she and her husband encountered in their marriage and her duties were now to her husband.

The bride had been reminded and understood the importance of being a virgin. If she was found not to be a virgin once she and her husband copulated, the young woman would be sent home to her parents. Her father would blame her mother for the daughter's indiscretion and for not watching their daughter and the mother would punish the daughter. Added to that, the bride price would have to be returned to the groom and his family.

Jay watched and admired the young woman. She appeared strong, mature and willing to take on the responsibilities of her new life, as her father-in-law escorted her to the table followed by the groom and his brother. The palm wine and dinner were served and the wedding celebration began.

While Jay, Trent, Rose and Webster and the others enjoyed the wine and the smothered chicken breast, wild rice and vegetables, Jay couldn't resist asking Trent his opinion on polygamous marriages. "If you lived in Africa and knowing you had the choice to have a polygamous marriage, which marriage would you choose?" Jay asked Trent as she sliced a thin section of the meat.

"I don't know, probably two or three. I guess it would depend upon my tribe." Trent flashed Jay, what seemed to her like a devilish smile, and winked at Webster. "What do you think, Nelson?"

"I don't have anything to say," Webster chuckled and looked at Rose.

"I would like to know your answer," Rose said, smiling and holding Webster's gaze.

"Me too," Jay agreed. She understood that Trent was right. The tradition seemed to have been changing and many of the marriages were monogamous rather than polygamous.

"Okay, guys, Rose and I understand that the men may have several wives for different reasons. One wife may help him with his business . . ."

"I understand, Jay," Rose said. "But speak for yourself."

Jay pierced the thinly sliced meat with her fork and stuck the food into her mouth. She understood that Rose didn't want to think about sharing Webster.

After dinner, a roll of drum beats began and couples began to dance while Jay, Trent, Webster and Rose observed and enjoyed the palm wine and the music and dancers, until finally Jay and Trent danced, enjoying themselves until late into the night.

Laughter filtered throughout the room and it seemed that everyone was talking at the same time and enjoying the wedding festivities, celebrating the couple's new marriage until it was late in the evening.

"Let's go," Trent said, reaching for Jay's hand and walking off the dance floor. "I'll see you later, Rose." Jay stopped at their table saying goodnight to Rose and Webster.

Seven

The night was comfortably cool, and Trent drew Jay close to him as they pushed their way through the crowd and to the edge of the sidewalk, waiting for the thick traffic to pass before they crossed the street to the parking lot. Automobile horns honked while the scent of diesel fuel filled the air. A distance away, Jay heard more music.

When they reached the Jeep, Trent drew her closer to him, and for a long time, they stood near his Jeep, gently holding one another. Jay lifted her finger and touched his firm lips, and he kissed her finger, sending a sensation through her. The thrill stirred her and lingered as if Trent had sent her an intense message. He kissed her then recklessly, ravishing her with sweet affection. Trent relaxed his hold on her as they stepped out of the embrace. "Trent Prescott, we should go home where we can be comfortable," Jay said, waiting for him to unlock the Jeep's door.

"You're right," Trent said, walking around to get in beside her.

Trent turned the radio on and started up the engine. The radio announcer interrupted the music with a special news report. There had been an automobile accident on the road that Jay and Trent took to the team's house and the road had been closed and would not open until the officers had taken information and checked the credentials of the three drivers involved in the accident. "That process can take all night. By the time everyone gives an accident report to the police it might be two o'clock before we get home," Trent said.

"We'll probably get home before two in the morning, Trent," Jay said, touching her finger to the button near the rearview mirror and turning on the light to check the time on her watch.

"We're going to my hotel room," Trent said, getting out.

By the time Trent came around the front of the Jeep and reached the passenger's side Jay was out of the car and hoping that the clothing shop she had seen in the hotel lobby was still open. She hadn't come prepared to stay away from home all night, and she needed an outfit to wear home tomorrow and a nightgown.

Jay and Trent crossed the street to the hotel again and she was happy to see that the shop was still open.

"I have to stop in here," she said, noticing that several of her teammates were at the registration desk ordering rooms for the night as she walked into the shop and headed for the nightgown rack. She walked over to the rack, not caring what color or length she picked and reached for long canary gown.

"I like that," Trent said, motioning his head in the direction of a row of sexy sleep wear.

"Trent, those are too uncomfortable to sleep in," Jay said, observing the sheer black, red and many other thong see-through nighties that were only for show, especially since the material was probably scratchy to the skin.

Trent's mouth twisted into an impish smile. "Baby, who said anything about sleeping?"

Jay returned his devilish grin and chose the yellow gown, and headed toward the shorts-sets, choosing an outfit that was more conservative than she normally wore and headed to the check out counter. While Trent pushed his hands in his pockets and waited for her, Jay paid the clerk.

Jay nodded to a few of her coworkers, acknowledging them while Trent's fingers grazed her waist, sending a shudder of shivers through her with his gentle touch. They took the elevator to his room on the third floor and entered his room that was cast with a veil of light. "Not having to stay in the team's house must be nice," Jay said, almost to herself as she scanned the beige love seat, silk green plants, cocktail table, a chestnut desk and chair at the far side of the room.

"When I need to get away from the team or in this case, this is my retreat," Trent said as he moved over to the bedside stand and stripped down to his trousers. Then he pressed the speaker button on his answering machine and began listening to his messages.

Jay allowed herself to study his broad chest for a second and then turned away. She wished Trent wouldn't undress in front of her. Just looking at how the band on his pants fitted neatly around his waist, his hips narrow, and how he had just enough bottom to make his pants hang just so was enough to drive her crazy.

Jay dropped her purse on the love seat, and half listened to his messages while looking out the window and thinking that she was looking at a nearby park, when she heard a message from Myers wanting Trent to call him, and another from one of their male co-workers.

Jay turned away from the window and began taking the gown from the shopping bag, when she heard a woman's voice. "Trent, the least you can do is call me. I understand you're busy, but that's not an excuse. You have my number."

Without warning, a ridiculous streak of jealousy spiraled through Jay as she was heading to the bathroom, and almost stopped in her tracks when she heard Sonya's voice.

"Trent, there is no law that says we can't be friends. But you know that we still love . . ." Jay walked into the bathroom and closed the door, and leaned against the vanity.

She was aware of where her insecurities came. Gladys had preached for years to her that most men weren't good, and would love nothing more than to have two or three women waiting in the wings, pining over them.

Jay had dismissed her grandmother's warnings, especially after she went away to school and made several casual male friends, and learned from listening to them that all men weren't as repulsive as her grandmother had wanted her to believe.

Nonetheless, Jay had to face the facts regarding her new lover. Trent Prescott had never given her any reason to believe that he held any similarity to the description she had learned from Gladys. Along with his other good qualities, he was kinder than she had once thought.

However, a sneaky quiet voice reminded her that

Trent Prescott probably mastered the game of love, and had no problem persuading women into joining him for a night out on the town. Jay closed her eyes, not wanting to think of what might happen afterwards. Still, another round of envious waves coursed through her and stopped to coil around her heart. Was she as ingenuous as Gladys wanted her to be, or should she have waited before she gave too much of herself to Trent?

The thoughts crossed her mind, one after another and she wondered had she made a terrible mistake. A thought more dismaying than the other swept through her again and she realized that she was in love with Trent Prescott, and was unable to control her rising jealousy.

She dismissed the frightening thoughts. She was stronger than she was giving herself credit for and prepared for bed.

She pulled the gown over her head and turned, resting her hips on the edge of the vanity, allowing memories of the passion they had aroused and ignited in each other and she couldn't imagine sharing him.

"Jay," she heard Trent outside the bathroom door.

She composed herself and brushed past him as she headed to the bed. Trent grabbed her arm. "I'll be out in a few minutes, so don't go to sleep," he said, making it sound more like an order rather than a request. She couldn't bring herself to speak. It seemed that her voice caught in her throat and she decided that not speaking to him may have been right at the moment. Letting him know that she loved him more than he loved her was not exactly the discussion she was prepared to have tonight. Besides, she'd had a long day that ended with fun and thinking about anything other than sleep was a waste of her time.

Jay was laying on her stomach in her favorite sleeping position when Trent returned and got in bed beside her. "What's wrong?" he asked her.

"I'm tired," Jay said, scooting farther down underneath the covers.

Trent raised up on his elbow, leaned over and looked at her. "You weren't tired a few minutes ago, so what's the problem?"

"Is there suppose to be a problem?" Jay asked. She had already admitted to herself that she was jealous and was determined to stay in control when she sat up and faced him. "If you think I'm one of the many women you can sleep with just so you can please your sexual appetite I want you out of my life now!" Jay said, hearing her own anger bristling in her voice, but she couldn't stop herself.

"If you're talking about those messages, I can explain and you already know about Sonya," Trent said.

Jay pushed herself up in bed to a more comfortable position and firmly planted one hand on her hip and raised a finger to Trent. "I don't play with little boys who pretend to be men, and I will not be added to your list of lovers." Jay turned away, feeling the tears settle into her eyes, mostly because she was angry at herself for her jealous outburst.

"Baby, listen. Lolita and I are good friends. I've known her almost as long as I've known Webster," Trent explained, telling her how he and Lolita had once lived in the same neighborhood in Canada when they were teenagers.

Jay looked straight ahead until she calmed down.

Trent squeezed her hands. "Sonya will do almost anything to start trouble. Jay, we're not going to fight," he said in a soft voice. Jay turned and looked at him.

"Sonya saw us downstairs in the lobby and she made the call a few minutes before we got to the room." Trent reached out and took the telephone. "Look at the time."

Jay looked at the time that Sonya's call came in and she was embarrassed by her own behavior.

"All right?" Trent said, locking his fingers behind his head. "Sonya knows me. She knows that when I come home at night the first thing I do is listen to my messages."

Jay was still quiet.

"I don't play games, baby." Trent looked at Jay. "Hm?"

Jay considered what he told her and she knew that Sonya had harassed her almost from the first day she arrived in the country. If Trent loved her as much as Sonya wanted her to believe why was she upset? "How many times have you broken up with her?" Jay asked.

"Once. That was it," Trent said.

"Did you forgive her?"

"I forgave her and I did it for me. I couldn't allow what she did to destroy me. Baby, I love you," Trent said.

Jay slid underneath the covers. They gathered one another close. "That's beside the point. How would it feel if Austin called and left a message for me?" Jay asked and raised up on her elbow to look down at Trent. "Hm?" She hit her finger against Trent's chest.

"I might have a similar reaction. I don't know." He held her finger against his chest. "I don't want Austin calling you."

"Those are my feelings about Sonya." She slipped her finger from his grasp and traced an imaginary line to the top of his masculine center, drawing a sluggish low growl from him.

Trent took her hand and squeezed it lightly. "I'm serious about us, Jay."

"I'm serious too." She made another trail to his chest and massaged gently until his nipples were hard as stone. "Hmm," Trent murmured softly. "But I don't think that I need to be loud and obnoxious, letting everyone know our feelings for one another." Jay stopped stroking Trent's chest and looked at him.

"Who's being loud and obnoxious?" He asked her.

Jay hadn't planned to tell Trent about Sonya's reactions to her and she still wouldn't. "I intend to love you in peace," she said, leaning down and kissing his chest while stroking the top of his muscular thigh.

"You should be careful where you touch me," Trent said, drawing her to him.

"And if I'm not careful?" Jay's smile was soft and seductive, as she buried her palms against his masculine center.

"This could happened," Trent said, tossing her over with one smooth move, and whipping the long gown up around her hips at the same time. Jay snuggled against him, promising herself that she was not losing control again, and she could never give him up. "Oh that," she said, brushing her lips against his hard chest.

Trent's answer to Jay was to trace his thumb along her cheek, and finally to the center of her lips. Slowly, Trent planted tiny kisses on Jay's cheeks and neck until finally he helped himself to her lips with a hungry and searching kiss. He hooked his fingers beneath the slender straps of her gown, pealing away the yellow material and displaying her firm breast. One hand captured her breast, stroking it lightly. "We will always be together," Trent whispered against her ear before he skimmed his mouth against hers, sending Jay further into a blissful and reckless state. Trent pressed his palm flat against her stomach and moved slow and gracefully to her thighs, stroking an irresistible flame and leading a sizzling trail to the *v* of her thighs and then burnt a path to her center.

Her heart pound as she savored every moment. They searched and explored one another for places not touched, and savory kisses hot enough to melt their souls.

Jay's fingers inched along his back taping slowly against his spine, igniting a rush of cascading emotions until he pressed her hands down against her side. "Stop baby," he said, his breath quickening and she felt the strength of his masculinity. When he composed himself, he moved a kiss to the center of her throat, drawing a breathless clamor from Jay that ended with his name. And he roamed to secret places exploring and searching and finally the scraping sound of paper split the silence and he returned to her, gently driving and exploring a world and lifting Jay to heights. Her blood felt like slow, hot liquid moving one fraction of an inch at a time through her veins while they danced and swayed to the tune of heady muffled babbled gnarls.

Jay and Trent basked in a glow of sweet intimacy, slept for a while and again took safe measures and continued to raise more flaming desire until they rose again to heights of ecstasy.

Jay and Trent wrapped themselves in each other's arms and slept.

Bam—bam—bam! Jay heard the rapping sound against the door, a sound that seemed to come from a long distance world. *Bam—bam!*

"Ahh!" Trent let out an angry clamor. "Who the hell is that?" he asked, sounding as if he was almost out of breath. Trent sat up and looked at the clock.

Another knock sounded against the door before he rolled out of the bed and crossed to the closet for a pair of pants.

"Myers, it's six-thirty in the morning? What do you want?" Trent asked.

Jay heard her boss mention her name and wondered why was she the center of their conversation at six-thirty in the morning, when she noticed Trent step out into the hall.

Caring less to hear more of what the men were saying, Jay dozed off, hoping to get another hour or two of sleep. Myers worried about everything that had to do with his project anyway, Jay mused. She dozed into a delightful sleep when she heard Trent and Myers voices raise in frustration. There was then only the firm thud of the bedroom door. "What's wrong?" Jay asked as Trent sat on the edge of the bed next to her. "What happened?" Jay asked again when his silence became too much for her.

"Myers wants to meet with you in an hour, downstairs." Trent looked at her and she observed the anger smoldering in his eyes.

"What does he want, Trent?" Jay asked. She thought that she and Rose had done a nice job on the interview.

"He wants to send you home," Trent said.

"Send me home for what—we didn't complete our project."

"Myers thinks that you will work better in the office," Trent said.

"That's not true. I want to know the real reason,"

Jay remarked flatly, getting out of bed and getting dressed for her meeting.

"Sonya made a written report to Myers, telling him that you couldn't get along with her and that the clash in the relationship was a problem." Trent stood and pushed his hands into his back pockets and paced around the room slowly, reminding Jay of a frustrated caged animal.

Jay wasn't the least surprised that Sonya would go to Myers and complain about her. Sonya had already proven that she was petty and determined to get Jay out of Nigeria one way or another. She had tried intimidation, embarrassment and had failed miserably at both. Now her only recourse to win the battle was to call their boss and make a false report.

Jay's eyes burned with threatening tears as she pondered her situation carefully. She was determined to stay calm in the face of the havoc Sonya had caused in her life. "What reasons did she give Myers for our problem?" Jay asked out of curiosity, wondering what other lies Sonya had told their boss in order to disguise herself as being an innocent, frustrated employee and not the employee with the problem.

"Sonya is threatening to resign and leave the Dancing Mask Project," Trent said. "Why didn't you tell me that you and Sonya had an argument the day of the parade and almost every other time you've run into each other?" Trent asked Jay.

"Maybe I should have mentioned the petty confrontation that Sonya picked with me, but what good would it have done if Myers needs her for the Dancing Mask Project anyway?" Jay remembered Sonya's warning and wished that she had paid attention to her. Sonya had made their problem seem bigger than it was and she was being punished for a conflict she didn't have control over. Jay struggled with her anger and the aching sobs that threatened her. She was determined to stay strong in the face of adversity and she would not permit anything or anyone to upset her to the point of tears.

Trent shook his head and crossed over to the desk and then back to the center of the room. "I told you that Sonya was a liar," Trent looked as frustrated as he sounded. "You didn't think I was telling you the truth?" He shoved one hand into his pocket and planted the other on his narrow hip.

"Myers believes her," Jay said.

"No, he doesn't. Sonya is staying only because she has already met with the tribe, and they know and like her. Because of that, Myers thinks she's the best person for the job," Trent replied.

"Okay," Jay said, heading to the bathroom to get dressed and then pressing her lips together to suppress the tears that blurred her vision.

"Baby, you're not upset because you're leaving?" Trent's voice reached her as she held onto the door knob.

Jay took her time answering him, but she couldn't allow him to hear the tears in her voice. "I don't like having to leave earlier than scheduled." She drew in a breath and slowly exhaled. "But I have a personal project that I intend to work on once I return home. So, in a way, it's good that I'm leaving early." Feeling more in control, but still angry, Jay turned to face Trent then, hoping that he didn't notice the tears in her eyes from the short distance across the room.

"I'll talk to Myers again and work something out.

That way, you can stay," Trent offered, moving toward her. "I don't want you to go."

"No," Jay said. "I can talk to Myers myself. It probably won't do much good since his mind is already made up. But we can always call each other." She went into the bathroom before Trent could get to her and locked the door.

Jay pressed her palms against the top of the vanity. One tear dropped from her eye and then the other. Anger and humiliation singed her. She freed her tears and allowed herself to cry. Her dream had come true, but not without a price that shouldn't have been paid and simply because she had chosen to love Trent, the remainder of her dream would be shattered. Myers wanted to meet with her and she would get the opportunity to argue her point, whether her point mattered to her boss or not. She was not going to wither because lies had been told about her.

Jay snatched a tissue from the tissue box, wiped her eyes and began her shower. She had fought a few battles in her life, but this was a fight that she didn't know if she could win. Her work for Myers had been good, so good that he had asked her to join the team. Although Trent had said that Myers didn't believe Sonya, it was the status of her own reputation that concerned her. Having Myers suspect that she was unable to work with the team could mean that she would never travel with Myers' research team again.

First of all, the whole matter was laced with lies. Could she tell her boss exactly what the problem was and hope he would allow her to stay and finish her work?

She considered the question, knowing that Myers was a determined man, but Jay didn't know if he was concerned with his employees' personal problems. Jay considered herself lucky that Myers wanted to send her home and was not firing her. Jay understood that Sonya would never have said anything to her if she and Trent weren't in a relationship and Jay wondered if Trent was worth it all.

Jay's tears mingled with the water from the shower spraying against her face as she remembered Sonya's last threatening words to her. *"We'll see about that!"*

Jay noticed Myers seated at the front of the hotel's restaurant when she and Trent entered. His glasses were perched on the tip of his nose as he read the morning paper. He held the paper to one side and lifted his cup and drank down whatever liquid he had ordered that morning.

"Good morning," Jay said, pulling back a chair and sitting, not waiting for Trent to assist her. Business was being taken care of this morning and she wanted to know from her boss exactly why she was being sent home, and whether Sonya had told him the real reason she had a problem with her. This was her career and she intended to defend it with as much mental strength needed to get the job done.

"Good morning, Jay," Myers said. He folded his newspaper in half before he placed it in the empty chair beside him. "Trent," Myers nodded, and placed his eyeglasses inside of his blue plaid pocket.

"Myers," Trent addressed Jay's boss and she detected the coolness in his voice when he spoke.

A waiter walked over and filled Jay and Trent's cups with coffee and asked for their order. "Coffee is fine,"

Jay said, and turned her attention back to Myers, not listening to what Trent was saying to the young man.

"Jay, I wanted to meet with you because there's a problem," Myers began as Jay recognized his usual speech when he met with the staff and someone who was in trouble.

"Trent told me that you wanted me to return home and I don't believe there's a valid reason." Jay sprinkled the coffee with sugar, understanding that Myers might not change his mind and she would go home, but not without a fight.

"I would like it if all of you could get along, and in this case, it wouldn't matter, but I cannot lose the project that Sonya is working on."

"The problem Sonya is having with me is personal." Jay glanced at Trent. "Trent and I are dating and she has had a problem with me ever since." She shrugged. "I don't believe that's a reason for her to resign or for me to leave my work." She raised her cup midair and looked at Myers over the rim.

"I know and I understand your concern, and I couldn't agree with you more. But you know that I can't take a chance sending someone else to work on Sonya's project when the people are already familiar with her. It's too late to change gears now, especially when the project is scheduled to begin soon." Myers looked at Jay and gave her a grim smile, then he glanced across the table at Trent. "Trent, I'm doing what's best for the company."

"We'll talk later," Trent said, and folded his arms across his chest.

"I understand the problem," Myers said, directing his comments to Trent. "I talked to Sonya when she asked for a transfer. I asked her would she have a problem working on this trip with you and she promised me that she had moved on. I should've paid attention when she insisted on heading a project. But Sonya works well and if I can't complete this project, I have a problem. Jay, do you understand?" Myers turned to Jay, directing his question to her.

"Yes, I do understand that you will have a problem," Jay answered, casting a glance across the dining room and paying attention to nothing in particular.

"You work well and deserve better, especially having to leave under these circumstances. So, I think you deserve a promotion. You will be working with Rose, assisting her with the information on all of the projects we have worked on here. You will travel and work with Rose on all other projects." Myer's aged lips edged into a smile. "When you return home, you will have some time off, but with pay, so that you can rest."

"Thanks," Jay said. She could use the extra time to work on Lees' and get it ready for opening.

"Now, I don't like discussing Sonya because she's not here to defend herself, but I would like to make myself clear. Sonya has a problem with you, which I believe will on occasion generate distraction in not only your work, but with her duties as well. Rose told me what happened and she and Trent recommend you highly," Myers said to Jay.

Jay knew that she had to thank Rose as she watched Trent unfold his arms and recline back in the chair.

"Once she returns to the States, I am transferring Sonya back to her previous position in Canada." Myers looked at Trent. "If there are no other comments, we're finished here," Myers said, as he continued to watch Trent.

It appeared that Myers wanted to talk to Trent. "Excuse me," Jay said, and headed to the gift shop, counting her good fortune. What had seemed to be a disaster had turned in her favor and she was more than satisfied with the results.

Before she walked out of the dining room entrance, Jay stopped walking to glimpse back at Trent and Myers. They were in another heated disagreement with Trent doing all the talking this time. Jay dismissed the men and walked to the gift shop.

She was satisfied with Myers' decision and that was all that mattered.

"Myers, you never take my suggestions," Trent said, eyeing Myers angrily. "I have suggested to you more than once to have a stand-in just in case something petty like this happens," Trent said to Myers.

"Trent, I understand that you're upset that Jay is going home." He grinned, flashing a set of white teeth. "But I'm glad you got back into the swing of things."

Trent didn't say anything to Myers even though he was pleased with the decision that Myers had made for Jay.

"You'll be home soon, and you and Jay will see each other as much as you want, and life will be sweet for you again," Myers chuckled under his breath. "It's nice to see you happy again."

Trent rubbed the back of his neck. As much as he wanted to fight with Myers for sending Jay home, he couldn't now with Myers stalling him after every other comment on how happy he was that he and Jay were lovers. Trent didn't need to be told how happy he was with Jay Lee. She was the best thing that had happened to him in a long time.

"I'll be right back," Myers said, leaving Trent to his thoughts.

However, it wasn't necessary for him to fight with Myers. Jay Lee had stepped up to the plate and defended herself and he wasn't surprised. Earlier, he had thought that Jay was going to cower since she didn't seem all that upset when they talked in his room. He was prepared to fight for her and let Myers know exactly how he felt about sending Jay home.

He also wanted to forget Sonya and her disagreements, and childish pranks. Once he had loved Sonya, and all that she was. She had held his heart, and in those days if anyone had told him that she was as nitpicky and scornful as she had been to Jay, he wouldn't have believed them. But after she trampled on his heart with her lies and deceit he believed that she would lie about anything. But Sonya's trick had worked against her when she picked a fight with Jay, Trent considered, as he waited for Myers to return.

He was certain Sonya thought that her game was the same when they were together. When Trent worked full-time for Myers, team members often came to him complaining about Sonya's intolerable attitude. Sonya would always smooth over the conflict saying that she was misunderstood. But with Jay, she had chosen a strong opponent and he knew Jay was a fighter. Trent imagined that any personal insults Sonya had lashed out at her were not acceptable to Jay.

Jay hadn't come to him complaining about her hurt feelings and how she couldn't work or live in the same house with certain members. She had protected herself and Trent believed that not only because of her work. But Jay's strength had earned her a promotion. Trent smiled to himself. He loved Jay for many reasons.

Trent looked up and saw Myers heading back to their table. He was sure he had to make Jay's reservation and complete all the paper work. After that, he had plans to take Jay out one last time before she left Nigeria.

Jay had never told him that she wanted to visit any particular place. He hoped she would be interested in his idea. "I'll get the paperwork started," Trent said when Myers was sitting across from him again.

"That's fine with me," Myers said. "I wish you would continue to work for me, Trent."

"I've already told you that I can't work for you anymore," Trent said, not wanting to get into another discussion with Myers about what was now becoming a full time venture.

"I mean that running from state to state, buying up old properties that no one wants because they're probably having a hard time selling is not exactly the career for you."

Trent spread his hands and tilted his head to one side. "Come on, Myers. Let's not get into this," he replied dryly. Myers would say just about anything to keep Trent working at the research center.

"All right, but you can't blame a man for trying," Myers grinned.

Trent checked the time on his watch. "You'll be here for the week right?"

Myers nodded yes.

"I'm taking Jay out for a few days before she leaves. You don't mind taking over?"

"Enjoy yourself," Myers said.

Trent walked through the lobby and headed toward the gift shop when he suddenly saw Jay holding up a dress twirling it in front of a mirror, and his heart swelled.

Eight

Three days before Jay left for New Jersey, Trent surprised her with a sight-seeing tour. They traveled to Northern Tanzania before dawn with plans to take a small plane from Kilmanjaro Airport for the fifty minute flight to an African game reserve.

With her camera loaded with the film she had purchased at the Serengetic lodge where she and Trent were staying, Jay snapped a shot of every animal that came into view.

Their last day and night together was painful for them and added to that, it was raining. However, Trent kept his promise to order a picnic lunch, having the basket sent to their hotel room complete with wine, music and roses. That evening, they went dancing and returned to their room early, both agreeing that they would rather spend their remaining time together making love. Jay knew she loved Trent and the time she would be without him once she returned home promised to seem like years.

The morning they were to leave for Nigeria, Jay could hardly bring herself to get dressed, knowing that at the same time tomorrow morning she would say good-bye to Trent. Jay knew they would call each other, but she liked seeing his face when she talked to him. She would miss looking into his eyes and watching his facial expression.

The next day, Jay and Trent were quiet as they rode to the team's house. Jay was missing him already. She pressed her hand into his, wanting to remember everything about him, the scent of his cologne, his smile and how wonderful she felt when he held her in his arms.

"Jay, are you sure you want to go home?" Trent eased the Jeep to the curb in front of the team's house and cut off the engine. His scrutinizing gaze met and held hers. "I can pressure Myers into letting you stay." Trent held both her hands in his and pressed his lips gently against her fingers.

The offer to have Trent pressure Myers into letting her stay through the duration of the project was tempting, but she had agreed with her boss that she should return home. Jay could hardly turn down the promotion Myers had offered her. "Thanks, but no." She leaned over and kissed Trent's chin and leaned back, observing the sadness in his eyes. "I'm the one that's supposed to be sad, not you." She smiled at him, then tweaked his chin playfully.

"I hate this and everything that's happened," Trent said to her as he rested his head against the back of the seat, and gave her a side glance before he got out and took Jay's luggage from the back of the Jeep.

Jay didn't wait for him to open her door. She wanted to go inside and finish packing before she changed her mind and took Trent up on his offer to pressure Myers into letting her stay.

Trent slipped his free arm around Jay's waist as they walked inside, stopping after every two or three steps to caress one another's lips. Trent blew lightly against Jay's ear, making her laugh. "Stop!" Jay said.

"Sonya, the love birds are back," Jay overhead Sonya's girlfriend signal Sonya to her and Trent's arrival. Within seconds, Sonya had joined her girlfriend on the porch.

Jay and Trent climbed the steps and spoke to the women as the moved inside the house, noticing that neither woman returned their greetings. However, she didn't miss Sonya's reminder. "I warned her."

Jay dismissed the ridiculous comment. She had so much to be thankful for and flaunting comments regarding a threat that had been executed in Sonya's favor was meaningless. "I'll see you tomorrow," Jay said once she and Trent were inside her room.

"If you need anything I'll be sleeping across the hall tonight," Trent said referring to his room. He leaned over and gave her kiss. "I might take you up on your offer," Jay chuckled and kissed Trent. "Goodnight," Jay said, still savoring the kiss they had just shared and the shuddering affects Trent caused inside her. She opened the door and Trent walked inside her room and turned on the lights. "Good night, baby," Trent said, once he checked that everything in her room was in order.

Jay watched him leave her room and her pent up tears refused to hold on any longer. Her throat ached from wanting to cry, and her heart throbbed for being the center of a foolish game with no reason and purpose.

However, Trent had made her leaving easier, doing everything he could to make her happy and forget about the mean distasteful lie Sonya had told. Jay wouldn't forget, but she had him to thank for keeping her content until she had to leave.

She splashed her face and eyes with cold water, washing the tears off her face and then began packing.

She lifted the lid off the small jewelry case and held the necklace Trent had given her. He had drawn sumptuous desires to surface, aspiring a special yearning she'd had no need for six months ago. He had brought her joy and pleasure and showed her that she could have fun, be happy and love and be loved. Nothing is going to stop me from loving him she mused, squeezing the necklace against her palm. She had traveled thousands of miles and found him and she wasn't giving him up.

Jay picked up the package that Carol had sent her figuring it was a scarf since her girlfriend had a fetish about wraps and hats and would pick one or the other up for her when she was shopping.

Okay Miss Carol, what color is this scarf? Jay gave the package an impish grin, knowing that Carol was probably up to having fun. Even from afar, it seemed that her girlfriend always had a way to cheer her up. Jay went to the vanity and took out the letter opener and returned to anxiously open the box. Even more than loving to travel, Jay loved receiving gifts. She hurried back to the bed and ripped open the package, removing the white envelope, and laying it on top of the yellow tissue wrappings. She then ripped the letter open.

Hello Jay,
There's no need for me to ask you how things are going. From the information Barbara gave me, girl, you're doing find.

*Barbara told me how you went to Africa and got yourself
a boyfriend. Anyway after that news, I decided to ship
you a little something to ease the transition along. I hope
you love it!*
Girlfriends forever,
Carol

Jay pealed the wrapping away. "No, she didn't, she
giggled, lifting the black silk and lace teddy from the
box and studying the skimpy attire. The scanty thong
underwear left nothing to the imagination. Carol was
too much, Jay chuckled, taking the teddy and standing
with it in front of the mirror. She held the seductive
outfit out before her. If she didn't have to pack, she
would've tried the teddy on. *I'll have plenty of time to try
this sexy outfit on when I get home,* Jay pondered, placing
the black teddy inside her suitcase and next to her underwear.

It wasn't long before she had finished packing and
sat down to call Barbara, letting her know that she would
be leaving Nigeria tomorrow morning and she would
need a ride home from the airport if she didn't mind
giving her a ride. Her next telephone call was to her
grandmother. Jay fished through her address and telephone book finding Gladys's girlfriend's telephone
number down South. She talked to Gladys for a while,
telling her she was coming home early and giving Gladys
Lee the least amount of information as to why she was
coming home, but didn't miss to tell her that she had
received a promotion. Gladys was happy that Jay would
be home soon and was even more excited that she was
opening the bed and breakfast as soon as she returned.

In the meantime, preparing Lees' Bed and Breakfast
for opening and her work at Myers Research Center,

promised to keep her busy with not much time to think
about Trent, and probably no time to plot revenge on
Sonya for hatching a plan to separate her and Trent.
Jay couldn't let the deed go unpunished. Jay pondered,
thinking of a suitable punishment to fit the deed Sonya
had sprang into action and couldn't come up with anything. *"I'll think of something."*

In the airport Jay circled her arms around his neck,
parted her lips and met his kiss. Her heart danced with
sensual pleasure as she explored his sweetness.

Trent slowly lifted his head inches from her tender
lips. "I'll call you every night," he said, tightening his
arm around her slender waist and drawing her closer
to him. "I love you," Trent said.

Jay pulled his head down and whispered in his ear.
"I love you."

Finally it was time for Jay to board her flight and
she left him with hope and the promise that he would
be home soon.

Nine

Eighteen hours later, Jay waited outside the airport entrance for her ride home. While wisps of crisp March winds played with the legs of her linen pant suit, memories of Trent toyed with her mind and she felt her heart swelling with desire and hungry passion. There was not a hint of doubt that he didn't love her as much as she loved him and she could hardly wait until he was home.

While Jay traveled home, she refused to think about Trent. Reminding herself how much she missed him only made her miss him more. So she had made notes on how she would decorate the bed and breakfast. Making notes for the bed and breakfast project didn't take much time, and she had slept, dreaming about Trent, her dreams filled with joy and sense of pure raptured bliss. Jay awoke from her nap knowing that she was the luckiest woman in the world in having found the right man just when she was about to give up on love and the affairs of the heart.

Jay took her sunglasses from her purse and put them on, shading her eyes against the dazzling sun. Without any further interruption, she rejoiced in her private glory of renewed hope.

Jay noticed Barbara's car rounding the curb and heading in her direction. She gathered her luggage.

"Hi," Jay spoke to Barbara when she was out of the car and walking toward her with outstretched arms. Barbara's shoulder-length hair was rolled into a twist and fastened together with a gold decorative hair ornament. "It's good to see you," Jay said, hurrying into Barbara's outstretched arms and hugging her godmother.

"I didn't know I could miss you so much," Barbara's saucy red smile complemented her walnut complexion.

"It's good to be home," Jay said, stepping out of the embrace and helping to load the luggage into the trunk of the car. "I want to hear everything that happened," Barbara said, closing the car's trunk after she and Jay had set the last pieces of luggage inside the trunk and they were both seated inside the car.

"I enjoyed the work and I had fun," Jay replied, more glad to be home than she thought she would be. But she was still excited and anxious to tell Barbara about the proposal parade, and the weddings she had attended, and how much she and Trent Prescott loved one another.

"Sound more like play than work to me," Barbara laughed as she drove slowly out into the airport traffic.

"Before I left, Trent took me safari sight-seeing, and of course, that was fun," Jay said, noticing that Barbara suddenly seemed far away and wasn't paying attention to what she had just said to her.

"Sight-seeing," she said. "I can imagine that was fun." Barbara glanced in the side view mirror and changed the subject. "Gladys can't wait until you get started on that bed and breakfast."

"How's Granny?" Jay asked, not missing the disquieting expression on Barbara's face when she turned to her and mentioned her grandmother. Jay didn't think she had any real reasons to be concerned about her seventy-year-old grandmother. Gladys Lee was as springy as any healthy senior citizen.

"Jay, you know your grandmother. As soon as she returned home from visiting her friend, she went off with the ladies to a church garden club meeting. She told me to tell you that she would be back soon."

Jay smiled, proud of the woman that had raised her. "I guess I'll see her when she gets back," Jay replied, hearing the strain in Barbara's voice. She seemed to have more important things on her mind, as if something was worrying her.

"Are you sure you're all right?" Jay inquired, concerned that Barbara might have a problem that she needed to talk about.

"I'm okay." Barbara glanced at Jay as she pulled out onto the main highway. "When are we going to get started on the bed and breakfast?" she asked.

"First, I need time to rest, but I was thinking next week would be a perfect time," Jay replied. She didn't want to wait too long before she started preparing Lees' Bed and Breakfast for opening.

"For someone that needs to rest, you are certainly glowing," Barbara said, sounding more like her old self now than she did seconds ago.

Jay was sure if after a day and a half she was still glowing, Trent had been responsible for the lasting effects. A smile captured Jay's lips as her memories wavered back to Trent. The effects of his insatiable kisses seemed to have stayed with her along with their promise to love each other forever.

Jay turned to Barbara, anxious to tell her about Trent, then decided that she would wait until she was home and had gotten comfortable. So instead, she kept the conversation practical. "Are you going to hire someone to manage the beauty salon when Lees' is opened?" Jay understood that because of a wrist injury that Barbara had years ago, she could not work in the beauty salon, but had offered to hire a qualified and skilled beautician to work in the beauty salon.

"I was thinking about hiring the beautician that worked for me a couple of years ago, but she let her license expire and I don't know if she's going to renew it or not." Barbara said, glancing at Jay. "I'm trying to find qualified beauticians, because I can't deal with those healthy fines from the department of regulation."

"It must be frustrating," Jay replied, glad that Barbara had at least agreed to manage the bed-and-breakfast, once Lees' was open for business.

"What happened to make you get sent home?" Barbara asked her.

"Oh," Jay's short laughter filled the cab. "Foolishness."

"What kind of foolishness?" Barbara asked Jay.

Jay's smile tapered off. She explained to Barbara the details about what had happened after she and Trent began their relationship. When she finished, Barbara didn't seem surprised and did not show any signs of disapproval either. She did not seem to want to know more about her and Trent's relationship.

"At least you're all right," Barbara remarked, heading toward Brigantine, a town not far from Atlantic City and then on to their small coastal town. "Oh," Barbara said, changing the subject. "I rode by Lees' a few days ago, and the house needs a little work." She flicked the right signal and changed lanes.

"How much is a little work?" Jay asked, since she hadn't visited the building for a while. The last time she'd stopped by Lees' was the day her grandmother closed the business two years ago since she had no particular reason for seeing the house.

"Cleaning is at the top of the list and replacing a few windows. The grounds need a lot of work and child, the front yard is a disaster." Barbara chuckled.

"I'm not surprised. But I thought we might need a new roof," Jay said.

"Earl said that the roof on Lees' and the cottage is fine. But we need a new parking lot," Barbara said, turning onto the street where Jay lived. Her husband, Earl Hilton had been a contract builder for years and knew exactly what work was needed.

"I can't thank Earl enough for helping out," Jay said. If it hadn't been for him checking the building and not charging her a price, she would never have been able to promise Gladys that she would have the building completed in a short time.

"Well my dear, you're home." Barbara pulled into Jay's driveway and shut off the engine.

Jay took her house keys from her purse and cast a glimpse at Barbara. She was staring ahead as if her mind was far away again and Jay speculated that something was wrong. She allowed her concerns for her godmother to taper and decided that she would wait to ask Barbara what it was that was troubling her. She got out of the car, and noticed that nothing seemed to have changed in the time that she had been away. Her tutored roof townhouse rose up over green manicured lawns, the same as all of her neighbors' homes in her quiet neighborhood.

Jay would never forget how proud she had been the day she could afford the down payment on her adorable townhouse. For years, the houses in the old neighborhood had been low income housing until a few years ago when a company bought and renovated the homes. The company then sold the homes at a reasonable price, one Jay could afford to pay.

Barbara popped the trunk to her automobile and Jay and Barbara removed her luggage.

"Thanks for the ride," Jay said, sliding the handles up on her rolling suitcases and climbing the steps to her small porch, while Barbara gathered her other luggage.

"Jay, you know that I don't mind doing anything for you," Barbara smiled, but this time her smile seemed more troubled than before.

"I love traveling, but there's nothing better than being home." Jay unlocked the front door to her home and walked into the cool foyer, rolling her luggage over the mail that had fallen through the door slot and laid in a scattered pile.

"I know what you mean," Barbara moved behind Jay, pulling the luggage into the living room.

Everything in Jay's living room was in order except for the thin layers of gray dust covering the cocktail and end tables, and the bookshelf.

She had given Barbara her extra house key, and hired a cleaning company while she was away. The dust on the furniture was a sure sign that she had arrived home sooner than planned.

"The cleaners will be here tomorrow," Barbara said, taking Jay's house key off the ring and laying the key on the coffee table. "I forgot to cancel because my mind was stuck on you returning next month even after you called me." Barbara set a suitcase down.

"Don't worry about it," Jay said, pulling her luggage across the room in front of the sofa. She dropped her purse on the cocktail table, while Barbara went to gather the mail from the floor that had fallen through the mail slot. Jay took out the African print material she had bought for Barbara while she was in Nigeria.

"I'm putting the mail in the kitchen," Barbara said, walking toward Jay's kitchen. "I love that material," Barbara said, smiling as she admired the black and gold printed cloth.

"This is your gift," Jay said, handing her godmother the material. "I didn't have time to do a lot of shopping the way I had planned." Jay took the mail from Barbara.

"This is beautiful," Barbara said, her face and eyes lighting up as she held the cloth out in front of her. "Thank you, Jay. This will make a nice outfit."

"You're welcome," Jay said. She took the letters and flipped through the stack seeing a letter with no postage and noticed Austin's signature scribbled across the center of the envelope.

"I'll open the blinds," Barbara said, laying the material down and crossing over to the window, letting in bands of golden sunlight, while Jay thought about lunch.

"What do you want for lunch, Barbara?" Jay asked. She could almost taste the homemade potato salad.

Barbara seemed lost in her own world and Jay wondered if she was ill, or if something had happened to Earl or any of her other family members. "Barbara?" Jay called out to her again.

"Yes?" Barbara turned and faced her and Jay didn't miss the frown gathering on her brow. Barbara was definitely in a difficult situation and Jay was more than certain that the problem must be a hard one to solve.

"Barbara, I know something is wrong. It's not Granny, so are you or Earl sick?" Jay asked, concerned that her usually happy godmother may have been suffering from a stressful situation.

"No. Earl and I are fine." Barbara's smile appeared forced and strained. "Did you ask me what did I want for lunch?" Barbara asked.

"Yes," Jay said, telling Barbara what she had in mind.

"Honey dipped wings and potato salad sounds good to me," Jay said, stilling the need to pry into Barbara's business.

"Okay," Barbara said, not sounding a bit enthused over her favorite food from the old fashioned restaurant they both enjoyed. "Godmommy," Jay used the pet name for Barbara when she was worried about her. Barbara had been both like a mother and an older sister to her and if she was upset, Jay worried.

"Jay, I do have something on my mind, but I'll tell you after lunch."

"Why not tell me now?" Jay wanted to know. Any time was good to her.

"You know I don't like discussing problems on an empty stomach," Barbara said.

"Okay," Jay said and ordered their lunch from the down home cooking restaurant that served the best food in town, then she sat on the edge of the sofa's cushion. "I wonder what Austin wants," she said, halfway to herself as she ripped his letter open with the edge of her fingernail. "He never ceases to amaze me," Jay looked up from the letter at the expensive painting Austin had bought for himself two Christmases ago, then given it to her after they broke up. He was as selfish as ever, she mused, looking away from the painting hanging behind the sofa.

"What is it?" Barbara asked Jay.

"Austin is being himself. He wants the painting," Jay said, crumpling the letter and taking it into the kitchen and dropping the letter in the garbage pail.

"You can do what you want, but I wouldn't give him anything," Barbara remarked, studying the gold splattered painting behind Jay.

"I think I'll give the painting to him," Jay said, loving the way the gold color on the painting went perfectly with her beige colored living room set and coral chairs. But having all ties broken between her and Austin was more important than having him hanging around asking for a painting that he should have taken with him when he moved his things out of her home.

Jay settled back onto the sofa and told Barbara about her trip. Barbara appeared interested in the details about the marriages and how mature the women were and the outfits they wore, the fattening huts and the food, but Jay realized that she seemed disturbed.

Their lunches arrived and Barbara opened the door and took the food to the coffee table and went to the kitchen while Jay paid the delivery woman.

Seconds later, Barbara was back with paper plates, plastic forks and a handful of wet napkin packs. "They usually don't send enough napkins with the order," Barbara said with a smile that barely reached her eyes.

It seemed almost impossible for Jay to wait until after lunch to hear Barbara's problem, but while she waited to hear the disquieting news, she planned to tell Barbara about her and Trent.

Jay kicked off her high heels, pulled off her jacket, and lifted a wing to her lips, tasting the honey before eating the meat. "Um," Jay groaned. "This is so good."

"Um-huh." Barbara said, picking up and opening the small wet napkin pack and wiping her mouth.

"Now, let me tell you about Trent," Jay said, digging her fork into the potato salad and lifting the fork, eating the salad.

"Jay, I'm happy for you but . . ." Barbara said.

"There are no buts. Trent is nice and I'm in love," Jay replied.

"That is what worries me," Barbara said.

Jay held the fork inches away from her mouth. "What do you mean?" Jay inquired, sinking her fork into the potato salad.

"I wanted to tell you after lunch," she said, "but you need to know."

"I need to know what?" Jay asked, the familiar nagging dreadful feeling captured her and she felt as if she was going to be sick.

"Trent is related to the Prescott family." Barbara informed her.

Jay felt the dizziness sweep through her and she felt as if she was going to pass out. "I told you his last name was the same as the family." She spoke in a voice that she didn't recognize. Barbara was mistaken, she mused. "He's from Canada," Jay said quietly. A flush of warmth replaced her dizzy feelings and swept through her. This could not be true. There had to be a mistake. Jay was filled with a confidence that didn't reach her heart.

"I know he's from Canada. Ernest told me." Barbara

lay the fork down on her plate and searched Jay's face. "When I called you, Trent answered your telephone." She laughed lightly. "I couldn't exactly tell him that he was not the man for you because of a family problem."

"But you said yourself, that he was not related to the family, Barbara." Jay knew then that she should have checked deeper into Trent's background.

"I know, but I mentioned Trent to Earl because I didn't feel right and I wasn't sure if it was because I had heard so much about the family from Gladys. I did not want to believe that these people were the reason my best friend, your mother, had died."

"What do you believe, Barbara?" Jay felt her voice drawing from deep within her.

"I don't believe that the Prescotts murdered your parents or had anything to do with their deaths. But the night after I had answered your letter, I told Earl that you had met Trent Prescott and the more we talked about the Prescotts, the more I thought I had not taken the time to actually find out if he was related to the family. So Earl said that he would ask a guy he knew that had known the Prescotts."

Jay realized that she was staring at Barbara, but she couldn't seem to control herself. After a while, she cast her gaze down.

"Earl found a man that knew the family and knew that they lived in Canada." Barbara sighed as if telling Jay was painful to her. "Trent's father is named Christopher Prescott."

Jay felt as if she had been in a dream that had turned into a nightmare and she couldn't wake up. She wanted to scream, but she couldn't open her mouth. She wanted to cry, but her tears were frozen. "Christopher?" Jay finally whispered the man's name that would end the love that she had known and would never know again.

"He's Trent's father." Barbara said. "Jay, I didn't know how to tell you this. But anyway, I looked for the Prescotts in Canada and sure enough, they live there."

"I thought you knew the Prescotts?" Jay said.

"Not really," Barbara assured Jay. "Your mother, Audrey and I had been friends when we lived and went to high school in Red Bank. When she married your father, we visited each other during the holidays, and especially during Christmas and New Year's. She never mentioned the Prescotts to me. When she died, Earl and I moved here so that I could help Gladys raise you." Barbara looked as if her memories were so strong, and she wanted to cry. "Everything I know about the Prescotts, I learned from Gladys." Barbara said.

The taste of honey and the small amount of food Jay had eaten suddenly seem to sour and she felt as if she was going to be sick again. "No. Trent can't be related to those people."

"Yes he is, Jay. But I still think that Gladys has her facts mixed up, because Earl and I heard from a very reliable source that your parents were hit by a drunk driver and the Prescotts weren't driving the car. As a matter of fact, Earl and I believed that they had already left town."

Jay Lee ripped open a wet pack and slowly removed the moist napkin and wiped her hands. "I love him." Jay said.

"I understand, but you have to think about what this is going to do to your relationship with Gladys." Barbara said.

It was then that Jay's frozen tears began to thaw and she was determined not to let her emotions show. Gladys had made her a promise that she would never speak to the family, and she had carelessly ignored the opportunity to question Trent further about his background. Without warning, he had stolen her heart and she had allowed it to happen.

"I should've checked sooner and tried to find the family for you, but one of Earl's aunts was in the hospital and I was driving down once a week to see her and taking care of a few things that needed to be done around her house. This is my fault." Barbara assured her.

"You did your best," Jay said, not blaming her godmother.

"I know you're tired, Jay. I can help you unpack now so that way you won't have to worry about unpacking later," Barbara suggested. It seemed that they both had lost their appetites for their lunch.

"Thanks, but I'll take care of everything," Jay said. She needed to keep busy and as tired as she was, she wasn't sure if she could sleep.

"Well, if you insist," Barbara said. "But I want you to be okay."

Barbara sounded as if she was speaking from a distance and not in the same room with her. "I'm okay," Jay finally said, picking up the plates and food and carrying everything into the kitchen.

"No, you're not okay," Barbara said, following her into the kitchen.

Jay set everything on the counter. She seemed to be destined to have been dealt an awful hand. Why had she followed her heart instead of her sound mind?

Wrestling with her conscious, Jay returned from the

kitchen and took one of her suitcases upstairs to her bedroom. She pushed the suitcase into the closet, promising herself that she would unpack later and sat on the foot of her bed. She didn't bother opening the blinds to light her dim bedroom. She closed her eyes hoping to stop the trail of thoughts that were haunting her. She was in love with her enemy, and she was unable to dissolve the dull ache at the center of her heart.

As numb as she felt, she was beginning to get restless as she forced herself to still her rambling thoughts. Nonetheless, composing herself seemed to have been out of the question, especially when she knew it was going to take a long time for her to stop loving Trent. Marching close behind that thought was the fact that she would be alone forever. Jay didn't care. If she couldn't have Trent in her life, she didn't want any man. Also she was not going to waste her time dating other men, hoping that she would forget Trent.

Another horrid thought captured Jay. Gladys promised that if Jay had ever met any of the Prescotts and become friends or even if she found out that Jay had spoken to a member of the family, she would disown her. Not having her grandmother with her because she was dead was one matter, but having Gladys Lee alive and disowning her was a serious issue, especially when she couldn't go to her grandmother when she needed her for anything.

Jay got up and moved slowly down the stairs to the living room and caught the handle of another suitcase. It seemed that every man that she liked had been chased out of her life because of her grandmother. Gladys hadn't wanted her with Elfin and Jay could imagine the tizzy she would be in knowing that she had met, worked and spoke to Trent, not to mention loving him.

"I won't mention to Gladys that you met Trent Prescott, Jay, but I think that you need to decide what you're going to do." Barbara's voice interrupted her thoughts.

"I don't know what I'm going to do, but I know that I can't forget him." Being honest with herself was one of the virtues Gladys had instilled in her, but Jay knew that Gladys would not understand or accept any excuse for what she had done.

"Honey, are you going to be all right?" Barbara asked her, peering at Jay as if she wasn't certain if she should leave her alone.

Jay didn't answer.

"I can stay with you tonight if you want," Barbara said.

"No, I'll be fine," Jay said, when the telephone suddenly rang. The jingling sound filled the room and seemed louder than she remembered. Everything seemed louder and brazen in her life after she learned that she had broken the family rule. Jay allowed her pondering to stall her from answering the telephone.

It was after the fifth ring that Barbara lifted the receiver and answered the telephone. "Hello?"

She held the receiver out to Jay. "It's for you," Barbara said and left her to her call.

"Hello," Jay spoke into the receiver and she hardly recognized her own voice. It was if she was chilled from cold weather and yet, it was spring.

"What's wrong?" Trent asked, and a sensual wave touched her heart.

"Can I call you back?" Jay asked, hoping that by

then things would make sense to her and she would have awakened from the terrible nightmare.

"No, baby, you don't sound well. Did you have a bad flight?" Trent asked her.

"I can't talk now," Jay said, knowing that she had to give him up after all.

"Why—who's with you?" Trent's voice broke into a whisper and was filled with concern.

"Barbara," Jay said, struggling to maintain a calmness in her voice.

"Barbara Hilton?" Trent asked her.

Jay smiled, remembering how Trent had answered her telephone in her room when she living in the team's house and had taken a message from Barbara. "Yes," she said.

"I understand that you're tired, Jay," Trent said, and paused. "I'll call you later."

For a moment, Jay listened to his soft breathing and she wanted to tell him the story that had been told to her about his family and how she had made a mistake in loving him. She also wanted to tell Trent that she didn't care who he was or what had happened in the past, but that she wanted him in her life. "We'll talk," Jay said, and held the receiver until the warning sound of the buzzer alerted her that the telephone was off the hook.

"Jay, I put your things away. I'll call you tonight," Barbara said.

"You didn't have to do that, but thanks," Jay said, feeling more alive than she had minutes ago as she walked Barbara to the door.

"I want you to go upstairs and sleep," Barbara smiled at her.

Jay nodded a "yes" to her godmother and doubted

that she would sleep because she was already having trouble banishing the sound of Trent's voice from her mind.

When Barbara was out of her driveway, Jay went to her room, closed the door and kneeled against the edge of her bed, allowing the tears that were partially thawed to come and she cried because she had to make a choice and whatever choice she made, someone was going to get hurt. But at the moment, her pain was almost unbearable.

Trent locked his hands behind his head and stretched out on the bed in his hotel room, giving Jay time before calling her again. She'd had a long trip and was exhausted and he understood.

However, the small voice in the back of his mind warned him that danger lurked. He closed his eyes and drifted into sleep, dreaming about Jay. He cradled her in his arms, feeling her soft fingers caressing his back, raising his masculinity to full height and his drowsy voice to a muffled growl. Then like a poorly developed photograph, she faded out of his sight.

Trent sat up and looked around his room. A brilliant morning sun shined bands of golden rays through the partly open blinds. He checked the time on the clock near his bed, realizing that he had slept through the time he had promised to give Jay another call. He was sure she was sleeping now and he didn't want to disturb her.

Tonight, he promised himself, he would talk to her and hoped that there was not a problem. But every fiber in his heart warned him that something had happened.

Trent didn't want to think what might have gone wrong. Nothing probably, he consoled himself, as the insecurities of how his last relationship had ended began to rise. He shut out the thought. Nothing would go wrong for him and Jay.

Ten

Another wedding was not what Trent needed this evening, but because he was being a nice guy and keeping a promise to Myers to travel to Africa to help out, he was stuck listening to the groom's father, brother and uncle when he would have rather been home with Jay, finding out from her whether or not she had a problem.

After the groom had asked for the bride's hand in marriage, she had accepted and her parents had agreed. Trent had to listen to the groom and his family offering the bride wealth in a stock of cattle and a generous amount of money before the groom took the bride home with him to his family.

He and several members from the team followed the party to the groom's house and joined the party that was given in respect to the marriage.

After the festivities, Trent went to the team's house where he was staying for the night and checked his messages before he called Jay. All week he had tried to call her and he hadn't got an answer and she hadn't returned his call. He was even more certain than before that there was a problem.

He took his cell phone, walked outside and

crouched against the tree facing the water, allowing the soft lapping waves to calm his spirit as he dialed Jay's telephone number.

The answering machine picked up his call and he hung up without leaving a message. He couldn't think of a reason why Jay would avoid his calls. Maybe she had rekindled her relationship with her old boyfriend, Trent considered, flirting with the unsettling realization that Jay going home and finding her old lover appealing could have been the problem. Maybe she was sick. Jay hadn't sounded right when he called her. But if she was sick, why hadn't she told him?

Nothing made sense to him, and his assumption of her rekindling her relationship with her ex-lover made the least sense of all after what she had told him about the relationship. *Maybe she has rekindled her love affair with her old boyfriend*, a tiny voice whispered in the deep crevices of Trent's mind.

Jealousy gripped Trent at the pit of his stomach and coiled before rising to his chest. He had made the mistake of trusting before and this time with Jay, he hoped he hadn't made another mistake. He dismissed the nagging intrusion that was attempting to dominate him. He believed that Jay loved him as much as he loved her.

Nevertheless, he was worried that something terrible had happened to her and he could hardly wait until he went home. And because of his impatience, the minutes and hours seemed to drag.

Trent closed the small cell phone in his palm and let his memories charge him. He was aware of his attraction to Jay when he had sat next to her on the plane. Instead of accepting his feelings, Trent had fought against his emotions, telling himself that he could never fall in love again.

He forced himself to keep his emotions in check because he had once too often been told that women weren't to be trusted. Then he met Jay, and for the first time since his broken engagement, Trent realized that his masculine emotions were alive and well.

Trent suspected that he was worrying too much, but he was determined to talk to Jay. It was then that he thought that she might have returned to work sooner than planned.

It was six o'clock in the evening in Africa, and he calculated the time in the States and figured it would be around one o'clock in the afternoon. Without further hesitation, he called Myers Research Center, taking a chance that Jay might have returned to work sooner than she should have. He waited for Myers' secretary to answer the telephone.

"Hi Trent," Myers' secretary, Shelly, said. "How are things in Nigeria?"

"Okay," Trent said, when he remembered that Jay said she had a project that she was planning to work on when she returned home. Trent was beginning to feel that he had made big mistake calling Shelly because nothing thrilled her more than to know everyone's business at Myers Research Center.

"Is Jay around?" Trent asked anyway just in case Jay had changed her mind about working on the project.

"No, she'll be back to work Monday, but I'll tell her that you called," Shelly said. "She should be home because I spoke to her about five minutes ago."

"Thanks Shelly, I'll call her at home," Trent said, ending the call and dialing Jay's home number again. She probably hadn't answered his call because she was talking to Shelly, he mused, glad that he hadn't allowed his assumptions to get the best of him.

"Baby," Trent said when Jay answered the telephone.

"Hi," Jay said, her voice was cool and distant as if she was speaking to a stranger.

"Okay, what's going on?" Trent asked, wishing that Jay was her usual cheerful and snappy self.

"I would rather talk to you when you get home," she said.

"I want to talk now," Trent said, not letting Jay put him off any longer.

The silence was almost too much for him as he waited for her to speak. "Are you still there?" Trent inquired, hoping she hadn't hung up.

"Yes," she finally said. "I don't think the time is right for us to talk."

"Don't put me off another second—I want to know and I want to know now!" Trent's voice was slow, harsh and even.

"I don't think we should talk now," Jay said again.

"Why?" Trent asked, refusing to let Jay dismiss him.

After a long pause, Jay finally spoke to him again. "We can't continue our relationship."

Trent heard her and it felt as if each word she spoke had been a bayonet piercing his heart and making it hard for him to speak. "Say that again," he said when he could finally talk.

"You heard me," Jay said.

"Yeah, I heard you and I want to know why and what made you change your mind about us," he said, recognizing the strain in his voice.

"It's too much for me to discuss now," Jay replied.

Trent couldn't believe that Jay had never felt the

same about him as he felt about her. Every fiber in his body and all that made up the special parts of his soul had told him that Jay was the woman for him and yet, he had been mistaken. She had never felt anything for him.

Trent swallowed the knot in his throat and knew he had to ask the forbidden question. "Are you saying that you never loved me?"

"No," Jay said.

"Then how can you turn off your feelings like that?" Trent asked, snapping his fingers. "Were you playing with me?"

"I wasn't playing with you," Jay said.

"So, what hell is your point?" Trent asked, feeling himself getting angry.

"I can't talk about it now," Jay said, "but it's best that we forget about each other and go on with our lives."

"Is that what you want?" Trent asked.

"No," Jay said.

"What do you mean—no?" Trent asked.

"I told you that I didn't want to discuss the reason now," Jay said.

"Baby, are you sick?"

"No," Jay answered. "We'll talk later, Trent. I have to go. Bye."

The dial tone cut into the thick silence. He knew he would have to be patient and wait until he saw Jay before he would learn what had caused her to change her feelings about them. Jay had all the answers and she wasn't sharing them with him. Again, Jay rekindling her relationship with Austin came to mind, and another round of jealousy began to cramp his spirit.

Trent finally concluded that he was the reason for

his obstacle and his problem was simple. He didn't have good sense. Hadn't he been cheated on before? One lesson hadn't been enough. It seemed he needed to repeat the course.

Trent knew that the three weeks and few days he had remaining in Nigeria was going to seem like a year and a day. But he would be patient and once he was in New Jersey, his first line of business would be to visit Jay.

If she thought she was going to break up with him on the telephone, she had been mistaken.

Jay Lee felt an unexplainable twinge of emptiness, a hollow gap that seemed to have opened inside her and could only be filled with her tears after her conversation ended with Trent. He had been relentless and without patience, trying to understand the true reason for her breaking up with him. A tear hung on the edge of her lashes and she blinked, allowing a liquid trail to wet her face.

Jay knew that she would probably never see Trent again, and the one time that she had been in love was gone forever. She should have stayed with her plan and waited before she began dating Trent Prescott. But she was attracted to his good looks, and his energy seemed like a pulling force dragging her to him. She like the way he had looked at her with his sweeping glances and when they had reached the point of lovemaking, afterwards without warning, she wanted to spend her life with him.

Jay didn't know how she was going to get through almost another year wrestling with the emotional withdrawal of dispelling Trent from her system, heart and soul. She'd had a hard time forgetting Austin, and she hadn't loved him a third as much as she loved Trent.

But now she would be impelled by her passion, pining and thinking about a man that she would never have in her life again. After she considered the promised downfall of her relationship with her grandmother if she ever found out about her and Trent Prescott's love affair, Jay knew that she had to choose her family.

Although her memories of her parents were indistinct to say the least, her memories of her grandmother still grieving after the years had stuck in her mind. Then the warning of her being disowned haunted her. Still, in Jay's heart, she believed that her love for Trent was right.

More tears choked her, but she braced herself. She was a strong woman and she would get over the pain that she had placed upon herself.

She splashed her face with cold water and got busy calling the cleaning company to clean Lees' Bed and Breakfast. She had taken care of all the paperwork to open the business and tomorrow she and Barbara were shopping for furniture. The rooms needed new bedroom sets after someone had helped themselves to most of the furniture. She also needed dining tables and bed coverings and the list grew.

As long as she kept herself busy, she wouldn't think about Trent. However, in the still of the night, Jay knew that she couldn't keep her promise. Last night she had lain awake, recalling the relationship she thought she had with Trent and how their relationship had been like a sweet dream that had ultimately turned into a nightmare when Barbara broke the news that the Prescotts had moved to Canada and not Delaware as Gladys had claimed.

All of her frightening instincts came to life at the mention of his surname when she met him. Why hadn't she followed the warning signs or paid attention? One question after another pounded her, as to why had she followed her heart, allowing her emotions to escort her down a path of passion. She had allowed Trent to wrap his arms around her soul, her heart, and her body. She had promised to never give him up, but now she didn't think she had a choice.

Jay discarded her concerns and turned her attention to more important matters like making sure she could find bed coverings at a reasonable price, and wholesale grocery vendors and other things that she needed. By the beginning of May, she hoped to have Lees' up and running.

She picked up the office supply catalogue and began flipping through the pages, looking at desks and choosing one that Barbara told her was needed for the office.

As she scanned the catalogue's pages, her thoughts threatened to reel her back in time. When she was in her teens, Gladys told her about the death of her parents and how they died. Jay forced the thoughts back to the corner of her mind. She would never have to worry about Gladys Lee finding out about her relationship with Trent.

Except for Barbara and the research team, no one knew that she and Trent had loved each other and her worries began to fade. Barbara promised her that she wouldn't mention her love affair to Gladys and the research team didn't know her grandmother.

Jay let out a sigh of relief, only to be dragged back to how fate had played a tricky game with her. This was just the kind of thing that would happen to her.

She had found Trent to be a challenge from the very beginning and he was more desirable than she had expected, making her heart reel and sway when they were together. And as luck would have it, he was related to her family's rival.

Life is not fair! Jay mused, wishing she'd never met Trent. *You can still date him, even love him.* Jay shook the irrational thought back to its hiding place. She could never betray her grandmother, her parents or herself to involve herself with a man like Trent Prescott, knowing that loving him was a disgrace to her family.

When she received his call, she wanted to tell him her reasons for breaking up with him, instead of waiting until he was home, mainly because she wasn't certain if she could face him and break up with him in person at the same time.

Jay lay the catalogue on top of her dresser and called Carol at work. She was getting hungry and was not in the mood to eat alone again tonight. She called Carol at work and asked if she could meet her at their favorite restaurant.

"Now girl, you know I can't wait to see you," Carol laughed.

"I'm sorry I didn't call sooner," Jay said, taking the gift she had bought for Carol while she was in Nigeria off the top of the closet shelf.

"I wasn't home anyway. I worked late for the past two weeks."

"Then you need a break," Jay said. "Can you meet in an hour?" Jay asked, tearing the tag off the gift and dropping it inside a gift bag.

"Yes," Carol said.

"I'll see you shortly," Jay said, hanging up and walking back to her room and laying the portable telephone on the nightstand.

Jay had met Carol her sophomore year in college. Carol was on the social committee and had invited Jay to a party one Friday evening. After that, she and Carol had become best friends.

Already in her late twenties, Carol had begun school late in life. While Carol was also a sophomore, her life experiences didn't compare with Jay's lack of knowledge in the social world after having lived a sheltered life.

However, Carol had been married and divorced and seemed to have all the answers to most of the important questions that Jay had no answers to, especially to her questions concerning men.

But this time, Jay wasn't certain if she could talk to Carol about Trent right now. The agonizing pain was still with her and she didn't know when she could talk about Trent without breaking down in tears.

Jay got up and went to change into a light-blue v-neck top and matching slacks. The spring evening promised to be nice and for a moment she wondered how it would feel to snuggle close to Trent on a spring night.

Jay took her purse and the gift and headed out to her car. She drove to the restaurant, fighting a line of five-thirty traffic and the will to stay strong and think about nothing at all.

She turned on the radio and heard a song that she and Trent both liked. Jay turned the radio off and slipped a CD in the player as if playing her music would be any different. She took the CD out and opted to drive in silence because the music she loved was the same music that Trent also loved.

Minutes later, she swung into the parking lot and headed inside the restaurant and joined Carol sitting in their favorite booth.

"Girl, I know you had fun," Carol smiled after they spoke to each other. Carol was tall, with a dark beige complexion and her shoulder length hair bounced with body when she swung her head from one side to the other displaying a pair of gold earrings.

"It was nice," Jay said, handing Carol the gift. "I hope you like it."

"Oh yeah," Carol said, holding up the Bantu mask. An array of other colors set atop its orange and rust background. "This is perfect, Jay. Thanks!"

"I loved your gift too," Jay said, observing how happy Carol was to receive her gift.

"Did he like the teddy?" Carol asked.

Jay was glad the waitress stopped at their table to take their orders, because she wasn't ready to answer Carol's question.

"Well?" Carol asked when the waitress left them. One side of her mouth pulled into a bright smile as if she was waiting to hear what Trent Prescott thought about the skimpy black outfit.

"He didn't get a chance to see the teddy," Jay said, observing Carol's arched brows raise a tiny fraction.

"Why?" Carol asked.

"I left sooner than expected," Jay said.

"I would like to meet him. When is he coming home?" Carol's eyes sparkled with excitement as if she could hardly wait for Jay to let her know when she was meeting Trent.

"You're not going to meet Trent because we broke up," Jay said.

"Come on, Jay, what happened?" Carol's voice was filled with concern.

Jay hesitated, but she was going to tell Carol sooner or later about the disaster she had gotten herself into. "He's related to the Prescott family," Jay said, telling her how Barbara found out for her.

"Oh Jay, that's not good, but then you never know Mrs. Lee might have softened in her old age."

"I don't think so," Jay said, waiting until the waitress set the fettuccine in front of them.

"I'm sorry," Carol said, spreading her napkin in her lap and swirling her fork around a string of fettuccine that was dripping with cheese sauce. "But I think you need to figure out a way to see him."

Jay didn't say anything. It was hard enough to tell Carol what had happened and she didn't want to speculate on how she would see Trent in the small town and still keep her grandmother's gossiping girl-friends from tattling. She was more than certain now that if Earl knew people that knew the Prescotts, her grandmother had friends that remembered the family as well.

Jay looked across the room and saw Mrs. Williams. The woman was one of her grandmother's friends and should have had a career as a gossip columnist since she thought everyone's business except her own should be public knowledge. "I couldn't see him with-out running into her," Jay said, waving a finger in Mrs. Williams's direction.

"I see what you mean." Carol chuckled. "But there are ways."

Hope picked at Jay's heart. She hadn't thought about dating Trent in secret and he probably would never accept the offer. Besides that, she doubted she would see him again after she gave him the reasons for breaking up with him.

"I don't think so, Carol," Jay said, and cast her gaze on the food before her while she told Carol about her work, and how she was sent home because of the tiff she had with Sonya, the woman that was once engaged to Trent.

"Well, I'm glad you're home," Carol said. "I didn't have a soul to talk to."

"I'm glad to be home too," Jay said, and sipped the soft lemon drink.

"I hope you can work something out with Trent."

Jay didn't say anything. A friendship with Trent was impossible and it didn't make sense to think of possibilities that would never happen. "Did you meet anyone while I was away?" Jay asked, smiling impishly at her girlfriend.

"Girl, please, I can't stop working long enough to meet anyone and you know I'm keeping my brother's children until he's out of physical therapy," Carol said.

"I didn't know your brother was sick," Jay said, and was also surprised that Carol was keeping Keith's three boys.

"Yes, he had an accident, and broke his ribs." Carol informed her of her brother's automobile accident. "When I go out now, it's to go to work, take the boys out, or to buy groceries."

"Your hands are full," Jay said, spinning another string of fettuccine on her fork.

"Girl, I'm so afraid that the middle child, Morris, is going to drive my car one night while I'm asleep. I don't know what to do with that boy." Carol chuckled. "He's obsessed with driving."

Jay knew she shouldn't have, but she laughed anyway. The boys ranged from the age of thirteen, twelve and eleven and Morris was twelve years old. "When are the boys going home?" Jay asked.

"The day school is out, I'm sending them home because my brother will be well enough by then to look after them."

Jay listened to Carol catch her up on the latest gossip she'd happened to hear bits and pieces of, like who was getting married or engaged and who had ended their relationships and divorced.

Jay listened, realizing that she had also ended a relationship and she felt her eyes tearing. Suddenly, her food didn't taste good any more and the drink seemed to have lost its lemony zest and she ignored her ringing cell phone.

"Jay, you need to think about seeing Trent and letting him know what's going on." Carol said to her when they had finished their dinner and were ready to leave the restaurant.

"I intend to tell him in detail how my parents were killed," she paused. "That is if I see him again." Jay gathered her purse and got up as she and Carol paid for their dinners.

"What if he doesn't know anything about what happened to your parents, then what would you do?" Carol asked Jay.

Jay shook her head because she didn't know what she would do. She only knew that she had to believe what her grandmother had told her.

Carol rose from her seat. "The only thing I can tell you is to follow your mind," Carol said as they walked to their cars.

Following her heart was the reason she was in trouble now, Jay mused as she slid behind the steering wheel and answered her ringing cell phone. Whoever was that had called her hung up on the second ring. Jay tapped into her answering service to see who had left her a massage. Austin had called leaving a message saying that he had heard she was back in town and he wanted to talk to her.

Jay shut off her cell phone. She had nothing to say to Austin Carrington. She wanted one thing from Austin and that was for him to stop by her home and take the painting.

Myers offered Trent the opportunity to leave for home early, telling him that he would supervise whatever work needed completing.

Two weeks later, Trent slid in beside his best friend, Webster Nelson and settled down for his ride to the airport.

"Did you find out what was going on with Jay?" Webster asked Trent.

Trent unbuttoned his dark blue suit jacket and loosened his tie that suddenly seemed too tight. "No, but I intend to find out," he replied.

"Maybe Sonya gave her a call," Webster said, and Trent didn't miss Webster's sideways glance as he dropped his house keys in his hand, giving Trent permission to stay in his house while he was waiting for renovations on his place to be completed.

The thought had crossed Trent's mind that Sonya might have called Jay. But Jay understood that he wasn't interested in Sonya. Now that he thought about Webster's comment, he wondered if Webster could be right.

However, Webster's suggestion was worth looking

into and he would find out if Sonya had anything to do with Jay's decision to shut him out of her life.

In the meantime, he was thankful that Myers was taking over, but not without reminding him that he had promised to work for him another few weeks and he would complete the job by running his office until he and the team arrived home.

Trent had no other choice but to agree. After all, he had promised Myers that he would work for him. However, if he and Jay couldn't work out their differences, he wasn't certain that he would be in the right frame of mind at Myers, having to work around Jay every day and not being able to talk to her.

There was always a solution to a problem and he would manage, thanks to Myers who had put him on the spot for a second time. If he had broken his promise and not supervised the team for Myers, he would never have met Jay Lee. He would have continued to heal from his wounds and his life by now would be whole again.

But Myers seemed not to have any mercy on him even after he told him that Jay broke up with him over the phone and again Trent wondered if Myers was playing games with his personal life, sending him home to work with Jay in the middle of a situation he wasn't sure he could handle. Instead of keeping quiet this time, Trent asked Myers if he was assisting him with his personal life. He had laughed as if his question was amusing.

Eleven

Early the next morning, Jay parked in front of the gift shop and crossed the street to Lees' Bed and Breakfast. She walked past the cleaning van parked near the embankment and headed up the walk to the bed and breakfast.

The building was old, but stood strong and steady and with a little work, would be in excellent shape in a short time, just as Earl had promised.

She picked her way across the scattered soda cans and fast-food sandwich wrappings littering the walkway as she moved toward the house and took notice of the grass. Brown patches and weeds growing wild sprinkled the yard. Jay made a mental note to order fresh sod, knowing that new grass would make the yard much nicer.

As she moved toward the house where she had spent most of her life and climbed the wide faded steel gray steps to the porch, she allowed the ambiance to settle over her as she noticed the broken porch swing where she, as well as the guests, had spent quiet moments.

"Earl." Jay called out to Barbara's husband.

"I'm in here, Jay," Earl answered Jay from the lobby.

Earl was tall, his skin was the color of a chocolate bar, and a mass of thick peppery curls covered his head.

"Do you think we'll be ready to open Lees' by the end of April?" Jay asked, hoping that the bed and breakfast would be ready for business by the beginning of May when the tourists came to town.

"Yeah," Earl said, laying a wrench inside his tool box.

She followed Earl, inhaling the scent of sanitizing solution that filtered out to her along with the distant conversation floating down to them from the cleaning crew who were working in the upstairs bed and bathrooms.

Jay ran a finger over the dusty brown registration desk, imagining how nicely the desk would look varnished in a flaxen color. "I think Lees' is going to be beautiful when we're finished." She brushed her fingers against her jeans, wiping off the dusk.

"I think so," Earl said, taking his tape measure from his carpenter's pants pocket and crossing into the dining room to measure the windows. "Barbara is taking care of the paperwork for the beauty salon and Gladys said that she kept the paperwork in order for the bar. I don't think we'll have a problem opening on time." Earl pulled the tape from the container and laid it across the window.

"In that case, I think we'll be open in time for the tourists," Jay replied, going downstairs to check the beauty salon furniture. She couldn't remember if Barbara said she was ordering new or used equipment, especially chairs.

The maroon chairs were just as she expected, mostly worn and the mirrors and floor covering needed replacing. The other equipment seemed fine.

"I think we can blow life back into this old place," Jay said when she was back in the dining room with Earl. Standing in the room where the guests had inspired her to travel reminded her that if she hadn't followed her dream, she doubted that she would have ever have met Trent Prescott.

Jay left the dining room then and stood in the lobby as a shudder raced through her when she remembered Trent's sensational passion. Jay forced herself to shut down her feelings because she needed to forget the mistake she had made, and without a solution to correct the mistake, she didn't want to remember.

However, forgetting Trent Prescott was a problem. For hours at a time, she would forget him and suddenly without warning, she was thinking about him again. When she promised Gladys that she would repair and reopen Lees', she had no idea how much the project would serve as an escape for her. She touched the necklace around her neck, stroking the small diamonds, and wished that she hadn't worn the jewelry Trent had given her.

Trent had not only given her his love, but his trust, and he expected the same from her. She had arrived home anxiously awaiting his return and like a boulder from the bottomless pit, her world had been smashed into bits and the best she could do was to wait for him and explain her reasons for breaking up with him if he chose to listen.

A tear caught in her throat and a grief-stricken sob echoed against the empty walls.

"Jay, it's very dusty in here, maybe you should wear a mask," Earl said, and Jay knew he had heard her strangled sob.

"I'm okay," she said, and went upstairs to check out

the bedrooms and hoped she wouldn't get in the way of the cleaning crew.

She reached the top of the stairs and looked over the railing down into the lobby, considering if she should varnish the floors or lay down carpet when her thoughts trailed back to Trent and how much she loved him.

I hope he understands, she mused as she peeked into bedrooms where cleaning women were busy soaking wallpaper off the walls and preparing the rooms for the paper hangers, when without warning, visions of Trent crossed her mind and she thought if she didn't stop herself she would go insane. Again she dismissed him from her mind and soon found herself waring against the impossible.

Trent had told her his deepest secret about how Sonya had been unfaithful to him. Even though she couldn't see the pain in his face because the room had been dim, she had detected traces of leftover anguish in his voice and she knew he had been hurt. When she last spoke to him, she had listened to him and heard the same wounded agony in his voice.

Jay walked to a nearby closet and opened the door and looked inside at the vacant shelves. She would do anything to free her mind from thinking about Trent, but the closet didn't help, but only reminded her of how empty her life would be without him and she sank down on the floor and cried.

"Jay," Barbara called her. "Ooh! I think these stairs grew since I last climbed them."

Jay wiped her eyes with the back of her hand and got up off the floor. "I'm in here," she said keeping her eyes lowered and hoping Barbara hadn't paid attention to the tears in her voice.

"What is it, Jay?" Barbara asked her.

She could never hide anything from her godmother and it didn't make sense to start now. Being upset in Barbara's presence would only prolong the anguish she was feeling. "I was thinking," Jay said, looking down at the hall floor.

"Jay, I can't tell you what to do," Barbara said as if she understood Jay's problem. "But you should talk to Gladys about this when she gets home."

"And have her disown me—she's all I have left," Jay replied.

"Jay honey, Gladys has disowned a lot of people in her day, but she's not crazy enough to disown you," Barbara replied.

"She hates the Prescotts," Jay said.

"I know," Barbara said to her. "But don't worry. Things will work out."

Jay couldn't imagine her and Trent's relationship working out, but she kept her thoughts to herself. She would deal with the issue if and when she saw him and continue to fight with her agony and hope that in due time, she would heal and move forward in a positive manner. "If we're going shopping for furniture we had better get started," Jay said.

"While we're out, we might as well stop at the home supply store," Barbara said, "and order the materials to redo the bathrooms." Barbara took a small pad from her pocket and showed Jay the measurements Earl had taken so that they would buy the right sized vanities and mirrors for the bathrooms.

Jay walked into a bedroom and checked the bathroom and agreed with Barbara. Not only did the vanities appear to have been installed during the Civil War, they were as chipped and tattered as the peeling wall-paper.

"Earl, we'll see you later," Barbara called out to her husband as she and Jay walked down the stairs and through the lobby and out to her car.

By the end of the day, Jay and Barbara had ordered the bedroom sets all the same style and shopped for bathroom furniture too.

Jay gathered a stack of wallpaper swatches and got out of Barbara's car telling her that she would see her first thing the next morning.

"Jay, tomorrow is Saturday and I have something I need to do. I'll see you Monday," Barbara said.

"I'll be over right after work," Jay assured her as she walked to her car.

Jay went home promising herself that she wouldn't think about Trent, but as she selected swatches of wall-paper for the rooms at Lees', she was unsuccessful in stopping herself from thinking about him.

Four-thirty and thirty minutes before Myers Research Center closed that Monday evening, Trent Prescott walked across the half-empty parking lot and into the quiet lobby and down the hall to the office he'd seen Jay popping in and out of when he'd stopped by to meet with Myers to discuss the African trip.

Trent was determined to talk to Jay and find out what had happened to make her not want to see him again. He raised his fist to knock on her office door when Shelly Clayton stopped him. "Jay didn't come in today," she said.

"Hi Shelly." Trent lowered his hand and pushed both hands into his trouser pockets and turned his back to Jay's office door. He knew Jay's address from the information on her file and the only thing left for him to do was go to her house.

"Hi." Shelly spoke to Trent. "Myers called and said you were coming home." Her wide eyes scanned his hand as if he was suppose to have been carrying something. "Did you bring the videotapes with you?" Shelly stepped closer to him.

"No," Trent said, moving away from the door, ready to leave and find Jay.

"I can give Jay a message Monday, but you'll probably see her tonight, uh?" Shelly asked Trent. She stood even closer to him, making it almost impossible for him to move around her without lifting her up and setting her aside.

"I probably will see Jay tonight," Trent said, making another attempt to move away from her.

"So it is true . . . I mean what happened in Nigeria with you and Jay?" Shelly asked Trent and took a step back away from him.

"Shelly, we worked," Trent said, moving around her. He had known Shelly Clayton for a long time and if he was right about his suspicions, he was in for a round of questions that he didn't want to answer.

"Oh?" Her ruby red lips circled into an O. "I heard that more than work went on over there. I am right, right?"

"Shelly, I don't have time to talk," Trent replied, aware that the gossip usually made its way to Shelly by email or telephone.

"Then don't talk, just listen," she said. "Maybe I can refresh your memory," she whispered as if one of the employees in a nearby office would hear her talking to him.

"Shelly, I have to go," Trent began walking away.

She grabbed Trent's arm and pulled him inside her office, and closed the door. "Trent Prescott, we have worked together for a long time, and you can't play dumb with me." She folded her arms across her chest, and studied him.

"I don't want to talk about it," Trent said.

"Sonya called me and said that you and Jay Lee were having a love affair," Shelly said, and waited for Trent to confirm the news. When he didn't say anything, she continued to inform him of all the details. "Sonya told me that when she found out that you were going to Africa she asked Myers to put her on your team. You know, she thought maybe you guys could get back together." Shelly paused. "But when you and Jay started going together, she said she picked a fight with Jay. And when she saw you and Jay going to your hotel room she told Myers that if he didn't send Jay home she was quitting." Shelly blinked with what appeared to Trent as pure satisfaction and smiled as if she was waiting for him to confirm the story. "Now, you tell me if that's a lie because Jay is home."

Trent rubbed his chin with the back of his thumb. "If you know all of this, why are you asking me?" Trent started walking away from her again when she dug her fingers into the sleeve of his suit jacket. "It never hurts to check," Shelly said.

"I . . ." Trent started to say he was leaving when Shelly interrupted him.

"I wished I could go on those trips instead of staying

cooped up in this office." She lifted her hand off Trent's arm. "I also heard that Rose and Webster called off their wedding."

"I don't know," Trent said, backing to the entrance of her office and opening the door. If Shelly kept him any longer, he might miss Jay, especially since he didn't know if she went out in the evenings.

"Since you don't know anything that happened in Africa, I guess I'll have to ask Rose if she and Webster are still getting married. I don't want to buy a dress for a wedding that's not going to happen."

"Shelly, if you'll excuse me, good night." Trent said as politely as he could to her, realizing that she was walking down the hall beside him.

Trent knew Webster and Rose were having problems, and if Shelly Clayton was telling him the truth, Trent was sorry Webster and Rose hadn't been able to work out their differences. However, he had his own problems to deal with, like the fact that Jay was dismissing him from her life as if their relationship hadn't meant anything to her. He was determined to find out what had cause the trouble and he wasn't stopping until he could patch things up between them.

"Okay, Trent Prescott, be that way!" Trent heard Shelly blowing wind between her teeth as he pushed the lobby door open. "Men are always pretending they don't gossip."

From her living room window, Jay noticed Austin Carrington maneuvering his expensive car into her driveway and she wondered if Austin had come for the painting. When he called her earlier in the week, leaving a message that he wanted the painting, she had returned his call and left a message for him telling him to pick the painting up the day before.

But it was just like Austin, doing what he wanted when the time was convenient for him and Jay wished he hadn't chosen this evening to intrude on her quiet time.

Jay watched him get out of his car. Austin was average height, wore his hair cut short, and his golden complexion was flawless. She watched him acknowledge her elderly neighbor across the street while he proudly straightened the lapel on his dark suit jacket.

Austin's impatience was annoying to Jay because he wanted instant gratification. On their first date, Austin had insisted that they become a serious couple, but she had refused. She needed to get to know him first. Jay realized well into their relationship that Austin wore many masks, and used his changeable personality for his own harsh and selfish reasons which ultimately compelled her to end their relationship.

Jay hadn't regretted the break up. She was happy to be free of the passionless love affair that Austin wanted her grandmother, Barbara, Earl and Carol to believe was perfect.

He rang her doorbell three times before she opened the door for him. "How are you, Austin?" Jay spoke to him.

"I'm fine," he said, stepping closer to her as if he thought she should invite him inside her home.

The expensive painting was the only connection left between her and Austin's failed relationship. After this evening, she didn't want to see him anymore. "I'll get the painting for you," Jay said.

"I want you to keep it," Austin offered.

"Austin, I wish you would take the painting. That

way, you will not have a reason to visit me." Jay turned away from Austin's dark gaze.

"Jay, at least you could consider being my friend." Austin moved closer to the door.

"Good night, Austin," Jay said, pushing the door.

"Wait." Austin stopped Jay from closing the door. "I was hoping that you had changed your mind about us while you were away."

"Austin, you know as well as I do that we are not getting back together," Jay said. Austin had once crowded her life with his infidelities and lies and even though she and Trent were no longer together, she had no room in her life for Austin again.

"Jay, six months is enough time for you to get over being mad at me," Austin said.

"Austin, I'm not mad at you, but we are through," Jay countered. "It's over," she said.

"Jay, I'm a different person. I changed while you were away," he said.

Jay rolled her eyes upward. "Please!"

"I know I've told you so many times that I've changed and I know that you don't believe me." Austin's expression was serious. "But I'm different and if you give us another chance you'll understand," Austin said to Jay.

"Will you please leave?" Jay said, pushing the front door. Austin grabbed the knob to keep her from closing the door in his face.

"Jay, you haven't been home long enough to have met anyone around here." Austin studied her closely. "You're going with someone from that team aren't you?"

"Good night Austin," Jay said, feeling a rush of tears racing up and settling in her eyes as she thought about

Trent and how they couldn't be together because of
an old dissension that had taken place too many years
ago. She lowered her gaze and composed herself.
"Austin, if you don't want the painting, we have nothing else to talk about."

"Okay, but I know a few of those guys working at
Myers and the ones I know, know that we were a couple. So you might as well forget about that little African
fling you had."

Jay gave the door a hard shove, closing it and shutting Austin out of her life forever. She hadn't considered her and Trent's love a fling. She pondered
Austin's opinion regarding the relationship and that
he suspected she was involved with someone from her
team. As she crossed the room and sat down on the
sofa she allowed herself to think of his threat to find
out which one of the men from the team she had dated
while she was in Africa.

A slow wave of apprehension swept through her as
the frightening thought crossed her mind. When she
and Austin were together, he had often partied at
nightclubs that some of the men working at Myers went
to. And she and Austin had gone to the same gym as
most of the team members. If Austin asked around and
learned that she had dated Trent Prescott, he would
most likely tell her grandmother.

When they first began dating, Jay remembered telling Austin the story about how her parents died. She
had given him the surname of the family Gladys had
told her were responsible for their death. Austin was
right, and she knew him and he didn't forget anything.
Jay was certain that he would find a way to use the
information against her if he found out that she and
Trent had been lovers.

Trent was out of her life, but not her system, and she wished that she were brave enough to defy Gladys and continue to date him anyway.

A trail of jealousy ripped through Trent as he watched the man that had just left Jay's house until he got in his car and drove off. He had just witnessed a lover's quarrel, and he thought he could trust Jay Lee. But he couldn't settle for the old truism that all women were the same because he believed Jay to be different. If she was different, why had he witnessed a lover's quarrel? It was clear to him that Jay was upset. He could tell by the way she had slammed the front door.

Unable to still the jealousy racing through him and pulling at his heart, Trent got out and crossed the street to Jay's house.

The harsh reminder that he had experienced with Sonya played in his mind again and threatened to make him relive the pain of the night he had walked in on her and her lover. So, why was he upset at seeing Jay with the man that just left her house? Trent searched for a justifiable answer to his own question.

Jay was adamant in their telephone conversation, declaring that she had not rekindled her relationship with her old lover. She assured him that their problem related to other matters and he didn't have the slightest notion what could be so horrible that it would make her not even want his platonic friendship.

Even though he thought, a platonic friendship between him and Jay was impossible. He loved her too much to put himself in an awkward position. It was all or nothing and Jay had better have an explanation that was to his satisfaction. He allowed the angry thought to grip him.

She was special to him, making him realize that he could give himself to her and love again. When she left him in Nigeria, he had felt empty as if there was a void inside him that could not be filled without her in his life. And he had stayed awake at night praying that she would have a safe flight home.

When she was home and safe he had called because he had a burning urge to hear her voice. Maybe what he thought was love for Jay was only physical passion. He dismissed that thought. But now he was facing the dreaded truth that he had denied the entire time he was traveling home. Maybe he had been wrong about Jay. Nevertheless, he couldn't put off learning the truth any longer. He would behave himself. Close contact always made him want to hold Jay. Trent took the two steps to Jay's porch in one swift move and rang the doorbell.

He waited patiently for another second or two and looked around her green yard and the cluster crimson buds that looked as if they were about to bloom before checking his watch and ringing the bell again. If Jay had seen him through her window and thought he was going away without an explanation, Jay Lee had made another mistake.

Once he knew why she didn't want to continue their relationship, he would go away and as much as he didn't want to, he would forget her. Living in the small town was not going to be easy, especially, seeing her and not being able to be with her. But he would manage. His work agenda was already complete with appointments to buy property or sell. So running into Jay regularly might not be a problem after all.

He rang the door bell again and this time planned to leave if she didn't open the door for him. Jay Lee was not going to waste his time. He wished her well in her life. He turned away from her door, ready to run across the street to his car.

The last ring from her doorbell brought Jay out of her closet. She had just pulled on a comfortable long sleeveless tunic, a house dress she lounged in when she wanted to relax and Austin was probably back to harass her again.

He was relentless, trying to get his way and most likely thought he could pressure her into taking him back into her life. A curse slipped across her lips as she walked down the stairs to tell Austin what was on her mind. Since he hadn't seemed to her to understand the door being closed in his face, this time she was going to tell him off and she didn't care if she hurt his feelings or not.

Added to that, if he wanted to find out if she had gone out with Trent while she was in Nigeria and then inform her grandmother on his findings he was welcome to do that too. But she would not tolerate his harassing and threatening her.

Twelve

"Austin, what do you want now?" Jay opened the door ready to give Austin a peace of her mind. "Trent!" And suddenly she ached to hold him. Jay stood before Trent and for a moment she checked him out from head to toe, from his fresh haircut, blue suit, matching blue shirt and tie, down to his buffed wing tip shoes. "I didn't know you were home," Jay said, stepping aside and inviting him in and not caring if he had heard the surprise in her voice. She knew he would be home soon, but not tonight. Jay lifted her gaze to his soft brown eyes.

"How are you?" Trent asked her, moving inside to Jay's living room.

"Not good," Jay said, being as honest as she knew how to be. "And you?" She asked Trent, still aching to wrap her arms around his neck and welcome him home.

"I'll let you know after we talk," Trent said, standing in the center of Jay's living room floor. "What's going on?"

"Everything that's not good," Jay said gesturing to the sofa.

"You're having problems with your boyfriend?"

Trent asked Jay as he pushed his hands into his trouser pockets, and seemed to rest his weight on the heel of his shoes.

"No, Austin is the least of my problems," Jay said. "I think I might have a problem with you."

"What kind of problem could you have with me?" Trent asked and before Jay could answer him, Trent continued. "I called you when I thought you were home, and all you could tell me is that you didn't think we should continue going together and I would like to know why."

Jay noticed the hard set in Trent's jaw and the lines etched between his brows. "Sit down," she offered, gesturing to the sofa.

"All right." Trent sat down and leaned back, stretching his arms across the back of the sofa. "I'm listening."

"I think I'm dating the family's enemy and if that's true, we can't date each other anymore." Jay didn't want to prolong what was about to end. And that was her love for Trent, but he had to know that she was loyal to her family.

"How did I get to be your enemy?" Trent asked, studying Jay.

Jay hesitated as she gathered her composure. She couldn't allow her feelings for Trent to stop her from telling the truth. "I told you that my parents were killed," Jay said.

"Yes, I remember." Trent eyed her carefully.

"Your family was responsible for their death. One of the Prescotts' actually ran them down with their car, or paid someone to commit the crime." Jay observed the frown that deepened between Trent's smooth brows.

"What?" Trent asked, the question appeared to darken his eyes.

"According to my grandmother, one of your family members killed my parents." Jay's voice faded. She cast a quick glimpse at him and he looked as if he was shocked at her information.

"No, that can't be the truth, baby," Trent moved to the edge of the sofa.

"Our families have been enemies for a long time," she said, telling him about the bed and breakfast and how her father had won the business and how Trent's family sought revenge and finally killed both her parents.

Trent leaned forward, resting his arms on his thigh and turned to Jay. "So you're Jay Lee. Lees' Bed and Breakfast." He looked at her as if he was shocked and couldn't believe that he had met her and was thinking that maybe they shouldn't be lovers.

"Yes," Jay said, with strict control over her urge to cry. However, she was glad that at least Trent seemed willing to agree that they couldn't be lovers any longer even if he had agreed silently with her. Jay felt much better knowing the horrible truth was out and she could get on with her life, even though it would be a long time before she would forget the time they had spent together.

"I remember something about that time." He leaned back and stretched his arms along the sofa back. "I was a kid, around eleven. My parents were managing the bed and breakfast for Uncle Flint, and I think he was planning to buy the place. I remember my father telling us . . ." He paused, as if he was gathering a clear picture of that particular time. "He told us that Flint had lost the business in a game of dice."

Trent continued to look at her. "I remember us having to move out of the cottage that was in the back of the building."

"I'm sorry," Jay said, realizing that Trent had been uprooted from his home and most likely it was painful for him and his family. But at least he had his parents, Jay mused.

"My father also said that the dice the man used was rigged," Trent added.

"I don't think so," Jay said, defending her father.

"Maybe not, but my family had nothing to do with your parents' death." His voice was strong, and yet warm, as he spoke with confidence while he defended his family.

"How do you know?" Jay asked.

"Because my daddy and Flint were the only brothers living in this town. I have two aunts. One lives in Delaware and the other lives in North Carolina. They could not have cared less if Uncle Flint lost his business. So why would any of my family kill your parents?" Trent asked her. When she didn't answer, he continued. "My daddy and uncle sure as hell didn't do it."

Jay was confused, but then why would Trent tell her the truth. He was a member of the Prescott family. In spite of those thoughts and their discussion, she still loved him.

"You don't know what your father did or didn't do," Jay challenged him.

"Baby, I know my parents and I know what we went through. My father is not a murderer, but if he was going to kill anyone, it would've been Flint Prescott for losing the business," Trent reached out and lay his hand on Jay's hand.

"I'm telling you what I was told," Jay defended her

source of information which had come from her grandmother, Gladys Lee.

"After Uncle Flint lost the business, we went to Delaware and stayed there for two or three days because our relatives did not want anything to do with us. If one of my daddy's army buddies hadn't gotten him a job in Canada, we would've been homeless, at least for a little while."

The information that Gladys had given to her on how her parents died was beginning not to make sense to her now, but one thing did. When she called Delaware while in Africa to check on Trent, a man answered the telephone, pretending he had never heard of the family before.

Jay felt a tear sting her eye and she turned away from Trent and blinked, refusing to cry. But something was not making sense, like why would her grandmother lie to her? And Barbara's claim that the family hadn't murdered her parents was much more acceptable. Still, Jay couldn't defy her grandmother. But Trent was like her, he loved his family, and she couldn't blame him for defending them.

"I can't see you anymore," Jay said, crossing her legs. "I don't think we can be friends."

"Jay, nothing you said to me is true," Trent said.

"Are you saying that my grandmother is lying?" Jay asked, determined to set the record straight. Gladys Lee was not a liar and she didn't appreciate Trent disputing the information Gladys had told her. "And can you prove to me that a member of your family didn't pay someone to commit the crime against my parents?"

Trent covered her hand with his and shook his head as if he didn't trust himself to tell her what he was thinking. "Jay, I understand family loyalty and all of that good stuff, but your information is not true. My family didn't have money to pay anyone to commit a crime."

Jay felt the usual familiar shivers race through her when Trent covered her hand, and his warm touch was almost spellbinding, making her want to plant herself in the cushion of his strong arms and ravish him with sweet kisses. She wanted to feel him next to her and bury her hands underneath his suit jacket and feel the strong muscles in his back, stroke his hard chest, and love him forever.

Jay banished the thought and stood up. Her legs felt as if they had turned to rubber and she let Trent steady her. She found her balance before he gathered her in his arms and moved away from him and to her front door. "I want you to leave." She held the door open, clutching the knob to steady herself.

"Baby . . ."

Jay didn't answer him. She tilted her head to one side and clutched the knob and prayed that she would have the strength to stay steady at least until Trent was out of her house.

"Baby," She heard him call her again and she wanted him to leave before she lost her right mind and told Trent that whatever happened years ago didn't matter anymore.

So she looked the other way instead of looking at him until finally, he left her. She held onto the door until he was inside his Jaguar and was driving away from her and out of her life.

Jay closed the door to her house and ultimately her heart. With a heavy sigh, and with her remaining strength, she moved slowly to the sofa prolonging her steps as if lingering would halt the throbbing ache in her heart.

She reached the sofa and sank down on her knees and without further hesitation, she allowed herself to cry.

Trent drove to the edge of the street and pulled over in front of a vacant lot and cut the engine and lights off on his car. He thought he was hurt when he found Sonya in a compromising position, but the pain of losing Jay Lee was almost more than he could bear. Her reasons for breaking up with Trent concerned a matter that he had no control over.

He pushed himself down in the seat and he stared straight ahead. He was dealing with a problem that didn't belong to him and he wondered what had he done to deserve this treatment. *God, what are you doing to me?*

When he finished questioning God, he turned the key in the ignition and checked the time on the dashboard. He had plenty of time tonight and taking the long trip home to clarify information that had torn him and Jay apart would give him plenty of time to think. His parents were going to explain to him what had happened between the Prescotts and the Lees. Trent pulled out into the street and headed to Canada.

Eleven hours later, Trent parked in his parents' driveway. From his parents' bedroom window, he saw the soft glow from the lamp and he figured his mother was up. He flipped the keys around on his key ring and let himself inside.

"Mother." Trent stopped at the bottom of the stairs

and called out to her before following the scent of coffee to the kitchen.

"Trent." Flora Prescott ran down the stairs and walked into her kitchen and stopped beside her son. "How are you?" Flora asked. She was a petite woman, with the same complexion as Trent. Her long thick black hair was pulled back into a ponytail, and her soft brown eyes were lit with surprise.

"I'm okay," Trent said, filling a mug with coffee.

Her son being *okay* was not enough for Flora Prescott. Added to that, when he spoke to her, he didn't turn around to face her. "What's wrong?" Flora inquired as she walked behind him and rested her hand against his back, nudging him to turn around and face her.

"I don't know. That's why I'm here to talk to you and Daddy." Trent pulled out a kitchen stool and sat at the counter. "I have a problem."

"Are you sick?" Flora took a coffee mug off the rack and filled it with black coffee.

"I'm not sick," Trent said, staring inside the steaming cup as if the hot liquid held answers to the questions he needed. "Is Daddy asleep?"

"He'll be down soon," Flora said, setting the pot down, and studying her son. "Trent, you know that I'm always glad to see you and Gwen." She slipped onto a stool at the other side of the counter. "But when you or Gwen shows up at this time of the morning, I know something is wrong." Flora took a spoon out of the drawer and scooped a small amount of sugar from the sugar dish. "I'm listening," she said, stirring the coffee slowly.

"What happened with the bed and breakfast?"

Trent looked up from the coffee mug he had been staring into.

"Trent, don't tell me that you drove all the way up here just to ask about that business." Flora said, and laughed softly. "It's been so many years since any of us talked about that place."

"I want you to tell me how Uncle Flint lost the business and do you know the people he lost the business to?" He tasted the coffee then and waited for an explanation from his mother.

"Oh well, let me see," Flora said. "Your Uncle Flint loved to gamble with dice and play cards. One night, he lost the business to Rollins and Gladys Lee's son . . . Rollins Junior. Why do you want to know what happened to Gladys and her family?" Flora was curious.

"I have my reasons," Trent said and straightened up. "How long did you know the family?"

"We've known Gladys and Rollins for years. I knew her son and his wife too when they were alive. Why?" Flora lifted the mug and sipped the hot coffee.

"How did Mrs. Lee's son and his wife die?" Trent asked his mother.

"Trent, we weren't living there when it happened, but my girlfriend told me that Rollins and his wife were struck by a car and that the driver was drunk."

"Are you sure about that?" Trent asked her.

"Of course I'm sure. Have you been talking to Gladys Lee?" Flora asked.

"If I had talked to Mrs. Lee, what would she have told me?" Trent asked.

"Knowing Gladys, she would tell you that someone in the Prescott family would've paid anyone to kill her son and daughter-in-law."

Trent rubbed his thumb across his chin. "Tell me that's not true."

"Trent, I don't know where all of this is coming from. But none of us was mad enough to kill anybody over that bed and breakfast," Flora said to her son, blowing on the liquid before she took a sip of the hot coffee. "At first I hated that we had to move," Flora said, "because we didn't have a place to go. But as I look back, it was the best thing that ever happened to us." Trent knew how proud his mother was of her own business selling bed linens.

Trent also knew there were records that would prove that an intoxicated person was responsible for Jay's parents' death. And he had to find a way to prove to Jay that his family hadn't paid anyone to commit a crime. "There was an altercation between our families. What was that about?" Trent asked Flora. He had to prove to Jay that his family was innocent even if she didn't want him anymore.

"Trent, I don't know why you need to know any of this, but Gladys Lee has had a problem with the Prescotts for years," Flora shook her head slowly as if she was trying to recall the years that had almost destroyed her family. "Why didn't you look for the police report?" Flora asked him.

"Because I would like to know why Mrs. Gladys Lee is upset with us after all of these years?" Trent pried, needing answers to his questions. If his family was innocent, which he believed they were, he needed to find the person who had committed the crime and a police report was not enough. Maybe then he could convince Jay that his family was innocent.

"Have we ever lied to you and your sister?" Flora asked Trent.

"No," Trent said. He couldn't think of a time that his parents had lied to him or Gwen.

"Gladys Lee has been spiteful, vindictive, and just mean for years." Flora chuckled and shook her head. "Gladys was once a nice woman," Flora added.

Trent was getting his questions answered and beginning to think that maybe his father was the man he needed to talk to about this problem.

"So what are all the questions for?" Flora asked.

"While I was in Africa, I met Jay Lee."

"Gladys's granddaughter?" Flora asked him.

"Yes," Trent said.

"It's been a long time. Jay is a woman now."

"Yes, she is and I love her."

"Oh no!" Flora got up off the stool. "You can't be in love with her."

"Why?" Trent inquired, watching Flora's brown eyes flash with angry.

"Because Gladys hates us," Flora said, and placed one hand on her hip and pointed one finger toward her son. She knew where Trent had gotten his story and Gladys was still lying and had probably raised her granddaughter to hate their family as much as she did. "You listen to me. You leave that woman alone."

Trent stood and walked to the window as if the early dawn held a reasonable solution to his problem. "I have to convince Jay that at least we're not savages," Trent said when his father walked in.

"Trent," Christopher Prescott spoke to his son and leaned against the counter. "It's good to have you back home, son," Christopher Prescott had a head full of thick wavy graying hair and matching mustache. He was built well for a man his age because he still worked out at the gym every evening after work. He had a couple of hobbies that he enjoyed and unlike his wife, he stayed out of his children's personal lives.

"I was telling Trent about the Lees and the Prescotts," Flora said and sat and crossed her legs the way she did when she was about to go into an explanation to one of her family members on a matter that concerned them all.

"You haven't settled down in Jersey and you're already having problems with Gladys. When will that woman let that lie rest?" Christopher poured himself a cup of coffee.

"The bed and breakfast didn't always belong to us," Flora looked at Trent. "Gladys and Rollins Lee owned the business first," Flora said, and she watched Trent while she told him the details on how the feud between the two families began.

"All right," Trent said, after he listened to his mother. But before he told Jay what happened, he had a few more details to take care of.

"I don't see what this has to do with Trent and Gladys's granddaughter dating," Christopher said to Flora.

"It has everything to do with Trent loving Gladys's granddaughter, Chris. She would probably have a fit if she knew her granddaughter was speaking to Trent," Flora said.

"Gladys knows she's not telling the truth. She's just looking for someone to blame for the mess she made," Christopher Prescott said.

"Still, I think that Trent would be better off not going out with Jay," Flora said.

"Flora, will you stop trying to run Trent's life," Christopher said.

Trent listened to his parents, bickering back and

forth while he thought about Jay, wondering if he could convince her. "I'm going to bed," Trent said, when Flora started talking about him as if he was still a teenager and needed protecting from the hottest girl in town.

"Gwen is using the guest room," Flora said to him.

Trent raised a brow. "Craig got a promotion and they're moving to New Jersey, so she's staying here until she moves," Flora added.

Trent unbuttoned the top of his shirt and headed to the den. "I'll sleep on the sofa."

He lay on the sofabed recalling his last visit with Jay before he slept and thought about all that he intended to do about the family feud that stood between him and Jay. He believed that she was hurting as much as he was when he saw her last night and he intended to straighten the havoc that Gladys Lee had caused in their lives. And he wasn't going to Jay or speaking to her until he had completed the task.

Once again, Trent needed Myers' assistance. He was certain that he would remain in his debt forever. But his concern was to make sure that he found the proof he needed before he spoke to Jay. Myers knew many of the officers from the precinct because he had taught most of them in his anthropology and psychology classes, the same classes he had taught Trent.

Trent needed to get his hands on Jay's parents' accident records and he needed the name of the man that had caused their death.

With what he hoped was a problem solved, Trent drifted off, sleeping until late the next day.

Thirteen

Late Friday afternoon, Jay stood back admiring the freshly painted bed and breakfast while the scent of fresh paint filtered the spring air. She had been so busy working at Myers' and helping to get Lees' ready for the grand opening that she hadn't had time to think about Trent during the day. Her nights were the hardest for her. She could barely sleep for thinking about him, and when she slept, she dreamed about him. The mornings after her restless nights she brewed strong coffee, and filled herself with caffeine to stay awake during the day.

Even though she passed Trent in the corridor at Myers' Research Center, they spoke to each other as if they had never been lovers. Trent would disappear inside of Myers' office where Shelly told her that he was working until Myers and the team returned from Nigeria. Trent must have known that her grandmother had been right and that his family had been responsible for her parents death. He was keeping his distance and she knew Gladys had been right. However, her feelings had not changed for him.

It was impossible to avoid Trent at work, but she was thankful that he was out of her life and she was waiting patiently for him to fade from that special place he had captured in her heart. But until those moments arrived, she would savor the sweet memories of their time spent together.

Jay turned her reminders of Trent off and thought of more pleasant things like how nice the grounds looked and how the cottage in the back of Lees' was more beautiful than she remembered.

Jay loved the way the flaxen varnish had renewed the old worn brown registration desk and how nicely the medium blue carpet complemented the lobby, dining room and stairs.

All she had to do now was to wait until the furniture arrived, order the groceries and the linens. In a short time, Lees' would be open for business.

Jay walked behind the desk and checked the equipment. Two new computers, telephones and fax machines were the added necessities to Lees' Bed and Breakfast that promised to make running the business easier than when her grandparents operated Lees' years ago.

She slid onto the thick cushioned stool, thankful that she'd almost completed the project and had fulfilled her promise.

Even though her weekends would be lonely, and every night she suspected would be the same until she would finally decide a year or so later to date again. She was also aware that it would take at least that long for her to get Trent completely out her system or to the point where she wouldn't go to go bed at night and spend a few minutes smothering her tears because she wished that they could be together.

Nonetheless, her life had to go on, and she had found solace in knowing that one day her dreams and memories of Trent Prescott would be another part of her past.

Jay reminded herself that all this was for the best. But if she had been strong enough to confront and defy her grandmother, maybe things would be different and she and Trent might be together.

Added to that, Austin had kept his promise to find out the name of the man she had dated while she was in Africa and of course a few employees who thought that a part of their job description was to inform him that she and Trent had been lovers while they were in Nigeria. Austin had called her with the news and the threat to tell Gladys about the affair she'd had with the man whose family her grandmother hated.

Jay dismissed her thoughts of Austin and turned on the computer and began making the food order in advance to make sure that the groceries arrived in time for the opening date, which was a short time away. She worked quietly placing her order and making a promise to find out more than what Gladys had told her about her parents' death. She was sure there were records to prove whether or not the Prescotts had been responsible, even if her grandmother had told her differently.

Halfway through her grocery order for Lees', she stopped working and gazed out the lobby's window, allowing her thoughts to waver to Trent, recalling the sound of his laughter, the effects his touch had on her, how his lips brushed hers, the firmness in his voice when he was serious, and the smoldering darkness that appeared in the soft color of his eyes when he was angry.

She returned to her work, reminding herself that she had made the right decision and although her heart was not listening to her reasoning, it only seemed to know her strong desire to continue the passion that she and Trent had shared.

Jay noticed the furniture truck pull up to the curb and stop, plucking her out of her memories of Trent. She was about to save the grocery order and get up and go to the kitchen to tell her grandmother that the furniture had arrived when Barbara walked in and stood at the edge of the counter.

"Jay, finish your order, I'll show the men upstairs," Barbara offered.

"All right, Barbara," Jay said. "Did Granny leave?" Jay asked Barbara.

"Yes, but she'll be back later," Barbara said, taking the furniture receipt from behind the counter to use as a check off list.

Jay made herself busy making a call to the wholesale linen company Gladys had used years ago while the furniture workers moved the bedroom sets upstairs.

Finally, the men finished their work and minutes later, Jay completed her work and was about to go upstairs and check out the bedrooms when Trent walked into the lobby.

"Jay," Trent called her and her first instinct was to wrap her arms around him and savor his warm and hungry kisses. Instead, she watched him cross the floor and stood on the other side of the desk.

"Hi," she spoke to him, wanting to deny the horrible information Gladys had told her too many years ago. "Why are you here?" She asked Trent, admiring how nice he looked in his tan shirt and blue trousers.

"I need to talk to you," he said in a low whisper, walking around the counter and standing in front of her.

"We don't have anything to talk about." Jay was determined to forget Trent Prescott, but his unstoppable strength made it difficult for her to ignore her feelings for him. Trent was always in her thoughts and now he was with her, instilling her with desire that would never be fulfilled.

She had lost family members once because of his family and she couldn't stand the thought of losing another. Still, the yearning desire to be with him would not go away. How was she ever going to get over the joy of loving him? Jay didn't have the answer to that question.

"Yes, we need to talk," Trent said reaching out and closing his hand at the side of her waist, igniting even more desire to change her mind and throw her worries to the wind and allow time to take care of all her problems.

"I'm listening," Jay said, losing her power to resist his gentle touch, as he moved his hand off her waist and pulled her to him.

"Can we go somewhere . . ." His voice faded as he lowered his head and almost touched her lips with his.

Her promise to forget him and live with the sweet memories they had shared diminished and was replaced with even more burning desire to be with the man she loved. If she listened to what he had to tell her, and know that after considering all he had to say to her without breaking her promise not to involve herself in his life again, she would give him a few minutes of her time. "I can't get away right now," Jay said, inhaling his heady cologne and wanting to hold him close to her. She couldn't take the chance and allow herself to fall in a trap only to fulfill her physical desires, knowing that Trent was probably as vindictive as all the other members of his family. She stepped out of his embrace and she wanted to ask him to leave. She held his gaze, searching his eyes and she didn't see a vindictive man, but the man she had fallen in love with months ago. "Where are we going?" Jay asked as she tossed her worries to the winds.

"Would like for me to wait for you?" Trent asked her.

"No," Jay said, knowing it wouldn't take her long to go upstairs and check the furniture, but she would rather drive her own car.

Trent held her hand while he told her the name of the restaurant he wanted her to meet him which was in a nearby town. He curved her in his arms again and Jay couldn't stop herself when she slipped her arms around his neck and caressed his mouth and Trent deepened the kiss.

The sound of glass crashing against the floor drew them apart. "I'll be ready in an hour," Jay said, figuring she might as well turn this time they had together into a date and if Trent was as serious about continuing their relationship as she thought he was maybe they could pick up where they had left off.

Her decision had nothing to do with disrespecting her parents' death or any disrespect for her grandmother and the dissension she held close to her heart. Jay Lee wanted the man she loved and giving him up was making her crazy.

"I'll see you then and when we finish talking, I have something to show you," Trent said.

Jay swung her head slowly, agreeing to listen to him when she heard footsteps and noticed that Earl was in the lobby.

Jay and Trent spoke to Earl and Jay turned back to

Trent. "Does this have something to do with our not seeing each other?" Jay asked.

"Yes, and I also have someone I want you to meet." Trent released her then and moved back, pushing his hands in his pockets, when they noticed Earl walking past them again. "I think you'll want to hear what I have to say, so don't be late," he said, and walked out of the building.

"Trent Prescott, was that an order?" If he answered her, she didn't hear him, the sound of more glass crashing against the floor captured her attention. Jay didn't bother checking. Earl had probably broken something else, she mused, thankful that she had ordered lots of dishes and glasses. She turned off the computer, declaring to herself that Earl had ten thumbs.

Jay grabbed her purse, not wanting to stop for her purse when she left for home, and hurried upstairs to look at the new furniture.

She was ambivalent as to whether or not she wanted to give up her relationship with Gladys, but she needed to know what Trent had to say and she wanted to be with him. She would sort through the dilemmas of her life later.

Jay walked out of Lees' not knowing what she would learn from Trent tonight and hoping that she was not making the biggest mistake of her life.

Gladys stood beside Jay's parents' graves, setting two bouquets on each. Then she went to her husband's grave and kneeled, sweeping a cluster of leaves and sprigs from the tombstone with her hands before she replaced the old flowers with a fresh bouquet. As she cringed over Rollins Lee grave, remembering his warning to her many years ago when Jay was a girl, Gladys wished that she had listened to him. But she was angry and hurt and she wanted to protect Jay from people that had pretended to be their friends when in reality they were nothing more than thieves, swindling her and Rollins for all that they had owned. Besides, Jay needed to be taken care of and Gladys wanted to make certain that there was enough money for her son to take care of his child.

Nevertheless, Rollins was a fair and honest man and she had loved him for his wonderful qualities, but she had disagreed with him again, when he asked her to live in the present times. She lived in the present, but she hadn't moved an inch mentally when it came to the Prescotts. And because of her adamant spirit and her need to resent, she had warned Jay that she would disown her if she as much as thought she was associating with the family.

Gladys had returned from her errand and followed Earl up the stairs to the kitchen after he had shown her the changes he'd made to the bar and the small beauty salon. She was about to go into the lobby to speak to Jay then go upstairs and look at the furniture when Earl knocked over a saucer. Gladys had made herself busy picking up the glass and was on her way to speak to Jay with the intentions of dropping the broken glass in the garbage container near the door, when she noticed that her granddaughter seemed to have been in a serious discussion with a man. She had stood in the hallway at the edge of the door that led into the lobby and listened to their soft whispers. Jay hadn't mentioned to her that she had met someone after she broke up with Austin, so she tried to get a better look and wished she had waited until Jay's friend had left because they were locked in an embrace, sharing a very intimate kiss. She had thought it was nice that Jay had moved on with her life until the man was leaving and Jay addressed him by his name. It was then that she knew Jay was involved with a man who was related to the Prescotts! She dropped the broken glass and it shattered against the tile floor again.

How Jay had met and fallen in love with one of the Prescotts, the very people she had warned her never to speak to was beyond her wildest dreams and she didn't know what to do. Gladys said a silent prayer, asking for an answer to a dilemma that might destroy Jay's love for her if she ever learned what she had done. Gladys rose from her knees and took a tissue from her purse and wiped the tears that had settled in her eyes.

She was old and had no one left in the world that loved her as much as Jay. At this moment she didn't know anyone she could go to except her minister and that was to confess her sins. But she was too embarrassed to tell him what she had done so many years ago.

Her minister would probably believe that she was as treacherous as Lizzy James said she was when she had refused to give her a ride to the bake sale and she had to take a bus in the snow. *"Rollins, I don't know what to do."* Gladys spoke out loud, her voice echoing against the quietness. She had made many mistakes, and had done plenty that she was not proud of. But this was the worst. And if Jay never spoke to her again, she didn't know what she was going to do. She needed time to think and the best place for thinking was with her girlfriend.

Gladys rose from her kneeling position and walked

to her car. She had no one to blame for her foolish mistake but herself. She had thought that Jay was safe from meeting the Prescott family. They had moved to Canada many years ago. Although a few still lived in Delaware, Gladys was certain that this young man she had seen today was Flora and Christopher Prescott's son. The Prescott sisters were married and didn't use their surname and Flint Prescott didn't have a wife or children and he was dead. Gladys clutched her pocketbook to her chest and moved slowly to her car.

Gladys couldn't go back to Lees' tonight. She was too aggravated with all the problems she had caused for herself. Also if Austin Carrington had been any good, Jay probably would've never met and fallen in love with Trent Prescott.

Fourteen

Jay sat across from Trent after they had finished their dinner while she drank cappuccino and listened to him explain how the Lees and the Prescotts had once been friends. But because Trent's grandfather hadn't kept the promise he had made to Rollins and Gladys, the Lees had lost the business to the Prescotts, beginning the feud between the two families that Gladys had kept bustling and blistering with hatred.

"As far as I'm concerned, baby, this feud has nothing to do with us," Trent said.

"Maybe not," Jay remarked, searching Trent's face in disbelief. She had never remembered when the business didn't belong to her family. "This just proves that my grandmother is telling the truth."

"Not the whole truth because my family had nothing to do with your parents' death."

"Trent, I'm sorry, but it's hard for me to believe," Jay looked over the rim of the coffee mug before she took a sip of the warm coffee. "I have never heard any of this before," she remarked firmly and set the mug down.

Jay noticed Trent's fixed gaze on her and his eyes held a pleading expression as if he was begging her to believe him and she wondered if any of what Trent had told her was true, especially the part about her father. But why would he lie?

She considered the reasons that he might refrain from telling her the whole truth. Like anyone, Jay imagined Trent didn't want her to believe that his family was as evil as her grandmother knew them to be.

However, Jay still found Trent's reasons disturbing even if he hadn't been dishonest with her before. Still, when she looked at him and met his warm gaze, her heart fluttered.

Jay looked away, unlocking her gaze from the tenderness in his eyes. If he had asked her to marry him at that moment, she would have accepted his proposal and eloped with him that same night. "I don't know what to believe," she said.

"Look at me," Trent said, reaching out and covering her hand with his.

Jay slowly turned away from looking at all the happy couples in the dining room and allowed herself to look at Trent.

"Have I ever lied to you?" he asked her.

"No," Jay said, wishing he would uncover her hand. It was hard for her to think straight when he touched her.

"Sometimes things happen between friends, baby," Trent said.

"I understand," Jay said, not wanting to think that her family was as much to blame as Trent's family had been.

"Jay, no one was hired to end your parents' lives and I can prove that to you," Trent said, taking his credit card from his wallet and motioning for the passing waiter to stop so he could pay for their dinners.

"If you say so," Jay said, once the waiter had left them with a promise to return with Trent's card and receipt. She was still digesting the terrible news that Trent had told her about her father Rollins Lee, Junior. Her father and Trent's uncle had been gambling buddies? She had never heard that from her grandmother before.

She sat quietly listening and fighting the urge to tell Trent what she thought of his so-called facts concerning her family until she couldn't resist keeping quiet any longer. She was still toying with the information that he had told her about her father. "You know, Trent, I can't believe that my daddy would hurt anyone," she said.

Trent leaned back in his chair and looked at her for a long time and she felt herself wanting to writhe under his gaze. "Jay, because of the games he and Uncle Flint played, we were almost homeless."

Unless Trent and his family were as wicked as her grandmother had informed her, she couldn't imagine him fabricating a story as disastrous as homelessness. "I'm sorry," Jay said, unable to dismiss the trail of questions slipping through her mind. Why hadn't her grandmother mentioned any of the details Trent entrusted with her? Jay pondered that thought while they walked out of the restaurant.

Trent circled one arm around her waist as he walked her to her car. "I'm telling you this because I love you," he said, and gathered her to him, but Jay refused his kiss. She needed time to think.

"Trent." She studied his face in the dim parking lot lights and knew that there was nothing that could change the message her heart was speaking to her. "I love you too. But I need time."

Trent tightened his arms around her until she could feel the beat of his heart against her breast. "We have to take care of this problem," he whispered against her ear and Jay shivered from the warmth of his breath against her skin.

At that moment Jay wasn't concerned with who had done what to whom. This was her life and she wanted to be with Trent, but things weren't adding up. She didn't know whether to believe her grandmother or the Prescotts.

Jay stepped out of his embrace and unlocked her car door. "I'll see you in a few minutes," she said.

Jay Lee planned to speak to her grandmother as soon as possible about the feud between the two families and she didn't plan to be delicate about the subject that had torn at her for years. Jay had so many questions to asked Gladys and her main concern was why hadn't Gladys told her the families were once friends.

Jay pushed the CD player button, filling the car with her favorite love song while she drove home, not wanting to think anymore about the disturbing news Trent had just told her. Tonight, she would have plenty of time to think, especially after she saw the proof Trent would show.

She pulled up into her driveway, got out of her car and waited for Trent to join her after he parked behind her car, carrying a black leather case.

"Jay," Trent said, once they were walking together to her house.

"Huh?" she answered, pulling her house keys around on the key ring and stopping to give Trent her undivided attention.

"Will you come to West Virginia with me?"

"I'll have to think about it," Jay said. "If I decide

to go, it can't be the weekend we're opening Lees'," she said, then added, "And I can't go Memorial Day." Jay would have loved to spend her holiday with him, celebrating the memory of the time they met and their new love but she didn't want to leave Barbara and her grandmother to open the bed and breakfast alone. "Trent, before I spend a weekend with you, I want to see the proof."

"Fine, but I'm leaving for West Virginia on Monday," he said, his voice crackled like a warm fire on a winter's night, as he assumed that she would believe his proof.

"I can't go with you on Monday, Trent," Jay said. She had to work and then go to Lees' after work and help Barbara to tie up any loose ends before they opened in a few weeks.

"Can you get away Friday morning?" Trent asked.

"I'll let you know," Jay said. She knew that Myers and the team were back now and Trent wasn't with the company anymore.

Jay pushed the key into the lock and for a moment, without warning, her mind went to Gladys and how if Trent were right, her grandmother had been dishonest with her. She had deluded Jay into believing that the Prescotts were their adversaries and there had to be a reasonable explanation. Feeling Trent's hand on the small of her back, she dismissed the thoughts and unlocked the door.

"I can't wait to get you inside," Trent said, lingering and parting her lips with the tip of his tongue as he searched her lips with a hungry kiss.

Jay pulled away, giving him a playful pinch on his wrist and walked into her home enjoying the light filling the living room with a warm radiant glow. She took Trent's hand and led him up the stairs to her bedroom.

Jay disappeared into the closet and undressed, changing to a short light colored lounge set and a pair of comfortable black bedroom slippers.

When she returned to the bedroom, she noticed that Trent had pulled off his jacket and was sliding the tape into the video machine, and was holding a folder. "Is that your proof?" Jay asked sitting on the love seat, preparing to see what information Trent could have found on the disaster that happened years ago.

"I think this should answer your question," he said, and sat beside her.

The older man stood next to a used tire sign and wore an exhausted expression. His eyes held a worried gaze as if he'd had a hard life, and when he lifted his hand to adjust his gray hat, Jay could tell that he had worked hard for many years.

"My name is Curtis Neal," he introduced himself and Jay listened as he spoke about the years he had spent in prison for striking and killing a young couple one Christmas Eve. "I was driving to a party my buddies were giving at the bar that evening. I knew I was going to be late so I drank before I left home, more than I should have. But I wanted to celebrate the holidays," Curtis Neal said. Jay noticed the wrinkled brown lines in his face began to pleat as if he was reliving the awful scene. "I was driving too fast and when I tried to stop for the red light, my car skidded on a patch of ice and right into a couple. I went to prison and my wife and children left me." Curtis Neal took a deep breath, and started again. "I got out of prison and no one would hire me, so I worked odd jobs until I got this business selling used tires. I would like to say I'm sorry to the young woman that is interested in hearing my confession. I am truly sorry that I caused so much pain in your life. I have never had another drink since that night."

The television screen beaded with snow and Jay turned to Trent. "You found the man?"

"Yes, with Myers' and Webster's help."

Jay realized that her boss knew many of the officers at the police station as well as Trent, but she couldn't believe that Trent would go to such lengths to prove that his family was innocent of the charges Gladys had claimed them to be guilty of.

Trent took a paper from the folder and gave it to Jay. "This is a copy of the newspaper clipping that reports the night of the accident and this is the clipping that was reported the day Curtis Neal was sentenced," he said, and Jay studied Curtis Neal's face in the picture. He was much younger and he appeared sad and worried.

Jay read the newspaper clippings, then gave the paper to Trent. "Where does Curtis Neal live?" She asked, just in case she wanted to verify Trent's information. She wanted to believe him, but her suspicious nature refused her.

"He lives about ten blocks from Lees'," Trent said and took out another stack of papers from the case. "I would like to show you that we didn't have any money when this happened and the deeds to the property that Flint lost including a copy of Prescott's Bed and Breakfast."

"Trent, no one keeps bank statements for years, except my grandmother." She chuckled softly. Her smile faded. She remembered the tire shack that sat back near the wooded area at the edge of town.

"My parents keep almost every paper that has anything to do with money and property. I had to make copies of these papers because they wouldn't let me take the originals." Clips of laughter followed every other word, as he pulled out the statements and passed them to Jay.

Jay looked at the papers. "Your father worked for your brother?" Jay asked Trent.

"Flint agreed to let my father buy the business. So he paid half the down payment and the other half of the down payment was supposed to be paid in six months. My mom took a part time job and before the deal was complete, Flint lost the business,"

"That was cold," Jay said.

"Well, I think we're all better off without the bed and breakfast," Trent said, taking the copies from Jay. "Now, can we continue where we left off?" Trent slipped his arms around Jay and touched his lips to her cheek.

Gladys had always told her to follow her heart and Jay knew that she was right in both her decisions. She would love Trent and she would talk to her grandmother. "I want to talk to my grandmother first, before I tell her that we're together."

"You don't believe me?"

"I believe you," Jay said, "but my grandmother is old and set in her ways. I don't want anyone telling her that we're going together before I get the chance to tell her first."

"All right, I guess we can see each other for a short time without telling everybody." Trent gave Jay a squeeze.

"Austin knows that we're going together and he's threatening to tell her if we continue seeing each other," Jay said, telling Trent how Austin had found out about them.

"I have one thing to say about the employees at Myers Research Center. They are nosy people." Trent said. "Okay, I can wait—but not for a long time," Trent said.

Jay's answer to him was to undo the buttons on his shirt and slip her fingers through a mass of curls laying against his chest. When she heard his breath catch in his throat, she kissed the center of his wide chest, stroking him gently, building a fueling flame that would eventually quench both their hungry desires. As Trent pulled her up beside him, his cell phone rang.

"Don't answer it," Jay said, not wanting a second of their evening together to be interrupted.

Trent answered the call and spoke briefly to the person calling him. "Baby, I have to go," he said, smothering a kiss on her lips. Austin Carrington had just called and threatened him, a matter he didn't take lightly. He intended to see Austin tonight and let him know the plans he had for him. He already knew from Jay that Austin was a swindler, loved to blackmail, and now he had just threatened to tell Gladys Lee that he was seeing Jay. "I'll call you," Trent said, taking the tape and folder from the love seat.

"What happened?" Jay asked as he was leaving her bedroom thinking that all he had to do was say the wrong things to the right people and Austin wouldn't be able to afford a bottle of beer let alone champagne.

Fifteen

Monday afternoon, Jay answered Trent's telephone call from West Virginia. She listened to his voice and she wished that she was with him instead of reviewing research videotapes from the African marriage assignment. "I'll be able to leave Friday morning," she told him.

"I'll have your plane ticket sent to you tomorrow," Trent promised Jay.

"Fine," she said, unable to refrain from smiling as she contemplated the joy of sharing the weekend with her secret lover. She was caught up in her own world, a special place that she and Trent shared together.

"I can hardly wait to see you." The sound of Trent's rich voice felt as if it had grazed her heart and she experienced the special warmth wafting her as always when he spoke to her in a low deep timbre.

"I still would like to know what the emergency was that made you leave me," Jay said, wanting to know why Trent had left her the last evening they were together.

"I don't want to get into it now, but I'll tell you Friday," Trent said.

"All right, I'll see you soon." Jay wrote the telephone number that Trent gave her to the house where he was living. They said their good-byes and Jay waited until she heard the click from Trent's end of the line before replacing the receiver on the cradle.

Jay returned to viewing the tapes and had barely begun before yielding to a worrisome thought. She was aware of the ramifications if her grandmother knew about her love for Trent. She hadn't had a chance to enlighten Gladys, telling her the information that Trent had given her regarding the family feud since Gladys had returned from her trip. Every time she wanted to talk to her grandmother about the old family altercation, Gladys always had more important things to do or she was too tired to talk and had plans to retire early in the evenings. Nonetheless, Jay was determined to confront her grandmother with the information and was willing to wait until she had time for her. In the meantime, she would enjoy a weekend with Trent.

Jay drew herself out of her pondering and pressed her palms against her chest realizing that the tape she was watching was half finished. She hit the pause button on the VCR remote and lifted her coffee cup to her lips, sipping the warm liquid and promising to stay in control of her rambling thoughts at least until she was finished working for the day.

She rewound the video because she had missed most of the taping. While she waited for the rewinding process to end, she wondered what might have been her decision while she was in Nigeria, if she had known Trent and his family were a part of their terrible past. Would she have mindfully respected Gladys's warnings—or would have dated Trent anyway? The question crept through her mind and lingered. She didn't know.

But she knew one thing concerning the matter . . . she wanted to tell Gladys what she had done and knew that even after her grandmother disowned her, she would never stop loving the woman that had made everything in her life possible and that included meeting and falling in love with Trent.

Jay gathered her purse and jacket and was ready to leave work to join Barbara at Lees' to continue tying up loose ends when her office telephone rang. "What do you want, Austin?" Jay asked, aggravated with Austin Carrington's harassment.

"Have you changed your mind about us?" He asked as if she had given him an indication that they would renew their relationship.

"Us?" Jay could hardly stand Austin. After all his lies and disrespect he had no shame insisting that they continue their relationship.

"I think Mrs. Lee would agree with me."

"Austin," Jay call him. She was not going to show him her fear.

"Yeah?" Austin voice held a hint of depravity.

"Go to hell!" Jay eased the receiver down and picked up her purse.

Austin must have thought she had been interpreting his refusal to rekindle their relationship as a joke, and to threaten her that he would report her affair with Trent to her grandmother only helped her to dislike him even more. He was selfish, conceited and obviously thought her world revolved around him. She considered this as she went to her car.

While Jay drove to Lees', she considered her compelling need to be with Trent. They would be alone spending a weekend together, free to go out without worrying whether or not anyone knew her and Trent and go to Gladys with the news that she was seen with Trent Prescott.

Jay drove to Lees' feeling warm and provocative, anticipating her wonderful weekend.

Several minutes later, Jay pulled up in the parking lot behind Lees' and got out, closing the car door with a soft firm thump. She looked with satisfaction at the cheery golden glow of lights illuminating from the bed and breakfast's new windows, while she crossed the lot to the back entrance.

Jay used her key and entered, walking down the hallway, passing the bar on one side and the beauty salon a few doors up next to the office where she walked in and noticed that Barbara was busy at work, reading applications. "You started without me," Jay said, sitting on the corner of her godmother's desk.

"Yes, I hired a cook, and three salon employees." Barbara held up three applications. "Two nail technicians and one hairstylist," Barbara said to Jay and reclined in the black leather chair.

"Good," Jay chuckled softly, noticing how nice Barbara looked seated behind the mahogany desk with her name engraved on the gold name plate.

Jay scanned the office and thought no one would have believed the room was once used for storage years ago. But Barbara insisted that the room would make a perfect office with just the right furniture and Jay couldn't have agreed with her more as she noticed the rich green plant setting atop the matching file cabinet. "I wouldn't have known how to choose a cook anyway and it's only right that you hire the salon technicians since you're the one with the license," Jay remarked proudly and sat in the nearest chair.

"License that I haven't used for a while," Barbara

gave her a facetious grin. "Did you see Austin?" She asked Jay.

"No, but I talked to him today. Why?"

"He left a few minutes ago. I thought you might've seen him in the parking lot." Barbara pushed her reading glasses farther down on the bridge of her nose and looked across the desk at Jay.

"What did he want?" Jay asked. Austin was behaving as if he didn't get her message. He had exhausted all of her patience when he called her and made another attempt to worm his way back into her life.

"He stopped by to visit, and to look at the work we did to the place," Barbara assured her.

"Oh," Jay said, not caring to discuss Austin anymore, but wanting to tell Barbara her plans to spend the weekend in West Virginia with Trent.

"Pass me about twenty folders and labels," Barbara said to Jay, pointing to the box on the table near the door.

"I'm spending the weekend in West Virginia with Trent," Jay said, lifting the lid off the folder and label boxes.

"So, you have decided not to break up with him," Barbara said, drumming the tips of her French manicured nails against the desktop.

"I've made a decision that I think will make me happy," Jay stated.

"So Gladys doesn't know about your trip or Trent?" Barbara asked Jay.

"No, I didn't tell her," Jay said, gathering folders and labels from the box and counting out ten of each for Barbara and setting them on her desk, then counted out ten of the same for herself.

"If she knew she would've had a fit," Barbara said,

reaching down beside her chair and taking out a stack of papers and invoices that needed filing.

Jay pulled her chair closer to the desk and began sticking the labels to the appropriate place on the folders. "Of course she'll be upset," Jay said. "But you know I haven't been able to talk to her about anything lately."

"Yes, she has been busier than usual," Barbara said. "She's been going to church services in the middle of week and having lunches with her girlfriend more than once a week after she returned from that trip."

"I need to talk to her," Jay said, telling Barbara how she wanted to tell Gladys what Trent had told her about the family feud.

"Oh," Barbara lamented while she worked on the folders. "You're serious about telling Gladys you're dating Trent?"

"Yes," Jay said.

"Well, looks as if you have made up your mind," Barbara said, and pointed a finger at Jay. "She'll get over the shock eventually."

"She will," Jay said. "Granny is a strong woman."

"Do you believe Trent?" Barbara asked her.

"His information makes more sense than Granny's story." Jay placed a label on the folder. "I want her to start from the beginning going into details. I don't want to know about how my parents were killed because of this place," Jay said, lifting her arm in a waving sweep over the office.

"Girl, you are really in love," Barbara said, and laughed lightly.

"You're right. But I've been taught to hate the Prescotts and it's time that Granny tells me exactly what happened."

"You know how Gladys dislikes being questioned about her decision," Barbara said.

"I'm not being disrespectful. But I would like to know more about the disaster than she has told me." Jay shrugged her shoulders and picked up another label from the stack.

"I don't think Gladys will abandon you. But aren't you afraid that she might keep her promise, Jay?" Barbara lifted a folder and held it as she waited for Jay to answer her question.

"If that's the case, I will deal with it when the time comes, but right now—I would like to hear what she has to say."

"All right," Barbara said. "Just be careful."

"I have called her at night when I knew she was home, and she has made one excuse after another. But maybe she is tired," Jay said, after a second of thinking about Gladys's busy schedule, "because I haven't told her what I want to talk to her about so I don't think she's avoiding me."

"Jay, you know how Gladys is. She's set in her ways and when she's ready to talk, she will." Barbara stopped talking and placing information on the new employees in the folders. "But I hope you're prepared when you tell her that you're dating Trent Prescott."

"Neither of us is married to anyone, and I will not continue to date him secretly any longer," Jay said.

"And you're willing to take the risk?" Barbara shook her head.

"Telling her is a big risk, but I'm willing to take the chance," Jay said.

"I guess I could do the same thing," Barbara said, taking a letter from the stack and frowning over the information. "You see, my parents didn't like Earl."

"I didn't know," Jay said, realizing that this was Barbara's reason for not taking Earl along on her occasional visits to her parents. As long as Jay could remember, she never heard Barbara speak much about her parents.

"After we were married, my parents were nice to me." She lay the letter inside the folder. "But they made it clear that Earl wasn't welcome in their home."

"Well!" Jay stared at Barbara.

Barbara stopped working and looked at Jay. "If I had listened to my parents, I would've been married to Bobby McGuire and putting up with his foolishness." She laughed and went back to her work. "So follow your heart and do what you think is best for you."

While Jay and Barbara finished working quietly, Jay allowed her mind to wander to the weekend she planned to spend with Trent. A familiar sensual feeling settled inside her and again she felt as if she could hardly wait for Friday morning to arrive.

"Barbara, I need a haircut," Jay said, raking the tip of her nails through her short crop of wavy black curls. "How's six o'clock tomorrow evening?"

"Jay, you're going to have to get over here on your lunch break if you want me to give you a haircut."

"I was planning to work during my lunch break since I'm not working Friday," she said.

"I'll call one of the stylists and she'll give you a haircut."

"I think I'll come over on my lunch break and work late instead," Jay said.

"She's good, Jay."

"Maybe she is good, but I'll feel a lot better if you give me the cut."

"And don't be late," Barbara warned Jay after a hearty chuckle. "You know I don't do hair anymore."

"I'll see you tomorrow," Jay said to Barbara..

Austin waited inside of the murky bar until Jay was in her car and out of the parking lot, before he slipped out the back. If Jay thought she was going to marry Trent the way Barbara had married Earl, she was wrong. He also had plans to inform Gladys Lee about Jay's romantic weekend with her enemy lover.

Austin walked out of Lees', pulling the door behind him and turning the knob to make sure the door was locked before he walked down the street to his car.

Trent Prescott had been forewarned. Austin reminisced over the night he had met with Trent, thanks to Sonya, who had her own personal problems dealing with Trent Prescott. Nevertheless, he was determined to put an end to Jay's brand new attitude.

He knew Jay had lost all of her common sense when he ran into one of the guys that worked at Myers and later, he had been introduced to Sonya at the club they went to. He had learned that Jay had met a guy in Nigeria. When he first heard the news, he thought that Jay had learned who Trent was and intended to settle the score in honor of her parents. He had been wrong again, especially when he saw her kissing him at an out-of-town restaurant that he followed them to.

And he didn't want to think about Trent Prescott. The man had nothing to say when he told him his plans if he didn't stop dating Jay. Trent hadn't taken him seriously. He simply planned to take Jay away for a weekend. Well, he was going to see to it that this little charade of a love affair would end. That way, he,

Jay, Trent and Sonya could get on with their lives together and Mrs. Lee would have the satisfaction of knowing that he was responsible for making sure Jay was sane again.

Sixteen

Late Friday night, Jay and Trent cuddled together on a pile of colorful pillows near the stereo, listening to love songs and drinking brandy, and enjoying the quiet time with each other in their cozy private world. Jay dipped her finger inside her brandy and touched Trent's lips, then with the tip of her tongue, she tasted the heady beverage. When Trent reached out for her, Jay playfully scooted away from him.

"You like to play, don't you baby—uh?" Trent set his goblet on the floor and reached for Jay, pulling her down beside him, droplets of brandy dripped from the tip of his finger as he sprinkled before he slowly kissed the liquid from her thighs. Each droplet followed by a kiss with the tip of his tongue raised sweet laments that slipped across her lips and out to him.

"Did you enjoy yourself tonight?" Trent asked her between kisses that he brushed against her lips sending waves of desire through her.

"Yes," Jay said, "But asked me now." She pulled him back to her planting a kiss of approval on his lips.

"Because it's hard for me to talk when you do that?"

"It is?" Trent asked, stroking his palm against her thighs.

"Ooh . . . don't . . . I don't know," Jay said, not wanting Trent to talk to her, as a few memories of her day with him return. Her day with him hadn't been an extraordinary day with a lavish lunch in an expensive restaurant, but was spent eating in a small eatery at the edge of town in the community where he was staying. Afterwards, they had taken a long walk, talking and stopping every so often, lingering and enjoying soft kisses.

Earlier in the evening, she and Trent had gone to the Soul Revue at a nearby club and she had enjoyed every minute of the live band playing old fashion soul music and the singers harmonizing soulful songs from the past. As always, she enjoyed dancing with Trent.

And now she nestled him closer to her, ending her evening with the promise of passion. A small cry slipped from her as he touched his lips to the hollow of her neck and she raised up, taking off the thick white terry cloth robe she'd put on after her bath.

Trent pushed his fingers underneath the thin straps, peeling away her gown and displaying soft firm breasts. He caressed them with a soft sexy gaze before he kissed one at a time. Jay felt herself reel from desire and she ached from wanting him and just plain, old fashion needs. She explored his back, his chest and slipped her fingers below his stomach, stopping at thick underbrush where she allowed her fingers to dance against his body and to the tune of the strangled husky groan escaping Trent. He caressed her with tantalizing kisses and she savored every second.

Trent got up and went to get the small packet that promised to protect them. He returned and kneeled beside her, opening the crisp cellophane pack, while

Jay savored the passion that was easing its way through her and to her heart.

Jay surrendered, meeting each impaling caress, and like sweltering kindle, the flames began to spread until they set bursts of raw sensation free into one another.

Jay knew she could never turn back. She was trapped by her own doing in an affair with a man who could be responsible for taking the last caring relative from her. She felt tears swell and roll to the brim of her eyes, and with the back of her hand, she wiped them away. "Are you all right?" Trent asked, looking down at her tenderly.

Jay was unable to speak and she nodded as they lay quietly listening to the still night and slow love songs, sipping brandy and loving each other.

The next morning after they returned from breakfast at a nearby restaurant, Jay found the coffee, and minutes later, the cottage was filled with the rich aroma of fresh coffee. She set the pot on the dining room table and filled both her and Trent's cup before taking her favorite section from the newspaper he was reading.

"You never told me what happened the night you left me," Jay said, not looking up from the newspaper.

Trent looked over the top of the newspaper. "Austin called me," he said.

"Why did he call you?" Jay asked, laying the newspaper down.

"He knows a few of those guys working for Myers—I guess they told him that we were going together." Trent turned his cup up to his mouth and drank coffee.

"What did he say to you?"

"He's going to tell Mrs. Lee that we're dating,"

Trent said, and picked up his part of paper and went back to his reading.

Jay wasn't concerned about Austin's threats. He was known for his blackmailing and threats and lies. "Oh," Jay said. "Is that all he said?"

"Pretty much. He talked a lot, but I didn't believe him," Trent replied. "What do you want to do to-night?" He asked, changing the subject, to make plans for their evening.

"First, we have to go to this restaurant," Jay said, showing the restaurant advertisement to Trent.

"All right," he agreed.

"And we can go dancing again," Jay said.

"Maybe we can go to that club down the street after our dinner, baby, because I'm tired from dancing last night."

Jay laughed. "Okay."

When they had decided on the events of their day, Jay finished reading the advice column and was about to look at the dress sales when she heard someone knock.

Jay looked over the paper at Trent and waited until he got up to answer the door before she went back to checking out the dress sale.

"What do you want?" Jay heard Trent speak in a low rumbling voice and then rose louder, sounding colder with each word spoken. "Why are you here?"

Jay got up and went to see what all the commotion was about when she saw Sonya standing in the door-way. Sonya reached inside her purse and took a small white pack and held it out to Jay.

"Pictures?" Sonya said, flashing Jay a wicked smirk. "Austin told me that you were here," she said as Jay moved closer to the door.

"How did Austin know I was here?" Jay asked.

"Yeah. How did Austin know we were here?" Trent asked Sonya and crossed his arms across his chest.

"Austin told me that he hid out in that bed and breakfast in town. He heard you telling a woman . . . I can't remember what he said her name was now." She pointed one short manicured nail in Jay's direction. "But anyway, here I am pictures and all." Sonya smiled at Jay.

"Is Austin with you?" Jay asked.

"Of course he's here. I wasn't coming to West Virginia alone." Sonya remarked harshly.

"You told Austin where Jay and I were staying?" Trent inquired and Jay noticed the hard line settling on the side of jaw.

"When Austin told me this news I remembered that you had this little place and I got the telephone number from information." Sonya appeared satisfied with a smug expression on her face. "Don't get me wrong. Austin and I are not dating."

"I could care less whether you're dating Austin or not," Trent said.

"I met him at one of our Friday evening parties," she said, looking at Jay. "The parties that you think you're too good to attend."

"Don't start with me," Jay said in a raised voice.

"Austin wants you back and he intends to show these pictures of you and my man to your grandmother. Austin wants her to know that you're dating the family's enemy." Sonya chuckled and Jay felt her anger leap to another level.

"Will you excuse us for a minute?" Jay said to Trent.

"Yeah," he said and went inside, leaving her with Sonya.

Jay pulled the door behind her when Trent was inside the house and placed her hands firmly on her hips.

"Trent and I are together. So why are you here?" Jay asked and waited for Sonya to answer her.

"Right, because you're hiding from your grandmother," Sonya said. "And when she sees these pictures, you're going to be on your own." She smiled and waved the photographs in front of Jay.

"Maybe, but at least I'm not running Austin down the way you're chasing Trent." Jay propped her hands on her hips.

"Trent will always love me," Sonya raised her voice.

"After he caught you in bed with another man?" Jay asked her.

"What . . . he told you our business?" Sonya asked.

"His business, Sonya. Now go away."

"I'm going to see how flip you're going to be when you don't have a family to turn to." Sonya turned and walked off the porch.

"It's like I told you before, Sonya . . . you're one simple sister."

Sonya slapped Jay, spinning her around. When Jay faced her again, she returned the slap, sending Sonya spilling off the porch. "Oh no, you didn't!" Sonya jumped at Jay and like two Persian cats they fought. Pictures of Jay and Trent were scattered over the yard and several neighbors were enjoying the free show as the women clawed at each other.

"Hey!" Trent pulled the women apart and stood between them with one hand on Jay's chest and one hand on Sonya. "Sonya, get off my porch and pick up those pictures. You can do whatever you want to do with them."

"Trent Prescott, you have not seen the last of me!" Sonya gathered the pictures and stuffed the photographs in the pack. "Your grandmother will see these," she said to Jay.

"Whatever!" Jay said, watching Sonya hurry out of the yard and head down the street.

Jay wanted to be the first to tell Gladys about her and Trent's relationship. But she knew Austin and he would get to her first if at all possible, and having Sonya waving the pictures around town would certainly upset Gladys.

"Trent, I want to be the first to tell Granny about us. I think we should go," Jay said.

"Come on," Trent slipped his arm around Jay's waist and closed the door. "When do you plan to tell Mrs. Lee about us?"

"As soon as I can get her to sit down long enough to talk to me," Jay said, going back to the dining room.

"Are you sure you want her to know about us?" Trent asked.

"Trent, my grandmother is always too busy to talk to me lately."

"The telephone works, baby." Trent's narrow gaze held hers.

"I want to sit down and talk to her face to face." She watched Trent walk to the window and turn around, looking at her with a narrow gaze. His mouth appeared tense and angry. Trent looked as if he was in deep thought.

"You don't intend to tell her about us or about the information I gave you," Trent said, pacing the length of the room.

"I want to tell her," Jay's voice came out as whisper and she hardly recognized her own voice. She composed herself. "But I have an idea," Jay said, and watched Trent. "We won't see each other again until I talk to her." She started walking to the bedroom. "So, I'm packing my things and I'm going home because I need to talk to her."

"What if she's still too busy to talk to you, baby?" Trent asked her and Jay could hear the anger in his voice.

"Then we'll just have to wait until she has time to listen to me."

"That means that we can't be together until Mrs. Lee decides that she has time to listen?" Trent touched Jay's waist.

"Yes," Jay replied.

"What?" Trent walked in front of her and stopped her from going into the bedroom.

"I know Austin. He loves to play games, and Sonya, I don't know." Jay pushed Trent, wanting to get to the bedroom. "But I don't want Sonya waving pictures in front of my grandmother and upsetting her until after I've talked to her."

"I agree with you, and I won't see you again until I can tell the world that we are lovers," Trent stated. His eyes were dark and almost black with anger. "I don't think you want to talk to Mrs. Lee about us." Trent's chuckle was tempered with his anger and his voice was cool and heartless. "I don't think it matters what I told you or how much proof I have shown you. You believe everything that you were told and you'll probably do anything to keep your grandmother from finding out about us."

"Are you saying that I'm using you?" Jay asked Trent. Jay's voice faded into a still whisper.

"What do you think?" Trent answered her question with one of his own.

"You invited me to West Virginia," Jay said, so mad she could hardly talk.

"Because we can't see each other in public."

Jay didn't miss the chill in his words. Jay pushed past him and walked into the bedroom.

"Where are you going?" Trent walked into the bedroom after her.

"I'm going home," Jay said.

"We're not leaving until tomorrow morning." He moved and stood over to her.

Jay closed her eyes, shutting back the tears. "You are going home tomorrow morning. I'm going home today." Jay pulled her luggage from the closet and began packing the few things she had brought with her and then made plane reservations before calling a cab.

"I intend to give you ride home." Trent stood behind her.

"I can get home without your help," Jay said when she had finished making the call for her ride to the airport.

"Okay, if that's what you want. We'll see each other after you have talked to your grandmother, but I doubt that will ever happen." He spoke to her and Jay heard a hint of indignation in his voice.

"You don't believe me because you don't trust me," Jay said, realizing that Sonya and Austin had accomplished the very thing they wished for: a fight between her and Trent. But she was not going to allow Sonya or Austin to flash some snapshot of her and Trent before her grandmother before she had the chance to tell her that she loved him.

"Cancel your reservation and the cab. I'll take you home," Trent said.

"No," Jay said, determined to get through the havoc alone. Going home tomorrow could be too late with Austin and now Sonya threatening her. What if her grandmother had a heart attack or worse because of her? She could live with being disowned by Gladys, but anything worse than that, Jay didn't think she could live with herself.

"Jay." Trent stood near the bedroom door, his back against the jamb and called her name over the sound of the cab's horn that was waiting outside for her.

"Excuse me," Jay said, as she pulled her suitcase to the bedroom door and waited for him to move out of her way.

When he didn't move fast enough for her, she placed one hand on her hip. "Move out of my way."

Trent moved and Jay hurried out to the waiting taxi with him following close behind her.

Jay flew home, disliking Austin more than she had when they first broke up. He hadn't changed the least bit and had joined forces with Sonya who Jay was sure loved nothing more than to drive the last pitch fork into her and Trent's relationship.

She was also mad at Trent for not believing her and thinking that she would never tell Gladys that she loved him. By the time Jay's flight landed, she was so angry she didn't know what to do with herself. However, there was one dispute Jay planned to settle. She would find her grandmother and enlighten her of what she had done and if Gladys Lee wanted to dismiss her from her life, she would accept her fate. But for once in her life, she would take a stand for the person she wanted in her life and not a man that Gladys Lee thought was right for her.

Once Jay arrived home and was comfortable in slacks and an old T-shirt, she called Gladys.

As usual, Gladys was ambiguous, not giving Jay a definite time that she would be available to listen to what she wanted to speak to her about. Not only did her grandmother seem to be avoiding her, Jay noticed that Gladys unlike her usual self, was not inquiring to know what she wanted to talk about. "Granny, are you avoiding me?" Jay was determined to set the record straight.

"No, Jay, I have a lot on my mind, but we'll talk soon." Gladys's voice sound fragile and quivered as always when something was bothering her.

"Would you like to tell me what's bothering you?" Jay was determined and relentless to discuss whatever was disturbing Gladys and if Gladys agreed to discuss her problem with her, she would listen and console her much as possible and then press her for information concerning the Lee and Prescott's feud, the seasoned dilemma that happened eons ago.

"No, I'll be fine in a few days," Gladys said.

"Have you spoke to or seen Austin?" Jay couldn't resist asking. As crazy as Austin was, he could've called her grandmother or had Sonya do his dirty work.

"No, I haven't seen Austin. Are you dating him again?" Gladys asked her. "No," Jay answered. "Are you sick?" Jay felt a dreaded panic rising inside her.

"No honey, I'm okay. I'm getting ready to go out and I'll talk to you soon." Gladys hung up before Jay could continue to press her for more answers.

Jay hung up at the sound of the dial tone that alerted her that Gladys had dismissed her, and she fought hard against the rising anger that was coiling inside her and sat on the edge of her bed. There was a problem brewing, and Jay intended to find out what was going on.

Trent Prescott paced the floor like a caged animal in his West Virginia cottage before he made a telephone call to Webster, dropping Austin's academic degree off to his boss Monday morning might shine a light in a new direction for Austin Carrington. Maybe now he would spend his time returning to college to earn the degree that he bought, instead of spending his time threatening Jay.

Seventeen

Trent walked into Myers' Research Center for the last meeting he would have with his old professor and boss.

He stopped at the open doorway of the conference room, catching a glimpse of Jay at work. He stopped, lingering for a few minutes and almost went in to speak to her, then thought better of his impulsive decision.

Trent suspected that Jay hadn't mentioned their relationship to Gladys Lee and he couldn't think of any other reason other than she didn't want him anymore. He had chosen not to call her and to wait for her to call him the weekend she walked out on him. His patience was beginning to exhaust him and he was thinking that he should move on. With that thought in mind, Trent wished that he could forget Jay.

Nevertheless, stopping by Myers Research Center reminded him of Jay, dredging deep into his memories and making it impossible for him to forget her. Why hadn't he paid more attention to her last name? Lee was a common surname and the thought had never crossed his mind that he would ever meet a member of the family that his family had problems with so many years ago. But as fate would have it, he'd met Jay Lee, and gave too much of himself to her. Now, he fought hard to forget her. But erasing Jay Lee from his memory was turning out to be a losing battle.

He needed time, and while he waited for the moment that she would no longer mean anything to him, he would return to his old ways. He would date and not tangle his emotions with affections and affairs of the heart.

The thought of staying a bachelor forever began to freeze in his mind and Trent considered the option to be the best choice he'd made in a long time.

Trent met with Myers and afterwards he headed to Rose's office to give her information that she needed from him. He passed the conference room again, and lingered once more thinking that he should tell her about the gift he had ordered for her. Trent decided against telling Jay. Maybe by the time she received his gift, she would be ready to talk to him.

Jay had kept herself busier than usual during the day at Myers and in the evenings at Lees' Bed and Breakfast after her ruined weekend with Trent. But all of her work hadn't kept her from thinking about him. As always, her nights were the worst.

In her fit of anger, she had physically fought with Sonya, after having Sonya flash a set of photographs of her and Trent together, hoping to bribe her into not seeing him anymore. It seemed as if Austin and Sonya's scheme was going to work. Gladys was not talking to her and was refusing to listen to anything she had to say and she had been careful not to think about him until Gladys knew about her relationship with Trent.

But now as she sat in the conference room, viewing tapes from the African proposal parade, and knowing she would see pictures of Trent in the tapes was not helping her at all.

Jay finished watching the tape on the proposal parade and slid another tape inside the VCR. The rolling drums from the proposal parade, hammering against cattle skin drums reeled her back to the past. Thinking back, Jay realized that maybe Trent was not suppose to be in her life after all.

She moved the tape forward, searching for the piece where she and Rose had interviewed Emma. Jay stopped and turned facing the door; she felt as if someone was watching her. She focused her attention back on the tape, considering that her imagination was playing tricks, and even if this wasn't true, she concluded that someone from the team was at the door and decided not to disturb her.

Jay studied the tape again, and instead of finding Emma's interview, she saw clippings of Trent and Webster. Jay stopped the tape and sat for a while, taking in every inch of Trent's features and physique. How had she made the mistake not to listen to the small inner voice that warned her to check his background further? Instead, she had listened to her heart.

She rolled the tape to the end, looking for the interview with Emma. While she watched for the tape for the meeting, she reflected on her childhood dreams. She had never thought much about getting married when she was a young girl. All she wanted to do was travel, but thanks to her grandmother, the idea of matrimony had captured her over the years, leaving her with thoughts of looking and finding a husband.

At one time, she had believed that she needed a

husband and she had accepted Austin's proposal. As their relationship grew farther apart, Jay Lee understood that she didn't need marriage to complete her life. Although, when she met Trent and fell in love with him, she believed she had found a life long companion, a good friend, and lover. She had dreams of spending her evening with him on warm summer nights, with flowers scenting the air, and enjoying liquid refreshments and listening to the sound of ice-cubes rattling lightly against their glasses. Except now she was beginning to believe that her dreams would soon turn into a nightmare, leaving no hope for her and Trent to ever share a life together without suppressing their love from her family. She wasn't certain how long Trent would wait for her and if he chose to move on, she knew that she would be doomed to loneliness and living the rest of life as an old spinster.

Jay removed the tape from the VCR after she didn't find the interview and checked the time. It was four-thirty, and if Rose wanted her to work late on the African assignment, she would be more than willing to take on the task.

"Rose, I can't find Emma's interview on this tape," Jay said, laying the tape on Rose's desk. "I can stay if you want me to look for the tape." Jay offered, looking around Rose's office at the group photographs Rose had blown up into posters with Trent, Webster and Myers standing shoulder to shoulder.

"Trent dropped the tape off a few minutes ago," Rose said, picking up the tape and handing it to Jay.

"Oh," Jay said, realizing that maybe her imagination hadn't played a game with her.

"Jay, it's Friday and I'm going home early tonight,"

Rose said, pushing away from the desk and standing up. "How are things with you and Trent?"

She jerked around facing Rose. "Not good," Jay said, not going into the details of her plan to wait before she continued their friendship.

"Are you ready for your wedding?" Jay asked Rose. Her June wedding wasn't far away.

"I'm not sure if Webster and I are getting married," Rose replied hotly. "I took your advice and stopped by his house to talk to him and Carol was visiting him."

"Carol?" Jay said, wondering how had her girlfriend met Webster and was dating him.

"Yes. Carol said that she was your girlfriend," Rose said and walked out.

The second the door closed behind her Jay picked up the telephone and dialed Carol's work number. "Carol."

"Hi Jay."

"Girl, why didn't you tell me that you and Webster were dating?"

"I'm not dating, Webster. Jay, you know I don't have time for a boyfriend."

"I wished you had told Rose."

"Jay, I was in the park jogging and out of the corner of my eye I saw the handsome hunk, that I know now was Webster Nelson, running beside me. And we eventually stopped jogging and started talking. Jay, you know me. I was thinking to myself was this my first time seeing him jogging in the park. Webster told me that he was in Nigeria. That's when I found out that you guys worked together. But girlfriend, he's a good-looking man."

"Rose thinks that you and Webster are dating, and she's blaming me."

"Jay, as soon as my brother's children go home the end of the month, I'll be free to party," Carol said. "How's Trent?"

Jay was quiet for a moment as she recalled her decision she had made not to see Trent until she talked to Gladys. She was beginning to think that she was never going to see him again. "I don't know," Jay said.

"What happened?" Carol asked.

"Trent is upset because he thinks I'm trying to keep our relationship a secret."

"You do have to tell her," Carol said.

"Yes I do. Austin and Sonya are waving around a pack of pictures, threatening to show them to Granny," Jay replied.

"Sonya . . . Who's she?" Carol asked Jay.

"Sonya is the woman that Trent was engaged to," Jay replied.

"Girl, we have to talk." Carol said.

"We'll go to lunch when you're free," Jay chuckled. She understood that Carol could hardly get away with three children to look after.

"You know Jay, after Austin, I think that you deserve a good man."

"I know, but I made the mistake of not learning who Trent was and I am still trying to deal with this problem." If she had been more careful taking time to know Trent's history . . . she dismissed her ceaseless pondering. "Carol, I have to go, but we'll talk."

"Yes, girl, and I don't want you to leave out anything, especially Sonya."

Jay laughed. If Carol only knew the fight she had gotten into with Sonya when she was in West Virginia.

Jay hung up and called Gladys. This time she wasn't

calling her to beg her for a meeting. "Granny, how are you?" Jay asked.

"I'm fine." Gladys sounded as if she were in a hurry.

"I was about to leave to spend time with Agnes. She's not feeling well," Gladys said.

Agnes lived in South Jersey and when Gladys visited with her friend in South Jersey she stayed at least three weeks. "You are coming to Lees' opening," Jay said. "I hope you're not going to miss the party."

"Yes, you know I wouldn't miss the opening," Gladys replied.

"I'll tell you when I see you," Jay said.

"I'll talk to you soon." Gladys hung up.

Jay wondered if Gladys intended to listen to what she had to say. She had ended the call quickly not giving her time to inquire further. However, Jay needed to understand the rival that had torn two families apart and ultimately threatened to end her and Trent's relationship.

Jay was terrified at losing the woman who had raised her. Gladys had kept her safe and loved her and taught her who she should love and not love. But her strong passionate need to love Trent had disjoined the lineage, the family member that she could go to if she was needed.

However she understood all to well now that if she wanted her grandmother's love, respect and loyalty she would have to break off her relationship with Trent. Jay realized that she would survive either choice that she made. She also understood that Trent was special and it wasn't just because he was handsome, a wonderful lover, but she enjoyed him thoroughly. His honesty was attractive and made him even so much more attractive. His promises were kept, he worked hard and

wanted nothing from anyone that didn't belong to
him. She may not have a choice. Jay only knew that
she would be banished from her family when she made
the choice that would cut all ties to her grandmother.
She was exhausted from the hate.

Eighteen

As usual, Jay kept to her daily routine, stopping by Lees' after work. She noticed that the cottage in the back of Lees' where she had stayed when she was a very little girl was freshly painted and surrounded with new green sod grass.

Jay walked around to the front of the bed and breakfast noticing the huge terra-cotta vases filled with blooming red flowers setting on each side of the front door. She had to admit that the scarlet flowers added an extra touch of beauty to the bed and breakfast's wide porch. She entered the lobby, noticing several boxes at the far end of the room, and assumed that the linens for the bedrooms had arrived.

"Hi, Barbara," Jay spoke and joined Barbara at the registration desk. All the rooms except one were booked for the opening week and Jay couldn't have been more proud.

"Hi," Barbara said, gesturing to the boxes across the room. "I think you need to take a look at those linens."

"I'll look later," Jay replied. She had plenty of time to inspect the order since it was still early.

"I think you should check the invoice, Jay," Barbara said, walking from behind the counter and crossing the room to the packages. "At least before Gladys sees the receipt."

"I don't understand the rush to check the invoice or the contents," Jay said, moving to the boxes and taking the receipt Barbara lifted from one of the boxes and held the paper out to her. "I know what I ordered. Sheets and . . ." Jay stopped talking and stared at the receipt.

Her heart fluttered as a trail of warmth swept through her. Why wouldn't Trent wait before he sent her a gift for the business? She pondered this question as she read PRESCOTT'S QUILTS, the company's name on the invoice. "Maybe Granny should see the package," Jay said to Barbara. At least if Gladys saw that the package was from Trent's mother's linen company, she would at least have a chance to tell her Trent's reason for sending the gift to her.

Jay took out a soft canary sheet set with matching floral pillowcases and admired the beautiful set.

"You're determined to tell Gladys, aren't you?" Barbara asked Jay.

"She'll be angry at me," Jay said. With the dissension that had poisoned the two families for so many years, not to mention the two conflicting stories, Jay was aware that her conversation with Gladys did not guarantee to be a pleasant discussion and definitely would not assure her that Gladys would give her blessings. But before she thought of all the heartache that was certain to take place while she informed Gladys how she had been disloyal to her, she had another pressing matter to take care of and that was to thank Trent for his gift.

Jay studied the invoice, paying attention to the price for the total order that was stamped Paid In Full, in bold blue letters at the bottom of the grand total, then read the exact number of bedspreads, sheet sets, and blankets recorded on the statement. She crossed the floor to the telephone to give Trent a call at his new office and thank him for the bed linens. His reception-ist answered the call on the first ring and Jay asked to speak to Trent.

"Trent Prescott, please," Jay said, and told the woman her name. After what seemed like two minutes, Trent was on the telephone.

"Thanks for the bed linens," Jay said after she had spoken to him and had noticed the coolness in his voice instead of his familiar warmth.

"You're welcome," he said. "Did you talk to Mrs. Lee?" Trent asked her.

Jay was quiet, but she should've suspected that he would ask her had she told Gladys about them. "No," Jay said. "She's out of town and . . ."

"Whenever you talk to her, give me a call," Trent said, and hung up on her.

Jay hung up and knew that Trent was serious. She had lost him.

The morning when Jay told him that he didn't want them to see each other until she had damage control with her grandmother, he was beginning to believe that she had never loved him. Today, he knew he had been wrong to believe that she was deliberately avoiding hav-ing a conversation with Gladys Lee.

Trent walked a few paces farther across the room, feeling the tension of his long day, and wondering when he would be free to love Jay without looking over his shoulder. He hated feeling helpless and being put in a position that he couldn't control. Trent realized that he was unable to solve the problem that he had no power over and it angered him.

He took his gym bag from the office closet, picked up his brief case and left the room. Jay was stubborn, strong and determined, and forcing himself to forget their problem was impossible.

Trent pondered that thought as he moved down the corridor and out of the building. Jay Lee was a powerful challenge, and unlike any woman he'd ever dated.

Trent drove to the gym, changed out of his suit and waited for the next available treadmill. He noticed Austin a few machines away.

"Prescott, what's going on?" Austin called out to him.

Trent felt the muscles in his jaw involuntarily working in slow motion, and added to that was a burning anger coiling at the pit of his stomach. "What do you want Austin?"

"Looks to me like Jay came to her good sense and dumped you." Austin grinned up at Trent.

"Like she dumped you?" Trent asked, and to keep from looking at Austin, Trent scanned the crowded room, seeing many unfamiliar faces and many employees from Myers Research Center. He was beginning to think that everyone in the small town owned a membership at the gym, including Austin Carrington.

Austin chuckled. "I think Jay and I might get back together."

"You can dream." Trent felt a streak of jealousy penetrate the center of his chest, and his black hatred for Austin caught root, and he wanted to destroy the man.

Austin laughed again, the pleased tone of his laughter rang out to Trent. "But my dream is not going to turn into a nightmare," Austin added with defiance, leaning his head to one side and looking at Trent.

Trent mustered control, containing his heated anger and the desire to knock Austin halfway across the room. He entertained that idea while a man on the treadmill stopped his workout and released the machine to him.

Without responding to Austin, Trent kneeled down on one knee and tightened the loose lace on his hightop tennis shoe.

"On the other hand, I know Jay will never go back to you, because I have a few pictures that I know Mrs. Lee would love to see." Austin stood close to Trent. "You see, Prescott, Jay can't afford to have you hanging around her. The price is too high."

Trent stood up and grabbed Austin's sleeveless top, slamming him against the wall near the treadmill. "She might not, if it's anything like the degree you bought." Trent shoved Austin away.

"You son of . . ." Austin swung his fist and landed it against Trent's jaw. "You got me fired!" Austin raised his fist when Trent struck him back, knocking Austin to the floor. They struggled, fell and rolled, hitting each other and cursing until Trent straddled Austin and raised his fist.

"Hey . . . Hey . . ." Webster and another guy ran to Trent along with one of the trainers and dragged the men apart. "What's wrong with you, Trent?" Webster placed his hand on Trent's back and walked him away from the gathering crowd.

"He started it," a woman pointed at Austin.

"The next time you guys want to fight, the sparring

ring is in the next room," the gym manager said, and walked away from the crowd.

Trent shook Webster's hand off his back and headed back to the treadmill next to where Austin was still standing. "Easy Prescott," Webster said, following Trent to the exercise equipment.

"I'm okay," Trent said, and cut his eye at Austin before he got on the treadmill.

"You bastard!" Austin yelled to Trent and headed in his direction.

"Hey—you," the manager said, walking back to Austin. "Get out."

Trent stepped on the machine, he adjusted the speed to fast, and started the running in place. The rubber soles on his tennis shoes slammed against the black rubber pad on the machine. *Slap . . . slap . . . slap . . . slap.* Trent's feet struck the moving black rubber, his strong muscular arms moving back and forth with the quick rhythm. He ran in place as if could race away his problems.

Trent slammed his feet harder against the floor. *Whap, whap, whap . . . shomp . . . shomp . . . whomp!* His promise to destroy Austin grew stronger. *God, don't let me kill Austin.*

A trail of salty perspiration rolled down his jaw, his neck and inside his shirt.

"Hey Prescott," Webster called him, and Trent slid off the machine, punching the slow button on the machine and curbing the speed. "Take it easy, man."

Trent held the bars on the machine and glanced over his shoulder, when he didn't see Austin, he turned and lowered the speed, slowing his heart rate.

"Are you all right?" Webster asked him.

"No." Trent answered, stepping off the treadmill

and burying his face in his towel, wiping the perspiration off his face. "Austin is threatening Jay."

"Yeah, well you don't have to worry about Austin," Webster said as they walked to the locker room.

Trent caught another glimpse at Jay moving between the leg and ankle weight equipment. Her gray spandex shorts and short matching top fit her like a second skin, showing off her flat stomach, firm thighs and displaying her firm breasts, and a solid set of firm arms and shoulders.

His relationship with Jay had been like a catch twenty-two. He was damned if he loved her, but only in secret. How was he going to spend the rest of his life without her? With that question in his mind he finished his shower and left the gym.

Nineteen

Thursday, the opening date for Lees' Bed and Breakfast had finally arrived and instead of being overly excited as Barbara and Gladys were, Jay stood at the window in the bed and breakfast window casting a blank stare with memories of Trent Prescott slowly careening through her mind. *"Trent."* Jay whispered his name, unable to dispel his image thinking that the black car that had just parked across the street belonged to him.

Jay had not seen Trent since the day she stopped by his office to thank him for the bedroom counterpanes. Later, she had caught a glimpse of him at the gym. She hadn't expected him to speak to her after she noticed Austin hovering around him.

She was barely able to complete her workout after she watched Trent grab Austin. She was relieved when Webster broke up the tussle. Jay knew Austin well. He had a habit of piquing one's nerves to the point of violence and afterwards, calmly standing aside and watching with pleasure as the person he provoked was accused of being the enemy.

Jay turned her attention to more pleasant thoughts, remembering the aftermath of the lingering passion she and Trent had shared in his office that same late afternoon.

However, seeing him at the gym had made it impossible to abandon the haunting bliss, and because of Austin's presence she had avoided him.

A row of street lights lit the streets and flickered and illuminated the evening dusk and Jay turned away from the window and crossed the floor to the desk. She sat facing the window, promising herself that she would talk to her grandmother tomorrow whether she was busy or not, making her aware of the special friendship she and Trent shared.

Jay was sure her grandmother would be displeased and probably hurt because of the choice she had made to love her enemy. Nonetheless, she was willing to take the chance and she would deal with the consequences later.

Another black Jaguar passed Lees' Bed and Breakfast, and Jay's heart fluttered against her breast. She didn't know why she was expecting Trent to the opening. He hadn't mentioned to her that he would attend the party, and Jay doubted that he would.

According to Trent, the bed-and-breakfast had been the place that he and his family had been forced to leave because of swindling, deceit and lies. Jay doubted that Trent would want to associate himself with memories of mendacity that caused him to suffer poverty and near homelessness.

A mass of tears clouded Jay's vision as she imagined how upset Gladys was going to be with her. So many years of warning her about the family that had murdered her parents and in the end, she had betrayed her grandmother and turned to a member of that same family for an undying love that she never knew existed, and a tale that held more certainty than that which Gladys had sworn to be true.

"Jay," Gladys walked to the desk and spoke to her, then rested her hands on the counter top, displaying a set of perfectly polished baby pink short nails. Her steel gray hair was cut short in the back and sides, the top fluffed back away from her face. The hairstyle seemed to have taken a few years away from her grandmother and she didn't look her seventy-two years.

"You look nice," Jay complemented Gladys, admiring the tan pantsuit she had given her for her last birthday.

"I feel good," Gladys smiled, and turned around admiring the lobby. "I am so excited that we're back in business," she said turning back to Jay. "If Rollins was alive to see this . . ." her smile faded. "He would be so proud of you." .

"I'm glad that you're happy," Jay said with intentions of broaching the subject on meeting with her grandmother first thing in the morning to discuss her relationship with Trent Prescott.

"I'm coming back to work," Gladys said and her face lit with a smile.

"That's good. Working will keep you busy," Jay replied.

"So, I told Barbara that I would assist her and that way she can spend time managing the beauty salon." Gladys smiled.

"You're the manager now?" Jay asked, raising one arched brow a fraction.

"I can hardly wait to get started." Gladys sounded so excited Jay wanted to forget that she needed to talk to her.

"How's your sick friend?" Jay asked her grandmother. She didn't want to hear any more excuses from Gladys, like leaving town for one reason or another when she wanted to talk to her.

"Agnes is fine," Gladys smiled at her granddaughter, then as if she had a terrible thought, her smile faded. "Jay, what is so important that you need to talk to me about?" Gladys frowned.

"Can we talk tomorrow?" Jay asked, observing Gladys's expression that reminded her of the how her grandmother looked at her when she wanted information when she was a girl.

"Jay."

"I need to know who killed my parents." Jay searched Gladys's face, looking for any expression that would prove Trent to be right, but instead, Gladys seemed calm.

Gladys slid her hands across the counter top and locked her fingers together and looked into Jay's eyes. "I was downstairs with Barbara a few days ago and I came upstairs. I saw you with a young man and I heard you call his name. So I walked out of the kitchen."

"Granny . . ." Jay started, but she was stopped by one of Gladys's uneasy glances.

"I know who he is Jay and I know that you're involved with him." She raised her brow.

"Yes," Jay said, remembering the crashing sound coming from the kitchen and realizing that she was right when she thought that Gladys had probably been avoiding her. "Why didn't you tell me that you knew?" Jay asked her.

"Because I had to think," Gladys said. "I thought he was a Prescott when I saw him. He looks just like his daddy . . . Christopher Prescott, when he was a young man."

Jay's fear that her grandmother would learn about her affair with Trent from the pictures that Austin and Sonya had taken was all for nothing. "I love Trent."

"I figured you did," Gladys said, and took a step away from the counter. "But we'll talk tomorrow. Lunch is at twelve, and I will remind you again of what I warned you about years ago. Then I'll tell you what you need to know." Gladys left Jay and headed down to the grand opening party that was being given for the guests and a few of their friends.

Jay propped her elbows on the counter and covered her face with her hands. She was going to be doomed and all because she was in love with the wrong man. She forced the waves of dread away from her. She was not going to allow herself to fret over losing her family. Even if Trent never spoke to her again, she would be fine without the love her grandmother had once had for her.

A flood of tears felt as if they had rushed to the brim of her eyes and stopped before rolling freely. She snatched a tissue from the box on the shelf underneath the counter and wiped her eyes. She had kept her promise, giving Gladys the business that she loved and making her happy again, and she then betrayed her.

The test of time loomed like a blackened cloud daunting a dangerous storm and Jay knew she would never be the same again. She was financially able, and needed nothing from Gladys and Barbara, but they had promised to be there for her when she was in need of a family.

Although any family would pale in comparison to Gladys's love. She had taken the place of her mother, reading bedtime stories to her, taking her to the park and soothing her when she was unable to sleep at night.

The Christmas her parents died, she had received her first bike equipped with training wheels, and her grandfather had walked beside her making sure that she rode safely to the park. But tonight reminded her of the times she had fallen when she was learning to skate, wobbling, and falling and getting up again until she was strong enough to glide.

The day she met Trent, she realized that she loved him before she learned the horrible news. And yet the love for her family would always run deep. She wouldn't stop loving Trent. She wondered what Rollins Lee, Jr. would think of the choice she had made now. She was torn between the love for her grandmother and her love for Trent. Jay swallowed the discomforting ache in her throat, being fully aware that she had allowed herself the privilege to bask in the luxury of Trent's affection, holding him dear to her heart.

He had introduced himself and she had ignored the tiny whispering warning in the back of her mind, and now her worst nightmare was unfolding before her.

Jay straightened, drawing herself out a depressive slump. She was strong and she would be fine. She reminded herself how she once had no friends and she had lived a life of loneliness as a girl and had survived. She would weather the storm again and this time she was older and much stronger.

Loud laughter and music from the party downstairs urged her to take part in the festivities that she had planned earlier, but because of her new revelations that Gladys knew of her and Trent's love affair, she wanted to be alone and nurse her rejection in peace. She dismissed all of her nagging thoughts and dialed Carol's number, hoping that she hadn't changed her mind about coming tonight. Jay let the telephone ring three times and hung up thinking that maybe her girlfriend had used the back entrance downstairs and was already enjoying herself and hopefully, not with Webster.

This was another problem Jay considered. Carol and Webster's budding friendship had nothing to do with her. However, Rose had directed all of her anger at her. How she had gotten herself mixed up into more personal problems within a matter of months was appalling to say the least, yet nothing could top the disaster she had caused in her life for loving Trent. *I will be fine,* Jay mused, getting off the stool.

"Hi," Carol walked in just as Jay was about to go down and join the party.

"Miss Carol." Jay greeted her girlfriend without her usual whimsical smile. Carol was dressed as stylishly as always, wearing a white knee length shorts-set and gold heels.

"Jay, this is the evening you've been waiting for so what's wrong?" Carol's spicy bronze lipstick trimmed with a trace of red liner complemented her smile.

"Granny knows that Trent and I are going together," Jay said.

"You told her?" Carol asked.

"No, she saw us together." Jay shifted on the stool and looked away from her girlfriend.

"Get out of here!" Carol planted her hands on her hips and leaned back.

"So, I guess I'll spend all my holidays with you and Barbara," Jay stated dryly, remembering that she had intended to tell Carol about her and Trent's mini weekend trip to West Virginia and been ruined when Sonya showed up at their cottage and Sonya and she had gotten into a fist fight. Her concerns tonight were about Gladys denying the man she loved and casting her out of the family because of it.

"Did Mrs. Lee tell you that she was kicking you out of her life?" Carol asked Jay.

"No, but she wasn't happy and usually my grandmother keeps her promises. She wants to talk to me tomorrow." Jay blinked back a tear.

"Oh Jay," Carol said, and Jay watched the water settling in Carol's eyes. "I am your friend through thick and thin, girl. You know that."

"I know, and I'm thankful for good friends." Jay consoled Carol after seeing the shock in her expression. "Let's go downstairs to the party," Jay said moving from behind the registration desk and crossing the room to lock the door, but not before she switched on the 'No Vacancy' sign. When she had arrived earlier that day, the new desk clerk had informed her that all the rooms had been reserved.

Jay took her purse and another tissue from the box, feeling a tear tittering on her lashes.

"Are you going to be all right?" Carol asked and sounded as if she were upset.

"I'll be all right. Stop worrying about me," Jay said, with such assurance she was beginning to believe herself as she and Carol left the lobby. She walked down the stairs with the urge to cry because she knew what tomorrow held for her and coming to terms with the reality that this would be the last time she would visit the place that had been her home.

Trent had entered Lees' through the back, an entrance he knew well, and walked into the bar, ordering a neat scotch and stood at the edge of the counter, lingering over the alcoholic beverage while watching the door for Jay since he hadn't seen her among the crowd.

Maybe she had decided not to attend the party, Trent considered that thought for about two seconds and changed his mind. Jay wouldn't miss the opening of Lees' Bed and Breakfast. He took another small swig from the glass and continued to watch the stairs. While he nursed his drink, he let himself reflect on his last encounter with Austin.

Trent had stopped Austin just as he was about to enter the back entrance to Lees'. Austin was his usual spiteful self, but his attitude soon changed when Trent told him how he couldn't afford to marry Jay even if she would marry him. He had bought his degree and his boss knew, that's why he was paying Austin minimum wage for the work that he trained him to do. The car he drove belonged to the company and there were more things that he hadn't told Jay, like the child support he was paying for a two-year-old.

Trent promised that he had proof of his findings and he didn't mind showing his information to Jay. Austin had left the premises and Trent doubted that he or Jay would be bothered with him anymore.

Seeing Jay walk into the room drew Trent back to the present and he clutched his glass as a spiral of pangs waffled his stomach and to his chest as he noticed her and the short red dress she was wearing. Tonight, Trent had no intentions to spend the evening without Jay. He observed a tall man approach her and wrap his arms around her waist and kiss her cheek. Trent felt as if a small missile had exploded inside him and one thought flashed across his mind. *War!*

Twenty

Jay had barely made it down the stairs and adjusted her eyes to the dim lights, scanning the room and observing happy guests and a few friends that Gladys had invited, when Elfin Mack grabbed her and pressed her to him. "Jay, baby!"

"Elfin where have you been?" Jay said, as she watched over his shoulder as Webster touched his hand to Carol's back and walked with her across the room.

"Been thinking about you," Elfin chuckled close to her ear, then he kissed her cheek.

"Man, please!" Jay laughed, and studied his face. Elfin had changed from the teenage boy that taken her to the concert years ago. He was a man with a mass of hard muscles and a smile that spoke success. "How have you been?" Jay asked before he could answer her first question and pulled out of his embrace.

"I've been fine, living in North Carolina and I'm thinking about moving back to town," Elfin Mack replied, giving her more information than she had asked for. "And you?"

"I'm all right," Jay exclaimed with joy at seeing Elfin, the man that Gladys had chased out of her life years ago.

"I rode by here hoping I would see you and found out that this place had closed and was opening again. What happened?" Elfin inquired, wanting to catch up on everything that had gone on since he was away.

"We closed after my grandfather died. So, I reopened Lees' for my grandmother," Jay said, proud of her accomplishments, but aware that she wouldn't be a part of the business after tomorrow. "Let me buy you a drink," Jay said, walking him to the bar's counter, when she saw Trent get up and move to another part of the room. "Earl, do you remember Elfin Mack?" Jay asked Earl after she had ordered white wine for herself and telling Earl to give Elfin whatever he was drinking.

"I don't think I'll ever forget him," Earl said with a pleasant chuckle and stretched out his hand. "What's going on man?"

"Regular stuff," Elfin gave Earl a handshake.

Jay drank wine and listened to Elfin telling her that he was newly divorced and moving back to New Jersey. Jay told him that she had just returned from Nigeria when he asked her about her work.

"Are you married?" Elfin asked her.

"No," Jay said, and glanced out into the crowd when she noticed Trent giving her a relentless gaze.

"Oh," Elfin said, and Jay noticed that he had followed her gaze to Trent. "He's a lucky man." Elfin said. "I saw a couple of people here that I haven't seen for a while. Thanks for the drink, Jay, and take care."

Jay nodded. "You too," she said, noticing him crossing the room. She set the wine down and tried to enjoy the music as she watched the guests when she noticed her grandmother laughing with her friends. It seemed to Jay that Gladys wasn't concerned about her being in love with Trent. But Jay knew Gladys Lee and she was like a hammer striking a thumb nail when least expected.

Jay got up and mingled, speaking to friends she knew and making sure the guests were enjoying themselves. Jay glanced around for Trent, noticing that he was involved in a conversation with Earl and Webster.

The battle Jay had fought to keep her and Trent's intimate relationship a secret had been futile, especially since she had just learned that Gladys knew that she was in love with the family's enemy.

Jay couldn't understand why Gladys hadn't mentioned that she was aware of her relationship with Trent. However, her grandmother always had her special way of attending to family business and this was probably another milestone that Gladys had given careful thought to and Jay didn't understand why her grandmother would have to give special thought to what she had done. She already knew she was no longer a part of the family. The thought of not having her grandmother in her life swept over her. But she couldn't hate what she had done, and one day she would come to terms with the cold fact that her grandmother hadn't loved her enough to forgive her for loving Trent and didn't want her around. She wished her grandmother well and all the happiness that God would bestow on her, but she had chosen a new life for herself, not without pain, but she had moved on.

Jay felt a rush of tears settling in her eyes and she quickly got up and hurried to the bathroom. Once inside, she composed herself. She couldn't live in the same town with Gladys knowing that she was not welcome in her home. She sat on the chair near the door and without another moment of hesitation she secretly made plans to leave town. Myers would probably be more than happy to give her a recommendation to work at one of the colleges that used his company's research.

She wouldn't travel as much, but at least she wouldn't have to face rejection from Gladys, even though no matter how faraway she traveled to begin a new life for herself, she could never run away from her guilty heart, and her feelings of betrayal.

Jay allowed herself to have a good long cry and when she was finished she walked out into the small club noticing that Trent had left. He hadn't spoken to her that evening and only acknowledged her with his intense glances.

She braced herself and began to mingle among the crowd, spending her last evening in the place where she had grown up and worked and had been loved and cared for. But because she had listened to her heart, she was destined to live alone for her entire life. And to make matters worse, Trent had seemed to discard her as if she were an old suit he no longer wanted, and she was glad that she hadn't gotten the chance to tell him that their secret love hadn't been a secret after all.

Around midnight, the crowd began to thin. Guests retreated to their rooms while old friends of the family left for home.

Jay could not fight her loneliness. After having a good cry, she had mingled between guests and friends attending to their needs and making certain that everyone was comfortable and enjoying themselves, mostly to keep from thinking about the two people she loved and had lost in one night.

Later, she gathered her purse and out of habit, she

gave Gladys a kiss on her cheek and headed out to the small cottage in the back of Lees' where she, Barbara and Earl had planned to stay for the first night of the opening. The three of them wanted to be close in case there was a problem.

Jay also was glad that she was staying at the cottage tonight. She was tired and going home to sleep in her own bed. The bed she had shared with Trent and made love until dawn would be impossible to sleep in tonight. She would think about him and Jay knew she wouldn't sleep.

"Jay." Barbara stopped her as she was leaving.

"Yes, Barbara."

"Did Gladys tell you that we were expected at her apartment for lunch late tomorrow afternoon?" Barbara asked Jay with worried concern measuring her voice.

Jay lowered her gaze. "Yes. She knows about Trent and I'm thinking that she might want all of us together when she disowns me."

"I don't know, honey," Barbara said. "I hope that's not true."

Jay walked out of the room, realizing that she had listened to her heart, a heart that had lied and now she was alone because Trent didn't want to be bothered with a relationship with her as she watched Trent leave the room.

Trent walked into Webster's guest bedroom, intending to sleep after he listened to his messages. He stripped down to his trousers and took out his cell phone.

Tonight, except for Jay and Webster he had been

between strangers and he hadn't expected to be a part of Jay's company. So why was he upset? For starters, he would've liked to have known who Jay's friend was. The man was probably someone Jay had known for years, but even suspecting that he was an old friend didn't make him feel any better.

If he had stayed seated at the bar, she probably would have introduced him to the man. He didn't feel like meeting any of Jay's friends so he walked to the other end of the club when he saw her headed toward the bar with her friend. Trent punched in the numbers to his voice mail. Listening to his messages usually took his mind of his present problems because there was usually a problem to solve, something he could sink his teeth into and forget whatever it was that was presently bothering him.

At least he hadn't felt his old insecurities rise inside him when he saw Jay with the guy which meant he was making progress in his healing. Still, he had to be honest with himself. He had recognized a smidgen of jealousy. While he listened to his messages, he considered the headway he had made since he had met Jay Lee.

He took a pen from the tray sitting on the dresser and scribbled the man's name and telephone number on a pad and erased the message, clearing his full voice mail and continued on to his next message, listening to Flora Prescott. He saved the message because he wasn't sure if he understood what she had said.

His last message was even more surprising. He held the telephone away from his ear, concentrating on the invitation that he had received. At this point, he knew that his mother wasn't kidding, not that she teased him about anything as serious as the message she had left him.

Trent shut off his cell phone and played back the events of his evening. He'd had a scotch or two while he watched Jay's friend play Don Juan and flirt with her. The music was good, but he hadn't listened much, but everyone seemed to be have been enjoying themselves.

However, the message on his voice mail had managed to bring one inquiry after another to mind. As he tried to figure it all out, questions swirled around in his head like a lazy ceiling fan on a hot day and nothing made sense. His intentions to sleep diminished and he was wide awake.

Trent pulled on his shirt and grabbed his cell phone and car keys. He had seen Jay going to the cottage around closing time while he was out back talking to Webster in the parking lot. He needed answers and he intended to find out what was going on.

But there would be time to figure out what he needed to know once he went to Jay. Right now, he wanted to make sure Jay was all right. Did she tell Gladys about them and had been disowned by her family or had Gladys Lee lost her mind? Trent fiddled with one thought after another until he could not stand another minute. Maybe he was worrying about Jay too much. He wasn't worrying too much he told himself. Jay was a woman with strong passion not only for him but for her work and other people. She hated liars, he knew that because Austin and Sonya had gotten on her nerves. Then there was her grandmother, the woman that had raised her and he wondered what Jay's reaction would be if her grandmother lied to her again.

Gladys Lee had accused his family for a crime that was committed against her family, one that took Jay's parents' lives, and because of her revenge, she was willing to disown probably the only person that truly loved her now. Her reasons weren't valid, Trent pondered. How could she deprive her granddaughter of love. Trent could hardly believe that Gladys would carry out her threat and he wanted to go to Jay even though he knew that she didn't need him, but he wanted to be there for her.

At a time like this, Jay Lee needed someone to lean on, someone to talk to and since he loved her and all of this was his fault, he needed to be with her when the hour of reckoning finally arrived. Trent began pacing as he always did when was upset, like a caged animal moving slowly from one end of the room to the other.

Twenty-one

Jay's old bedroom in Lees' cottage had been painted in soft lavender and trimmed with purple borders, a big difference from the damsel pink that Gladys had found appropriate when she was a girl.

Sleeping in her old bedroom in Lees' cottage hadn't stopped Jay from thinking about Trent Prescott. Even though she was exhausted, sleep failed her so she lay in her bed refraining from thinking about the pain that she would encounter tomorrow after listening to her grandmother remind her of her promise and finally she was prepared to say good-bye to all the people that cared and loved her.

Jay began to drift in and out sleep as one promising nightmare after another rose to the surface. Her first visions of Trent floated across her mind followed by visions of her grandmother's angry glare.

She turned on her stomach and shifted around until she was comfortable when suddenly the door bell rang. Remembering that she had forgotten to bring her house coat, Jay waited for Barbara or Earl to answer the door.

In her rush to get to Lees', she had grabbed the bag she had used when she went to West Virginia and was sleeping in one of her favorite nightgowns that she hadn't worn while she was visiting Trent.

The bell rang a second time and Jay lifted herself to sitting position, preparing to gather the sheet from her bed and wrap herself in it when she heard footsteps past her bedroom door, followed by a cantankerous and loud grumble and Jay recognized the familiar sound of Barbara's voice when she was upset.

Jay lay back, deciding that whatever was going on. Barbara and Earl would handle the problem.

However, the soft knock on her door assured her that she had been mistaken and she slipped out of bed, grabbing the top sheet and wrapping herself in the lavender material.

"What happened, Barbara?" Jay asked when she noticed Trent standing behind her godmother.

He didn't wait for Jay to invite him inside her room. He walked in and pushed the door shut behind him and circled her in his arms. He then walked her to her bed and sat her down.

The sheet that was suppose to have covered her fell around her in a crumpled lavender heap, exposing her firm round breasts and smooth skin. "What?" Jay asked watching Trent wet his lips.

"Mrs. Lee left a message for me," Trent said, widening his stance and resting both hands on his hips. "Did you talk to her about us?" Trent asked.

Jay thought it would be enough to have Gladys disown her over lunch. But she had taken deeper measures, inviting Trent to witness her humiliation. But the day of presumption had arrived and Jay was certain that Gladys wanted to show her how wrong she had been to fall in love with their enemy. "I didn't tell her;

she knew." Jay realized the warm shiver racing through her was brought by Trent's heated gaze.

Trent unbuttoned his shirt halfway and sat next to Jay. "How?" He asked.

"The day you stopped by the bed-and-breakfast," Jay said, filling him in on the details of Gladys's findings, as he sank down beside her. "And today," Jay said noticing the time on the clock, "she's kicking me out of the family." She blinked back tears, determined not to cry and savored Trent's warm embrace and his heady cologne.

"You'll have me . . . if you want me," he said, nestling her close to him.

Jay lifted herself from snuggling against his comfortable chest and studied him. "If I want you?" Jay asked Trent.

"Well," Trent said and cupped her chin in his palm. "Who's the guy that was all with you?"

"Elfin—I told you about the concert I sneaked off to with him one night when I was a teenager." Jay laughed lightly.

Trent kicked out of his shoes and propped one foot on the bed. "And?" Trent's voice was husky against her lips.

"We knew each other in high school," Jay said, experiencing another shuddering sweet shiver race inside her and she yielded to the building burning passion.

"Is that all?" He lowered his head further, touching his lips to hers.

"Hmm," she moaned softly as he caressed her lips with a soft kiss and gathered her closer, so close that she felt his masculinity against her.

"Baby, I didn't mean to come between you and your

family. But I'm here for you," Trent said, holding Jay away from him.

"I'm glad that you're here for me, but it's not your fault. I knew this would be the result of the choice I made."

"I feel responsible," Trent said.

"I don't want you to be here for me because you're feeling responsible and guilty." Jay assured him.

"No, I want to be with you. I don't understand your grandmother."

"She's set in her ways, and at this point, I don't think she will change her beliefs." Jay reassured herself as well as Trent.

"I'm sorry," Trent said, nestling her close as she felt tears sting her. "You have me. I'm your family."

She calmed herself and relished Trent's warm gentle caresses against her back and she didn't care if she had a family or not as long as she had him.

She loved Gladys Lee with all of her heart, but she would not allow her to chase another man out of her life. She would choose whom she would spend her time with, give her heart to and love forever. "Hmm," Jay said, unable to respond properly because his kiss didn't allow for conversation. She felt his hand slip over her shoulder, peeling away the sheer black gown and without warning, he kissed her taut breast until she felt as if she would skid out of control.

Jay lay back as he released his hold on her and watched as he discarded his clothes, taking safe measures, he joined her, his touch was light against her thigh as he stroked her building an ardent flame and before he ended, each scolding trail told her in details what he was going to do to her.

When he finished, he lifted the sheer black gown,

unveiling and feasting his gaze shamelessly on her. True to his word, Trent Prescott kept his promise. His kiss was hungry and burning like hot metal searching to find more sweetness to drink. He grasped her waist and inched downward, trailing with the tip of his tongue, stopping at the hollow of her throat, and onward to her cleavage, slowly building a fire of passion.

He gently stroked her soft flesh and her blood simmered as she thrust slowly levitating herself forward and caressed his muscular chest. She yielded her touch to his warm skin and made a path, raising a masculine snarl that escaped him as they savored each other, arousing a wanton roaring flame.

When she could stand no more, she slipped her fingers in the waist band of his pants and watched with pure satisfaction as he reached inside the pocket and pulled out two small packs and dropped them beside her before he discarded his pants and boxers in one long sweep.

Keeping his promise, he lifted her to the edge and planted one foot on the bed and the other on the floor, and with unabashed anticipation, she draped her long legs over his broad shoulders and embraced him as soft palpations of torridly iron met with silky crevices, deepening with each delightful caress until she drowned in a sea of pleasure that she hadn't known before.

They climbed together a rocky hill, each peak bringing pleasure of pure sweet ecstasy and Jay felt herself spin and reel as their bodies careened forcing her to cry out in blissful delight, enjoying the throb of waves and the tortured look on Trent's face as he drove deeper into founded crevices one inch at a time. They climbed to another explosive peak, a greater level than she had been with Trent and she wanted to tell him, but she couldn't speak.

Trent wrapped her in his arms and they became one body, one heart and one soul as they skidded and swirled out of control into a sea of sweet passion and joy.

Jay swallowed back a tear of pleasure and slipped her arm around Trent's waist, pulling him back onto her.

"Marry me, Jay," Trent raised up and searching her gaze as if he was looking for signs that she would be his wife.

Jay pushed Trent off her and raised up on her elbow. "Are you sure you want to marry a woman without a family?"

Trent drew her to him. "I want to be your family, Jay," Trent said, pulling her underneath him. "If we leave for Maryland now, we'll be there in time to get married and back in time for Mrs. Lee's luncheon."

Jay's answer was to kiss Trent and she did, filling herself with the sweet taste from his lips until they were almost breathless. She was satisfied knowing that she had made the right choice living her life with a man she knew would bring her pleasure.

"I have something for you," Trent said, getting up and taking a small black box from his jacket pocket and returning to her. "Will you marry me?" Trent opened the box, flashing a beautiful diamond engagement ring and wedding band.

"Yes, Trent!" Jay smiled and didn't fight back her happy tears. Later after a shower together, Jay and Trent tipped out of the cottage, leaving a note for Barbara that Jay would see her at lunch.

Two-thirty the next day, Trent dropped Jay off at her

house promising to join her later at Gladys's for their late lunch. He also told her that Gladys had invited his parents to her luncheon. They were in town helping Gwen and Craig settle into their new home. His mother and Gladys ran into each other in the shopping center a few days ago and Gladys had invited them.

Jay didn't know why her grandmother had chosen to make a big deal. She soon decided that Gladys must've thought that the more Prescotts there were to witness her denying her the right to the Lee's family the better.

The inevitable could no longer be prolonged. However, Jay would have preferred that Gladys disown her over the telephone, that way she and Trent would not have to had rushed back to her humiliation.

But with Gladys, business was taken care of in an appropriate manner. Jay pondered as she dressed in a hunter green calf-length skirt, matching shoes and beige tank top.

She and Trent were married now and having her grandmother's blessings was a dream that would never come true. Jay pondered that idea while she carefully applied her make-up and afterwards raked a brush through her short hair. Jay took the necklace Trent gave her while they were in Nigeria from the jewelry box and held it in her hand. The necklace was a token of his love for her and she loved him as much as he loved her. Jay hooked the necklace around her neck and stuck a pair of large gold earrings into her ear.

She was prepared to accept her fate and humiliation gracefully. Even if she had not known Trent the way she knew him now and he had come to her with the information regarding her parents' death, she would have believed simply because his information made more sense to her now than Gladys's.

However, Gladys had given no choice but to believe all that she had told her over the years. And like any child that looked to a parent for guidance and information, she had believed her grandmother to be correct in her knowledge. Jay knew no one that would know what had happened years ago to her parents.

If she hadn't met Trent Prescott, she would never have seen the proof that cleared his family from the cruel accusations that Gladys had labeled the Prescott family.

Jay was beginning to believe that the Prescotts had suffered far more than she and her family, and yet Trent and his family had risen like the phoenix from hot ashes and moved on with their lives.

Trent didn't seem to hold any grudges probably because his parents never taught him the animosities that Gladys had inspired in her. She had been promulgated with knowledge that was too much for a small child to bear and Jay wanted resent her grandmother, but she would wait and listen to what she had to say today.

Although, she had to move on with her life regardless of what her grandmother said or denied. She would love her from a distance because this was her life and her beliefs and she would not be bound to a family that was filled with deceit and hatred and had ultimately destroyed their relationship.

Jay took her purse and the gift she had brought from Africa for her grandmother and left for lunch. She hoped that Gladys would like the small leather black elephant and the table cloth. Then she wondered if Gladys would accept the gift.

Twenty-two

Jay used her key to enter Gladys's home, inhaling the delicious aroma of seafood while she studied Austin seated on the couch in a relaxed manner. She dropped the key in her purse. "Why are you here?" Jay asked Austin noticing the smug expression on his face.

"Mrs. Lee invited me to lunch," Austin said, raising from the sofa and moving toward her. "How have you been, Jay?" Austin asked her.

"Fine," Jay answered snapping her purse shut and moving toward the kitchen where she heard Barbara and her grandmother talking. She needed to return the key she'd used to let herself inside the apartment, and the gifts she had for her. She also wanted to tell Gladys that she and Trent were married.

Jay cast a disgusting glance at Austin and she wasn't surprised that her grandmother had invited Austin for lunch so that he could witness her being disowned for no other reason than to embarrass her. Her grandmother probably wanted to assure her that Austin was the right man for her. But Jay had long passed the stage of intimidation and she held not one iota of chagrin because she loved Trent.

She watched him reach inside his suit jacket pocket and pull out the pictures she had seen while she and Trent were spending time away from home.

"Mrs. Lee promised to look at these." Austin slipped the top picture out and held it for Jay to see.

Jay was almost impressed with Austin's surety. He was determined to force her back to him as if she was his concubine and a slave to a passion that she no longer needed or wanted from him.

"Excuse me," Jay said, going to get the door when she heard the bell ring. When Gladys hurried to open the door and spoke to whom Jay suspected were Trent's parents.

"Flora and Christopher come in," Gladys said, and stepped away from the entrance of her door allowing the couple into her living room.

Jay noticed that Trent favored his father, but had his mother's soft brown eyes. She was a petite, unsmiling woman Jay noticed, paying attention to Flora's beautiful features. Her black hair was pulled into a stylish bun and her make-up was light and flawless.

"Jay, this is Flora and Christopher Prescott." Gladys gestured to the couples. "These are Trent's parents," Gladys said, with a smile that assured Jay that her suspicions were correct. Her grandmother had a plan.

"Hi," Jay spoke to Trent's family, focusing her gaze more on Flora than Christopher Prescott.

"How are you, Jay?" Flora said, and stretching out her hand to her.

"I'm doing well," Jay said, wondering if Flora and Christopher knew that there was an additional relative in their family.

"I've heard a lot about you, Jay over the past weeks," Flora's firm handshake was one of an honest woman.

"It's nice to meet both of you," Jay said.

"And this is Austin Carrington," Gladys said, introducing him. "Have a seat. Lunch will be ready soon, but first we're going to talk." Gladys left the room as the Prescott family sat down.

"Barbara!" Jay heard Gladys call her godmother and waited for Barbara to join them before she sat in her favorite chair.

"Why are these people here?" Austin whispered to Jay.

"Lunch." Jay shrugged and sat in the chair near the window, and watched Austin nervously find a seat next to Gladys's favorite chair.

"Well," Gladys said looking at her guest and pressing an imaginary wrinkle from her full-bodied peach-colored dress.

"Gladys, if you're up to your old tricks again, Christopher and I are leaving," Flora said, and Jay noticed a stubborn frown ruffle her black arched brows.

"I invited you here because we need to talk," Gladys promised, and Jay could hardly believe that her grandmother wanted to speak to the Prescotts, and added to that consideration, the two families were in the living room, and behaving like people from modern civilization.

"If the food is fitting to eat," Flora snapped.

Jay was beginning to think that she had thought too quickly summing up the actions of her grandmother's lunch guest.

"Flora," Jay noticed Trent's father nudge his wife.

"Flora Prescott, you know I am a good cook," Gladys snapped back, and Jay let out a groan. Everything was happening exactly as she suspected when Trent told her that his parents had been invited.

"I know that you are a good cook, Gladys, or at least you were until you lied on us." Flora's fine features crinkled.

"That's what I wanted to talk about," Gladys said.

"Now we're getting to the meat of the discussion," Flora replied. "You don't want your granddaughter involved with our son."

"I didn't get to that part yet," Gladys replied, and lifted her gaze to meet Flora's.

Austin got Jay's attention when he cleared his throat. She looked at him and he winked at her.

Austin was an insignificant part of her of past, so she looked away.

"I can't tell Trent who to date because he's a man. But Gladys, I'm telling you if anything happens to my son, I am personally coming down here and there is no telling what I am going to do to you."

"Will you let me finish, Flora?" Gladys said, switching her gaze to Jay.

"Flora, let her finish," her husband said, and patted her hand gently.

"All right," Flora said and sat back, crossing her shapely legs.

Barbara walked into the living room followed by Earl who was on his way out the front door. "I'll be back, Barbara," Earl said after speaking to everyone.

Barbara nodded and spoke to Trent's family and sat near the door.

"I want to talk about my son and Jay's father," Gladys said, looking around the room and settling her eyes on Jay. "She's nothing like her daddy," Gladys said. "Her courage has brought us to this point." Gladys continued to study her granddaughter.

"Uh!" Flora groaned, when the doorbell rang.

Barbara got up and opened the door for Trent. "Hi," he spoke and then sat in a chair next to Jay.

A rumble of greeting floated out, filling Gladys's living room.

"Hi," Trent said and smiled down at Jay.

"I saw Jay and Trent together and for the first time I knew I had to speak out." Gladys said.

"Are you still a part of the family?" Trent leaned over and whispered to Jay.

"So far," she whispered back to him.

"Flora, you and Chris know that my son was not the best person in this town," Gladys said, and looked at Jay.

"Yes, Gladys, we know," Christopher said.

Jay didn't feel the odd shiver coursing through her as she had the night that Trent informed her of the dirty deals her father had been responsible for against his family. But over the years, according to Gladys, her father Rollins, Jr. had been perfect.

"I played a part in Rollins Jr.'s ways and actions. I knew that he was not nice . . ." Gladys paused and stroked her palm across her chest. "I'd turned my head or closed my ears to anything I saw or heard that he had done when he was a boy." Gladys let out a sigh as if admitting the truth about her only son was the hardest task she had ever taken on. "Junior stole from people . . . not with guns or anything, but he tricked them into thinking that he was an upstanding person and gathered their confidence and learned about all of the valuable things they owned and . . ." She stopped again and wiped an uncontrolled tear.

Jay eased to the edge of the chair, ready to comfort her.

"Are you all right?" Trent leaned into her, and she answered him with a slight nod.

"The day my husband borrowed the money to pay the tax on Lees', the Prescotts and Lees' were very good friends." Gladys waved her hands toward Flora. "Times were tough and Rollins couldn't repay the debt to your father." Gladys directed her comment to Christopher. "I knew Rollins had signed a paper agreeing that if he didn't repay the loan on the date required that he would lose Lees' Bed and Breakfast to your family."

"Gladys, we know what happened. You don't have to tell us," Flora said.

"Jay doesn't know," Gladys gave her granddaughter a weak smile, and Jay noticed her grandmother's eyes were filled with tears.

Jay turned to Trent and they held each other's gaze for a minute. "Did you tell her?" Trent leaned down and whispered to Jay.

"No, I didn't have time. Did you tell your parents we were married?" Jay asked him and he nodded a "yes."

"That's right, Mrs. Lee. Let them know," Austin said.

"Be quiet, Austin," Gladys said, and continued her confession. "I knew that Flint and Junior loved to play with dice." Gladys drew in a long breath and let out a heaving sigh. "I wanted my business back so bad, I would've done just about anything." She glanced at Jay. "So, I asked Junior to help me and he agreed. I bought a set of rigged dice and . . ." Gladys wiped her eyes again.

"When Jay's parents were struck and killed I suspected that maybe old-man Prescott might have had something to do with their death. But after I saw the police report I knew better. But I taught Jay that your family was our enemies and if she spoke to any of you I would disown her."

Gladys let out another heaving sigh, and Jay went to sit beside her. She couldn't stand to see her in agony.

"The day I saw Trent and Jay, I realized for the first time that she was happy and in love. I want all of you to know that Jay and Trent have my blessings."

"Ah man!" Austin said.

"Austin, please!" Gladys said.

"I turned years of friendship into a hateful lie and I deceived Jay." Gladys patted Jay's hand. "I'm sorry that I taught you to hate the people that had been our best friends."

"It's all right, Granny," Jay consoled her.

Gladys reached inside her dress pocket and pulled out an old police report. "This man was drunk when he . . ."

"I know," Jay squeezed her grandmother's hand.

Jay glanced at Trent across the silent living room and watched his smile.

"Thank you, Gladys, for straightening out this foolishness because you had my children thinking that we were murders." Flora looked at Christopher as if she was surprised that Gladys Lee had finally set the record straight, clearing her family's name of all the wrong she had accused them of committing.

Gladys turned to Jay. "Honey, will you forgive me?"

Jay circled her arms around Gladys and kissed her cheek. "Granny, you know I love you and yes, I have already forgiven you."

"Flora?" Gladys asked.

"Gladys, we forgive you."

"I was so angry that Chris Prescott took our business. He already had two more businesses and that little vegetable farm. He knew that the bed-and-breakfast were our only means of income and I hated him for making us struggle and I was mad at my husband for years because he signed those papers. I did the only thing I knew how to do at the time to survive."

"Gladys, I probably would've done the same thing too," Flora said, locking her fingers together and placing her hands in her lap. "Because I can tell you, right my father-in-law was not a saint." She said and then added. "Of course, you know by the time Chris's daddy died Flint had lost all of the property."

Trent's chuckles filled the room and the others joined in with his laughter.

"Jay, you're wearing a wedding ring. You got married?" Gladys asked, and switched her gaze from Jay to Trent.

"Yes, we did get married," Jay said.

"Why didn't you tell me?" Gladys asked

"Gladys, you probably didn't give Jay time to tell you," Barbara spoke up for the first time. "Congratulations Jay," Barbara said, her smile appeared to light up her face.

"Flora, did you know?" Gladys turned to Trent's mother.

"Trent told me this morning," Flora smiled at Trent and Jay. "Jay, I would like to welcome you to our family," Flora said, and Jay couldn't believe the day she was supposed to be ousted from her family she had gained a family and the approval and confession from her grandmother.

"I have better things to do with myself," Austin said, and got up, dropping the pictures in Jay's lap as he walked past her and out the door, while everyone got up and headed into Gladys's dining room, taking their place at the table.

Finally, Jay had gotten the chance to give Gladys her gifts. She stopped her grandmother before she went to the dining room. "These are for you," Jay said, and watched Gladys marvel over her gifts.

"Thanks, Jay." Gladys hugged her, and removed the tablecloth from the package. "I'm covering the table with this cloth now," Gladys said. "Come on honey, let's eat."

"Jay, you did the right thing when you married Trent, because he needed a wife." Flora said, once she was seated at the table and helping herself to Gladys's jumbo curry shrimp and passing the platter to Christopher.

"We know," Trent said, eyeing Jay with a smile in his eyes that hadn't yet reached his lips, as everyone at the table helped themselves and enjoyed Gladys's fried chicken, jumbo shrimps, and tiny baby ribs smothered in gravy, mashed potatoes, tender mustards, corn bread, dinner rolls, apple pie with whipped cream and ice tea with thick lemon slices and several bottles of red and white wine.

"Gladys, I know you didn't cook all of this food," Flora said.

"No, but I supervised," Gladys said. Then she placed her hand across her chest. "Oh my God! I can be a great-grandmother." Gladys laughed out loud. Trent and Jay exchanged glances as well as everyone else at the table before they ate.

"That's right," Flora said, and Barbara agreed with her.

"I am so happy, Jay," Gladys said, not acting like the

woman Jay had been raised to know when one mentioned the Prescotts. "You and Trent have to get started as soon as possible because I'm in my seventies."

"I have a grandchild, but I'm always happy to get another one," Flora said to Gladys and directed her comment to Jay and Trent.

"As far as I'm concerned, I'll be Jay and Trent baby's grandmother," Barbara said.

Trent leaned in close to Jay's ear and whispered. "We can go home and work on that now."

Jay was ready to go. She hadn't had much sleep and with all the excitement of opening Lees', getting married and her grandmother's confession, it was almost overwhelming. "I'm ready when you are, but not to work on starting a family," she whispered back.

"There's nothing wrong with practicing." Trent's grin was mischievous.

While Gladys, Flora and Barbara argued over who was going to baby-sit Jay and Trent's baby because the child was not going to a daycare center, and how Flora was living in Canada and couldn't baby-sit anyway, Jay and Trent eased away from the table and out to their cars.

Later that evening, Jay and Trent Prescott melted together, filling each other with love. She had been determined to love him no matter the price she would pay because she knew that her heart would never lie.